CAVE OF STARS

CAVE
OF
STARS

George Zebrowski

HarperPrism
A Division of HarperCollins*Publishers*

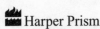Harper Prism
A Division of HarperCollins*Publishers*
10 East 53rd Street, New York, NY 10022–5299

COPYRIGHT © 1999 BY GEORGE ZEBROWSKI

ISBN 0–06–105299–X

HarperCollins®, 💥®, and HarperPrism®
are trademarks of HarperCollins Publishers Inc.

FIRST PRINTING: SEPTEMBER 1999

DESIGNED BY JACKIE MCKEE

Printed in the United States of America

Visit HarperPrism on the World Wide Web at http://www.harperprism.com

Library of Congress Cataloging-in-Publication Data
Zebrowski, George, 1945–
     Cave of stars / George Zebrowski. — 1st ed.
          p.   cm.
     ISBN 0–06–105299–X
     I. Title.
     PS3576.E35C38 1999
     813'.54—dc21
                                                                99-24459
                                                                CIP

99 00 01 02 03 ❖ 10 9 8 7 6 5 4 3 2 1

For Barry Malzberg, Cassandra's lover,
Who also instructs Athena and Apollo.

*"The life of reason is our heritage
and exists only through tradition.
Now the misfortune of the revolutionists
is that they are disinherited, and their
folly is that they wish to be disinherited
even more than they are."*

—George Santayana

*"Reason's heritage exists only through a
flawed tradition, and can everywhere be seen
subverted. The good fortune of revolutionaries is
that they are disinherited, and their salvation is that
they seek to be even more disinherited.
The past should be remembered if it is still at work in
the present, for good or ill; but if it is all used up and
has nothing more to say to the present, then it cannot
summon the future and should be forgotten.*

*What may be left of it is a kind of dramatic
beauty which elicits from us a painful love of the
past, a love that also imagines some hidden wisdom
or virtue is still there; but what remains is only a
memory, or a false memory of things once
familiar but now gone. Will our futures go the
same way of impermanence? We shall see."*

—Richard Bulero
Against the Past

1

All this began some twelve light-years from the Sun, in the year of 2331, on the fourth planet of Tau Ceti, in the third century after the death of Earth.

2

Warm wind threw salt spray into Ondro's face. Dark clouds stabbed the sea with lightning. Rain swept across the reef, raced the breakers and dotted the half-moon beach with a million drops. He held his face up to the wash, inhaling land odors from the shower, imagining the continent where all that would have been his went on without him.

He had taken to going out to the beach just before a storm, to be alone when reproaching Josepha. *Are you alone now, my love? Do you suffer for what you did?* Had she done anything?

He sat down as thunder rolled over the sea. A bolt burned the sand near him, but he felt only a feeble fear at its illusory show of purpose. Those who had arranged his end would not be so easily cheated. The lightning seemed to know enough to avoid that. It both amused and dismayed him that the other exiles preferred inevitable drowning later to a quick, merciful bolt sooner. Hope breathed beneath their daily resignation. They could not help it.

What was reason, after all, but a gray counsel. Tomorrow the ocean might dry up and they could all walk home—and be met halfway by white horses to ride the rest of the way.

He clenched his teeth and shook with the sudden tropical chill as low clouds pulled in over the island. He shivered into sorrow, then lay back and stared up into the hurrying gray masses, seeing Josepha and himself in their first moments together, regarding each other with interest, even wariness, as if each already knew what was to come—she looking tall and slim, long dark hair down her back, he stocky, light-haired, healthy—and felt love for their shy innocence, and despair for the wreck of himself now, for what she was now. *Kill me today,* he said to the approaching storm. *Today.*

Her disappearance a week before his arrest, her failure to search him out in prison, had convinced him that she had been a loyal cleric's daughter. Her dark-eyed looks of devotion and tender words had been false from the start, his love for her a leash placed around his neck by the secret police; and instead of the consummation of a marriage night, he had been given only the memories of longing for her pale body.

They had met in their first year at New Vatican University, among the sons and daughters of the professional class—merchants, artisans, engineers, lawyers, and physicians—who had come for their grudging chance at learning, even though their choice of professions was restricted to that of a student's parents.

He had trained in architecture and had planned to return as his father's apprentice. Josepha had studied theology and moral law, hoping to become a lawyer. She had told him that she was being sponsored by a papal official who wished to remain anonymous. Later, she had confided to him that this official was probably her father, but he had been skeptical; the illegitimate children of clerics had been known to make exaggerated claims about their anonymous fathers in the hope of advancement.

In their second year, Josepha had drawn him into a clandestine group that had access to the restricted papal library, where he had learned something of Earth's history, and had come to believe that the papacy had to be abolished, by force if necessary. The very existence of the concealed library, cut out of the rock beneath New Vatican, had convinced him of the urgent need for change. Knowledge that could change the world for the better had been hoarded for three centuries. There was no need for people to work so hard on farms and in the townships. A better and longer life was possible. The endlessly repeated idea of a difficult daily trial as preparation for a life beyond the world began to seem cruel to him, and his faith had been replaced by contempt for the Church. The life it had made for its people was the Way of the Cross, with no reward but death for the common man, while the elite enjoyed temporal power. The fact that the library could be penetrated had convinced him of the regime's fatal weakness.

At the center of the papal library sat a duplicate of the control room from the starship that had brought the original refugees from Earth. The ship itself had been left in high orbit around Ceti IV, but the duplicate control room had been built to transfer from orbit the ship's artificial intelligence and database. Yet millions of books had never been printed out and could be viewed only on aging equipment. The corridors around the central bank were filled with thousands of hastily bound volumes that had been retrieved as they were needed, or as a hedge against failing information storage, or because a cleric had become curious. Pornographic volumes lay tucked away here and there, and sometimes, when Ondro looked for them again, he found they had disappeared. His overwhelming first impression had been that almost no one knew what was in the library anymore and that this amnesia would one day become com-

plete. No one knew if the artificial intelligence still spoke to anyone, but he doubted it; the heavy door to the central control area
was locked, and it appeared not to have been opened in many
decades.

The official doctrine of the Church was that slow changes
were best. The catastrophic example of Earth's brief technological history was to be avoided by educating only a small technical
class that would maintain a stable economic government under
the Church's moral guidance. In practice, the official doctrine of
change meant no change at all.

The library group became a revolutionary cadre at the end of
the second year, when Ondro's brother Jason had arrived, but its
only aim was to continue learning against the day when the
papacy could be brought down. The creation of effective cells that
would include members in high positions would take many years,
perhaps longer than the lifetimes of the original members.

"We're being too cautious," Jason had said one day. "We
should strike at the top as soon as possible, take their lives with
one blow. They've been secure so long that it will come as a
shock, and before they can rally we'll have control."

"But what if public support fails?" Josepha had asked.

"The public will know nothing about it. We'll simply replace
the gang at the top, and the others will follow, scarcely realizing
there has been a change. Then we'll start replacing from the top
down, keeping our group a secret, so that we can continue no matter what happens."

It had all been so halfhearted, Ondro realized with a renewed
dismay as he sat in the downpour. Renunciation was the only
balm left for his regrets and lingering ambition. Here there was no
future to build, no past to tend. The night's starry immensity
seduced him into a sublime self-sufficiency, and by day the sunlit

intimacy of trees, sand, and water lulled him into forgetfulness.

But a durable peace eluded him. Thoughts of death brought back the icy resolve of his first convictions. He still wished for the end of Bely's theocracy, the death of Bely himself, if necessary, and would gladly plot again if he were ever given a place from which to strike.

But that place was not here. These islands were only sandbars. Sooner or later a hurricane would sweep the entire archipelago clean of life, as it had done in the past. Josephus Bely, His Holiness Peter III, who hid the knowledge that would topple him inside a rock, had chosen these islands as the final place for both criminals and political exiles, where the great sun-engine of weather would do his killing for him.

3

The whispering snake had coiled in Josephus Bely's sleeping brain for nearly twenty years. *The end is coming,* it hissed. He opened his eyes to darkness and hated his bodily decay, because it strangled his faith in the life to come. *The end is coming!*

And it would be final. The hope that had made him deathless during his youth of faith was fading, and he feared that this growing faithless emptiness within him was a punishment for the lingering imperfections in the papal succession from Old Earth, and for the changes—the changes, the poison of the changes that seemed to come with a wind from hell!

He struggled up from his bed and crossed the cavernous room to the open windows. Great white clouds sat over the sleeping city of two- and three-story wood and brick buildings that huddled around the open spaces and tall towers of the palace and cathedral.

He stepped out on the terrace and filled his lungs gratefully with the night air. *There is a life beyond this one,* his tingling body said as it was chilled by the brine-spiked breeze from the western ocean. *The changes, the mortal changes,* his mind insisted, *they have destroyed you!* All clerics, including popes, had fathered sons and daughters by selected females at one time, to increase the numbers of the refugees from Earth. According to the Jesuit geneticists, the arriving community had been just large enough to survive; to hold back any reproductive potential would have needlessly limited the gene pool's diversity. The women's faces had been covered at first, so that no cleric would know his offspring.

But in his time he had known his daughter's name, fathering her with a Sister of Martha long after he had become bishop. The anonymous reproductive duty of novices for the priesthood should never have been extended beyond the time of ordination. The personal need had lived beyond the immediate one of community survival because the geneticists had only made temptation easier to accept with their more-the-merrier view of the gene pool. Every breach of celibacy should have been punished after the danger had passed, yet still the Jesuits insisted on adding to the population. Some of them had sought to modify and even abolish celibacy, but they had lost the fight. *Corruption, corruption,* he cried within himself. Three centuries of papal rule had committed and then practiced error, he told himself, clinging to the fact of his daughter's existence and wondering if God was on the side of the burrowing heretics who sought to overthrow religious rule. The Church was no longer the Church. The City of God had died with Earth, and he was an impostor . . .

Suddenly he saw the universe through heretical eyes, as an

unbounded, self-sufficient infinity requiring no creator, in which afterlife was the dream of what could be only when natural life learned to preserve itself. Survival into ages of greater knowledge and skill was the real hope of heaven. Religious imagination was nothing more than a denial of the simple fact of decay, and faith a yearning that had mistaken the means of salvation, which would come from within, from the powers of the human mind, alive and teeming with secular sins.

Was it so? Or had his loss of faith thrown him into a pit of fear and delusion? Was it so? He might imagine anything at night and think it true. Night was the devil's cloak, covering the light of his waking mind, letting out the demons from below.

Struggling with his doubts, he turned away from the darkened city, found his cold sheets, and fell dead into his dreams, where he lay buried in the ground, falling apart while overhead the stars burned. He became dust, but was still conscious, enduring as the stars finally aged and new ones were born, and he became part of the unfeeling everblack, then nothing. Without flesh, there was nothing, nothing at all, his flesh whispered. You must have it to live, to become yourself, and you must raise it up renewed to be saved. Even the old doctrines couldn't make up their mind about what would be saved, spirit or flesh.

They didn't know. They had never known . . . oh, dear God, my lost strength, they had never known. . . .

4

As she waited in the wood-paneled audience chamber, Josepha looked around anxiously at the walls. The carvings of angels and devils battling each other with the weapons of history were cut deeply into the brown-stained wood and accented with black and white. Nowhere in the room, she realized, did the vast, convoluted depiction show a victor. It was a common feature of Jacob Kahl's prolific works.

She began to struggle with a sudden fear. If her cleric father knew of her involvement with the cadre, he might try to use her to track down the other members of the cell, if they had not all been arrested. To have ignored his summons would have placed her under suspicion.

She took a deep breath and sat still. Maybe this was about something else entirely. After all, she had never been commanded to appear before any authority or to come to this audience chamber for the kin of clerics.

"Welcome, daughter," a male voice said from behind the screen.

"It was by your order, wasn't it?" she asked, unable to control her trembling as she gripped the arms of the chair.

"Of course."

"But why?" she added.

She heard him sigh. "I know you wanted him, daughter, but he betrayed us all. And he would have blocked your way—"

"What has he done?" she demanded in a breaking voice.

"Don't you know? He sought the overthrow of the state."

"Ondro? Impossible. I know his family."

"He was not alone, daughter."

"Where is he?" she asked, afraid that she would hear that he was dead.

"He has been judged. I don't know the details. You're well rid of him."

"Where is he?" she shouted, realizing that Ondro's life was

over, that all his hopes for his profession would never be realized. No one in the cell had expected sudden arrest by the state, at least not before they were all established in their chosen paths. It had been a kind of game, meeting once a month to discuss the latest revision of the revolutionary council's program for the future. No one knew who was on the council, or when it would call the cells to action. We were all fools, she thought, talking of revolution but also dreaming of personal power. How many other conspiracies waited in Bely's vast, decaying bureaucracy? Who was the council, anyway? It might be a cardinal or two, perhaps even a single individual telling the cells what they wished to hear. Maybe there was only one cell. Bely himself might have started the whole thing to trap dissenters as they appeared.

She had come to the cell meeting and found an empty room. The chairs and table were in disarray, and the lock on the door was broken.

She had fled in panic, wary of contact with any of her friends from the group, afraid to find out who had been caught, fearful that some of those who had been arrested might be released to lure others into giving themselves away.

There were rumors of a cardinal being assassinated right here in the papal palace.

Later, she found the summons under her door in the college dormitory. It was the first message she had ever had from the man who claimed to be her father.

Quietly, she got up and came around to his side of the screen. "Tell me!"

The old man sitting there looked tired. "You must not . . ." he began, swallowing as he looked up at her. His obvious distress gave her confidence.

But as she looked at the pitiable old man who shrank from her gaze, she saw something familiar in the gaunt face, and her pity turned to surprise as she recognized the pontiff himself, by whose order she had escaped arrest—and who by being here now confessed himself as her father.

She stood in silence, unable to speak.

"What will happen to Ondro?" she asked at last, struggling with the pontiff's revelation, wondering if it might be a lie. "If you are my father, then you must tell me!"

"You cannot understand. . . ."

"Then explain it to me."

He shook his head and sank deeper into the heavy cushions of his chair. "Go back to your studies. Forget . . . or risk joining him in punishment. Do you want your life to end here and now? I have other hopes for you."

"What are you saying?"

"Forget these associations. Remake your life, and we will talk again."

5

Paul Anselle's nightly walk through the papal palace was a bodily form of worry, when his reason—free of daylight's restraints and glaring practicalities—paraded his dilemmas before him, then reproached him for not having done more with his power and influence. He sometimes felt frozen at his center, transfixed inside an outer shell that spoke and acted with no feeling for his fellow human beings.

He preferred order to justice, because he was deeply suspicious of human nature, even if order's peace was held by duplicity and manipulation. Only long periods of quiet might provide the foundation for lasting progress, he told himself.

He insisted to himself that a religious state had to oppose secular happiness to some degree; by its own theology it had to accept a measure of misery in life, as a testing process, and allow evil as the occasion for moral choices. But that was only the theological facade. The secret of the Church was that it sought to give human life a structured decency based on an authority beyond question, by which to maintain itself in power by divine right. It did not matter that God's authority might be doubted by the most intelligent; what mattered was that the ideals of a good life would be observed by most people. Simple minds needed justification from an unimpeachable source; they would doubt ethical values that merely proclaimed themselves. The Church's great fear was that the flock might come to believe the dictum, "If there is no God, then everything is permitted."

Paul had long ago concluded that the world moved according to hidden currents, and that these were not God's mysterious ways. Bely, who was not a fool, knew that the growing secularization of Cetian society was a threat to the Church. The old dogmas were being worn away. The sky had not opened recently to destroy the world, as had happened to Earth more than two centuries ago. A difference in kind was creeping in with increasing population, among whom practical behavior was always the best measure of unbelief. One had only to observe how much of life went on without reference to doctrinal belief.

Paul's hope was that the scaffolding of theology would one day fall away and reveal the genuine sympathies of human ethical ideals, as real in themselves as if given by God.

But Paul knew that this would not happen in his lifetime, if ever. Too many heretics were in exile, scarred beyond recovery, and he was a minor Merlin who thought for himself only in private.

Ironically, his inner independence and knowledge of the past only helped him to serve Bely better; few understood so well what was at stake on all sides, and almost no one knew the nature of the roles that were being acted out.

There could be nothing for him during a revolutionary upheaval. His power would not survive a transition, even if he lived through it, because no one would see his true self, or trust him. The time to have allied himself with change was long past. And he knew that his younger self would not have understood the harm that revolution would have brought, and would now be struggling to regain the noble ends that had been destroyed by evil means.

He felt pity for Bely. Secretly, the old man clung to the impossibility that his daughter might succeed him if she excelled in her theological studies; but this was a delusion born of pride and biology, and Paul had not tried to argue the hope, which would fail without his opposition. She could not ascend to Bely's position while he lived—no one could, unless Bely resigned—and she would be ignored after his death, no matter what arrangements Paul made. The cardinals could promote only one of their own, and no woman had ever been a cardinal.

Paul expected the number of Bely's delusions to increase with the pontiff's failing health. At any time now, Paul expected Bely to trot out his trump card, the legend of the one female pope, which had somehow survived along with the transplanted Vatican. The cardinals were watching very intently.

Had Ondro cultivated Josepha to spy on her father, or had the two youths simply fallen in love? There was no evidence that Ondro could have known that Josephus was her father, because

Paul was certain there was no way he could have discovered the fact.

Paul had not spoken to Josepha for nearly a year. They had become friends during her girlhood, when he had become her protector at Bely's request. She had been only four when her mother had killed herself.

Lesa Eliade, Josepha's mother, had been a woman of great faith. Paul remembered the warmth he had seen in her eyes, the kindness with which she had treated even the humblest of people. She had come from a farm a hundred kilometers south of New Vatican, after her family had died of influenza, to become one of the Sisters of Martha, who served in the papal palace by washing the robes and linens of the cardinals and priests, dusting the papal treasures, scrubbing the floors and cooking the Pope's meals— and bearing the children of clerics who could never officially claim them.

Josepha had been only four when Lesa had been found hanging in her room, from a noose made of a silken sheet bearing the Pope's crest. The Papal guards had been quick to remove the body, and the other Sisters of Martha had denounced the woman who would be condemned to eternal damnation as a suicide; but Paul had wondered how sincere their condemnations were, how many of them might have sympathized with Lesa.

Paul knew what had brought that kind and beautiful creature to take her own life. Josephus could never have acknowledged her openly, but he should have made a private place for her in his life. Instead, as he ascended in the hierarchy, he had stopped seeing her and was soon disavowing her to the few, such as Paul, who knew of the affair. He had broken her heart, and seeing him become Pontiff had almost certainly crushed her faith—that and knowing that her daughter would inevitably be taken from the mother who loved her to be trained and educated and used to serve her father's ambitions, as were all the children of the Sisters of Martha. And because Josepha was a woman, the ambition of her secret father would not be a high one.

Paul had been the one to find Lesa's suicide note, before ordering the guards to removed the body. "We're all alive in hell," she had written, "but what have we done to deserve it?"

Paul had thought a long time about Lesa, and his view of her had not changed over the years. The woman who had worked so hard to forgive her fellow human beings, to understand their needs and weaknesses, Bely's included, had possessed a genuine faith. She had deserved the storied life to come, but her faith had been shattered, leaving her with no hope of salvation, or fear of eternal punishment. She had looked into the abyss, and had gone willingly.

And the agony of it was that Josephus had loved her; that much seemed certain to Paul, because Lesa had loved him, and in the early days Josephus had confessed to him his love for her. So what had happened? Ambition. He could not take her with him. He would not even risk that ambition for a secret life with her, and it would not have been a great risk. Nothing at all, in hindsight, in a world where faith was dying. Lesa's faith had told her that Josephus would confess his sin and not turn away from her and their daughter. But as he buried them far from himself and the papacy, she despaired of her faith and its chief representative before God. It was all Josephus could do to see to it that his daughter was well raised and educated; but her life preyed upon his faith, as it had upon his dead love.

Paul had never told Josepha any of this; she had been too young to remember much about her mother, but rumors of Lesa's suicide had followed Josepha Bachelard, the name Paul had registered to hide her past, to the halls of Saint Elizabeth's, the girls school where she lived and was educated. Suspicions about her identity protected her at the school; but she found happiness there for herself, by proving that she did not need privilege. Paul had seen this plainly during his frequent visits, about which Josephus always demanded detailed reports. His daughter liked and admired the nuns who taught her, especially the scholarly Sister Perpetua, and they in turn treasured the girl.

But in time Paul had seen signs of distress in Josepha's dark eyes, as if she knew everything and could see what was to come. She never spoke of any close friends among her schoolmates, and Paul suspected that her mother's suicide had somehow become known, and had tainted the girl in their eyes.

It saddened him now to think of what state she was in following Ondro's disappearance, even though he knew that she was strong.

Paul always tried to think in historical terms, which promised him, to a degree, that he was looking at the flow of facts without the interruptions of generational life. He knew himself as one of the last in a long line of scientists and engineers who had come to Tau Ceti on the colony ark from Earth. A kind of Masonry still existed, but it was one more of engineers than of scientists, of practical people who knew how to keep things working; basic inquiry and research were not their interest. But it was their influence, together with that of the merchant-businessmen, that had brought the decline of otherworldliness as the basis for law and ethics. Their sons and daughters had an alternative—in business, engineering, and in architecture—to farming and basic industries, and to the pieties of life in the Church's civil service.

But the old vision of a powerful, technically advanced Earth had not been completely erased. There was life beyond the Tau Ceti system, in the mobile worlds, where three centuries would have certainly brought new developments. Something was stirring in the people of his world, Paul thought, and it was more than the historically common crisis of religiosity. It was akin to the millennial tremors of Earth's history, the hope of a Second Coming, perhaps even a rise of a secular ideology that might replace traditional faith and rule without fear and self-loathing.

But these feelings of change, he reminded himself, had been around for more than half a century, feeding on scraps of history and imaginative possibility. Everything could be accomplished in the realm of pure possibility—but what was likely in the existing climate of power and politics? How far had the tide come up to the City of God? And how long would it take to sweep it away? Delay would bring less social disorder, but it would be too late for him. He would not live long enough to participate in any progress.

He came to the great north windows of his wing of the palace and looked out at the night sky. A tall, gaunt figure stood on Bely's terrace across the courtyard. It was the old man—and Paul suddenly wished for the sky to be pulled back, so that his old friend might see the face of his God and be assured once and for all.

Paul watched the night-orphan, as he had so often over the years, until the wasting shape wandered back inside; then he turned and began his own slow search for his distant bedchamber.

He imagined, as he walked, what Earth's sunspace had endured in the years following the ruins of the home planet, as groups of survivors had struggled to reorganize. The remnants of Roman Catholic Christianity had modified a vessel into an ark and set out to find a new Earth from which to prepare for heaven. Other ships had also sought the nearer stars, while mobile worlds went out to reproduce themselves, forsaking natural planets.

The fragment of humanity that had come to Tau Ceti IV burned away the native life on one of the two continents and seeded the soil with the alien biota of Earth. Three centuries later, fifty million human beings lived in conditions that had been set to prevent progress beyond Earth's early twentieth century.

The other continent was still an alien, mostly unexplored wilderness, blamed for every new disease and the object of superstitious fear. It was also thought to be rich in metals, which the merchant-businessmen knew were the key to economic growth. The rapacious settlement and exploitation of that continent would make a great crusade one day, only awaiting an ambitious pope to give it his deadly blessing; and by so doing he would also prolong the Church's power.

Bely knew the need for metals, but he also knew and feared the unstoppable developments that heavy industry would hasten; but when it came to a choice between being swept away or accepting change, his successors would choose change.

No signs of native Cetian intelligent life had ever been found, probably because the invaders had arrived too early or too late. But this world would certainly never develop any, now that man from Earth was here to prevent it. The issue was an obscure one, but he thought about it from time to time, imagining the vast aborting of the alien unborn that had already taken place.

He stopped before the door to his quarters and felt a moment of sympathy for Ondro and his brother Jason. The two Avonmoro brothers had longed for something new to intrude into their world, bringing impossible changes, loosening the mortar of time and fear that had made a changeless wall around their hopes.

The knowledge for change waited in the vast library of the ancient information storage and retrieval system below the palace. But unused skills also required teachers, and there were none. The trades passed on only much-used techniques that required minimal understanding, enabling the world to function, after a fashion, but without progress.

He entered his apartment, closed the heavy wooden door, and turned the key in the wrought-iron lock. He stood there for a few moments, looking at the dimly lit carvings of angels in the wood, and was sick with the loss of sweet possibility that he had known in his youth. He turned away, hoping that there was still enough night left for him to find sleep's mercy.

$$6$$

He was a fool to have doubted himself, Josephus thought as the anemic glow of dawn lit up his windows. When Josepha had refused to leave, he had tried too hard to explain to her why Ondro, however honestly or unwittingly, had become part of a larger threat. The revolutionary cells had to be cleaned out once in a while, because their aim was to work from within over long periods of time, threatening one day to elect a pope from their own ranks.

He should not have admitted to her that he also blamed himself for the liberal decisions of his early years in office, among them the order to release to the schools the record of Earth's heritage. The past's corrupting examples had taken their toll, forcing the Church to share its control of science and technology, especially medical knowledge, with too many people. And as new students came up through the schools and were able to compare their world's accomplishments with the record of Earth's achievements, the taste for change could only grow, ignoring the fact that Earth had destroyed itself and that the aim of a simpler life was to insure survival of the means to attain the eternal life of heaven. If this decay continued, he had warned, then a successful revolt against the Church would become possible. Under pressure, the cardinals might even select a heretic pope to be a tool of the educated class, in the mistaken belief that they were serving the Church's survival. Earth's history would repeat itself as religious guidance of life slipped into secular hands and the material world became the sole object of life. Humanity would become blind to the life beyond life, deaf to the values of the world beyond the world.

"My life will have been for nothing," he had told her, hearing his own words as they must have sounded to her, hollow and self-important, but truthful.

"But I love him," she had said to him, tearing at his father's heart with her eyes.

"Love cannot exist for long outside of the knowledge of right and wrong. Surely your studies have taught you that?"

She had glared at him, declaring that the substance of his words meant nothing to her, shaking his convictions as only a youthful gaze could do, because it could only look ahead.

"It's not such a bad place where I have sent Ondro and his brother," he had added. She could not marry, of course, if she were to have any chance of rising to the rank of cardinal and succeeding him. Women had never risen beyond the station of parish priest, even though the Church had opened the way for them on Old Earth.

"Where is he?" she had demanded, as if questioning a child, and he had felt the falseness of the fatherhood that he could not deny or abolish.

"I cannot tell you, daughter."

"I'll find out. Someone must know."

She had left the chamber before he could give her his general blessing, leaving him with the weight of her resolve. It would not help her; even if she learned where Ondro was, she would not be able to rescue him.

As he lay in bed and looked out at the brightening sky, he remembered the generosity of his youth and the ways his own compassion had been used against him, leading him to give away too much of the Church's authority to others. Perhaps it was still not too late to reverse the changes. But was his faith strong enough to help him apply the means?

7

Ondro came to the top of the hill and looked down at the makeshift village of wooden houses and grass huts. In a dozen lifetimes these islands could not grow an economy powerful enough to build a navy and invade the mainland; even if there were enough ore to develop metalworking, there would never be enough food to feed the growing population that would be needed. The power pyramid was just as rigid here as it was back home. The criminal hierarchy here was largely based on force and physical brutality, while the political prisoners paid obeisance to intellectual and rhetorical skills. There was little contact between the two camps, although there was no question in his mind that the criminals could easily overpower the politicals had there been anything for them to gain besides the occasional sexual demand. Idleness born of changeless decay maintained a stable hopelessness.

He sat down and thought bitterly of the documents he had signed to avoid torture, deeding away his father's land and house to blanks on paper, to nameless members of the religious oligarchy who had told him he would have no need of his property where he was going—so why suffer pain? Bely was probably just as corrupt as his authorities, or deluded about their actual behavior.

The odor of fish reached him on the rise, telling him that a fresh catch was sitting in the shed near the shore. A small field of scrawny grain was coming up on the far side of the village. The chickens were clucking away in their fenced area. The fruit trees were expected to do well this year, but he missed the potatoes, carrots, and beets of the mainland. He would probably never taste them again. The distant hope in the thought made him smile; that he would certainly never taste them again was the truth that his errant thoughts insisted on denying with modifiers. If he had his grade school teacher's blackboard on which to diagram sentences, then he might be able to root out all hope from his thoughts. Yet again—not might, but would root out all hope. Hope makes a man deathless, someone had once written; he should have written that it makes him a fool before the fact of death, to go forward into the abyss with any hope at all.

Jason waved to him from their hut, then started up the hill. His brother was still losing weight, Ondro noted, and he was taking more frequent naps. He had given up inside himself, and there was no way to call him out again. Together they had planned great waterworks, had dreamed of redesigning cities, and that was one reason they were wasting away here. Too much change would have rearranged the world, taken power from its masters; change could only be slow, conserving the positions of the powerful, preserving against the evils of revolution. But occasionally, some secret violence had to be done to internal enemies.

As he watched his brother struggle up toward him, Ondro found it hard to believe that Jason had been the vocal theoretician

of the cadre. "That's why we're both here," Jason had confessed
one day, admitting guilt but showing no repentance. "I should
have known they wouldn't have let us change the world so easily.
They don't need new cities and more people. Too hard to control.
There's enough herd to keep the masters on top."

That Jason was gone.

"Hello, Ondy," Jason said as he came up to him, smiling for a
moment as he had when they were boys, and sat down next to him.
Together they surveyed what world was still theirs.

After a while Jason smiled at him. It was the second time
today. Ondro felt a jab of hope.

"I wonder if we had it in us," Jason said with a show of
energy, "to carry through with our plans."

"You seemed ready enough," Ondro said, ready to play along.

"We would have risked poisoning our ends with necessary
killing, as the old historians say. Or is that just another bit of pre-
ventative teaching, to keep us quiet in our chains?"

"Who knows," Ondro said. "We might have sacrificed a
whole generation to reach better times. Maybe slow changes are
better, no matter how long they take."

"What if they never come?" Jason asked, his voice reaching
for strength.

"Single generations, facing death, are never patient," Ondro
said. "We lacked the belief in the life to come, to make us patient."

"We had our belief in the future," Jason said, "in what was
possible. And we held that belief with clear knowledge of how we
were being held back. We had no time, no chance, to make our
own mistakes, to commit our crimes, to try new ways."

Ondro said, "You might as well say it. I got too close to some
cleric's daughter, and that got us here. She may have even led
them to us."

"I don't blame you," Jason said. "Who could have known that she was the small hook with which they would pull us out into the open? Who knows, they may have arrested her, too."

Ondro glanced at his brother in surprise. Jason had only rarely speculated about Josepha's role in the arrests. There had been no word from her or about her after the arrests, not even a rumor among the prisoners about what had happened to her. Ondro was relieved that she wasn't here—but where was she?

"What did you see in her, anyway?" Jason asked.

"I don't know," Ondro replied without any of the emotion he expected to feel. "With all the show of fervor she put on, she still seemed innocent of politics. Just a theological student with no future except the one that her nameless father might one day give to her."

"You felt sorry for her," Jason said, but without the reproach that might have asked, "We're here because you felt sorry for her?"

"Maybe I did," Ondro whispered, hoping for a physical blow from his brother as a sign of his improving health.

Jason laughed. "She was beautiful. I'll admit that much. If you had to get a leg up, she would have been a painless way to go. You might have achieved a position of some use."

Ondro looked at him and didn't know what to say, thinking that his brother was getting confused in his argument.

Jason saw his questioning look and said, "You think now that you might not have been of much help to us if you had married her, that you would have deluded yourself with the idea of slow change, of leaving things as they are. Oh, I admit we might not have been better than Bely. We're all the same inside, but Bely's hereditary hierarchy added worse to bad from the start. Just look at their rules. They stand justified by the story of a crucified god who rose from the dead—and one of their rules is an injunction against doubting that yarn. How's that for self-serving convenience?"

Ondro took a deep breath, feeling reassured.

"The simple human trust in experience and health," Jason continued, "which is all that faith is—a kind of shorthand—is made into a cosmic system of trial and redemption in a life beyond this one."

"I'm not surprised that we all try to make something of the abyss around us," Ondro said. "Goodness brings life and evil inner death, does it not? And are we not judged, whether we admit it or not, by our motives and our deeds? And then do we not have to live with what we have made? I'm not surprised that we dream of a place beyond life where all wrongs and sorrows stop, and where every question is answered."

Jason's wasting face smiled at him and said, "Well, yes, but I don't have to believe it's all true. I'll sit here and judge motives and deeds, and I'll grant you that we are what we have made of ourselves, at least to a degree—but beyond life there is nothing that will damn us or save us, and Bely rules here, with promises he cannot keep, with fears that only serve him and his. Maybe we should have played his game and waited for slow changes—but for our impatience we'll die here. With patience we would have died in our father's house, still being patient."

"You're probably right," Ondro said.

"I hate how they separated you and Josepha," Jason said sadly, suddenly drained. "I wonder if she even knows what happened to you." His voice trembled as he said, "It was just your luck to be my brother. They might have let you off more easily if I hadn't been such a firebrand. I could have left you out of it."

"I'm more like you than that," Ondro said, "and that would have prevented me from just going along to get along. Sooner or later . . ."

"I know, I know," Jason said feebly.

Ondro gazed at the sinking sun. Something of his brother's fading rebelliousness entered him, and he resented his own humanity—the flesh that was doomed to die, the mind that struggled toward the light and never quite attained it. There was no help anywhere, despite the longing that reached out and pleaded with the nameless, irredeemable fact of living that seemed to be both wakefulness and dream.

"Storm's coming," Jason said, and lay back where he sat. "Feel the drop in pressure?"

This one will finish us, Ondro thought, and a part of him welcomed it. A blind rage readied to break across the sea and drown the island exiles; yet it would still be a crime, committed by Bely with nature's innocent hand. *We'll be dead forever,* Ondro thought, thinking of his bones rotting in the sea, where in a million years he would still be dead, still counting up to forever.

"You know," Jason said in a whisper, "I'm looking forward to it."

"Paul," Josepha said in a sad, trembling voice, "are we still friends?"

She had come to his quarters very early in the day and had been admitted because she still had the pass he had given to her. He gazed at her as she sat before his desk in the dark, heavily curtained study, and remembered the young girl he had visited regularly at the convent school so he might report back to her father. For some time she had imagined that he was her father, despite his denials. Well, now she knew, and the critical look on her face sent a chill into him.

"Of course we're friends," he said, "and I hope we will always be."

"You know why I'm here," she said sternly.

He sat forward and put his hands on his desk, under the green shaded light. "Do you care for him that much?"

She nodded. "This should not have happened."

Paul sighed and sat back. Like her mother, Josepha was a good Christian, and her ethics were a reproach to her father. "But what do you imagine I can do?" he asked.

"Free him."

The trembling was gone from her voice; she was determined to have her way.

"And who else? His brother, his friends? Would you abandon them? If it's right for one, then it's right for all to go free."

Her eyes squinted at him. "How many are there, Paul, and where are they?"

"Too many for me to be just. And you would wish me to be fair?"

"That's just a clever argument for doing nothing," she said coldly, and the intonations reminded him of her father's voice. "You could get him out. I don't ask you to be fair if it means abandoning him. One thing at a time."

Paul sat forward slightly. "So I get him out. Does he then take up where he left off? Not likely. Are you two then prepared to live in obscurity, just to be safe? That wouldn't be much better than the life he has now. Keep in mind also that his release would be traced to me. I would have to send a ship, with armed men, to separate him from the others, and I could not conceal any of that."

"Then you won't help me," she said softly.

He was silent, trying to control his feelings, to seem kind when he could not be kind. "I'm sorry," he said, hating the effort, watching her hands grip the armrests. "I know what I can and can't do," he said as she got up, turned her back to him, and stood very still.

There was nothing she could do. She was the last of her group, free and powerless. But he asked the question anyway. "What will you do, Josepha?"

She turned and faced him, and the look of fury on her face dismayed and frightened him.

"Whatever it takes," she said. "With your help or without it."

And my help can only be nothing at all, he did not say, fearing that he would not be able to save her from suffering. No one would listen to her now or help her, because this generation of rebels had been dealt with. Bely would officially deny that she had been one of them, but he would not help her. No one would help her.

"Is it worth being a swine, Paul?" she asked. "Is it worth what you get for it? What do you get for it, Paul?"

It was a good question, and he didn't have the stomach to try answering it. As with all the best questions, it had no easy answer, and perhaps no answer at all. How could he tell her that rebels either joined the regime and did what they could or were exiled or killed? God, whether he existed or not, had only creatures to do his work; and if he was *not,* as was likely, then the creatures had only themselves to do what had to be done—and they were left an even smaller arena of power: what could be done. The window of human freedom had always been too small for any man's liking; but it was better to see through it, better to reach out and do what could be done, than to miss the chance completely and do nothing.

That's what I get, he wanted to say as he looked up at the woman who was killing the girl he had known.

"This is what you get?" she asked. "This study, these quarters? A little food? Someone to serve it to you? Someone to clean your rooms and do your wash, like my mother did, so you can hide from everything and lie to yourself about the good you are doing? Jason and Ondro were right. It's all for holding us back from a better life, to keep you and the others at the top."

He had no strength to answer her, but finally he said, "Leave your pass with me, and don't come here again. I don't want to hear from you or know where you are. That will afford you some safety."

She stepped closer and dropped her pass on his desk. "You're just a coward!" she cried, fixing him with her gaze.

He looked away and started to say, "If it helps you to think that of me," but was unable to continue and covered his face.

He wanted to tell her that he was trying to save her life, that after Bely and he were gone she would be without protectors; and for a moment he imagined her death, and saw himself trying to explain to her after the fact that he had tried to prevent it . . .

The stillness became a desert between them, and when he looked up again, she was gone.

9

The late-breaking storm had been mild, passing quickly. Ondro came out to the beach at midnight and spotted the Sun of humankind's beginnings where it rode high among the stars along with bright Vega and Sirius, and once again felt himself a stranger to Tau Ceti IV, the world of his birth, now reduced to an island in the sea.

He had thought too deeply about the violent transplanting of a fragment of humanity to an alien world to feel completely at home. Increasing knowledge had chased that childhood complacency from his mind. Granted, no adaptation of colonists to an Earthlike world could be perfect; the life of Earth itself had not been a perfect fit to any era of its past; but it was the absence of nearly all written discussion after the first fifty years of set- tlement that he had found suspicious during his explorations of the papal library. An unsettled continent sat on the other side of the world, and he wondered what waited there for human- kind. His deepest feeling was that humanity's hold on Tau Ceti IV was precarious, and becoming more so, unless medicine pro- gressed.

Weed and driftwood from the storm washed up along the beach. Crabs stole across the starlit sand. He began to walk, enjoying the night, emptying his mind of the past that sometimes seemed like a bad dream from which he would awake. His own past seemed to be the dream gone bad of other pasts which stood like walls around his time. Lifetimes were prisons to begin with, walled by the shortness of their stay. The time in his father's house had once been an eternity of secure waiting for his life to begin; now it seemed an instant of ignorance, opening into a minefield of knowledge.

His father, who had finished bringing up his boys after his wife died of influenza, had said to Ondro: "Find your own place in this world. Love your architecture. Your buildings will outlast the big problems you love to worry about." His father had seen into him, Ondro knew, and had warned him about nurturing the thoughts that had exiled him to this place. "The world's problems are too big for you or any one person to carry around on his shoul- ders. Your mother read too much, thought too much, and it made her very unhappy. I think she was glad to die."

His father, Ondro thought, had been an example of a leg- endary Earth animal, the hedgehog. The hedgehog knew one big important thing, while the fox knew many things. His father would have said that his son Ondro knew too many things for his own good.

Jason, who learned just as quickly and saw as far, kept his thoughts to himself, and this seemed to reassure their father. Jason's love had been theoretical mathematics, but their father saw him only as a valuable partner in their future architectural business. He had also died of influenza before he could see his boys finish university—or see them imprisoned.

Ondro stopped and looked toward the horizon. An unfamiliar bright star hung low over the sea. He sat down and waited to compare its position to known stars, and saw that it was moving slowly, as if it were an inner planet or an asteroid coming sunward on a cometary orbit. He was sure that he had not seen the object before.

After a few more minutes he felt sure that the object's motion was too swift for a planet or an asteroid; it had to be much nearer to show such obvious change of position, perhaps even near enough to be in a wide orbit around his world.

He watched until the new star fell below the horizon, certain now that planetary rotation alone could not account for all its movement. The more he thought about it, the more he felt that its motion was a sun orbit; but there was no planet only a few hundred thousand kilometers sunward. So maybe it was an asteroid coming in on a cometary, and had just missed Ceti. He knew what that might have meant, and shuddered at the general ignorance of his world, which could have done nothing to prevent being wiped out in a matter of moments.

He sat there, thinking of the lurking diseases that waited to thrive in human bodies, and of the inheritable flaws that hid in the poorly understood structures of the human genome. He mourned the short human lives that rarely exceeded a century; and he despised the mockery of education dispensed through the schools of a transplanted vestige that stood uneasy on its rock of insistence.

10

It sometimes both puzzled and impressed Voss Rhazes that humankind existed in any large numbers outside the mobiles. He knew only his own habitat, but he had taken for granted from his earliest years that the reproducing mobiles were the primary form of humanity derived from Earth and the true future of the species. His mobile had met only one other, its originator. The estimate was that there had to be at least two dozen others, and perhaps half of these had reproduced.

But the scattering of ships in a thousand-light-year radius of Earth had brought into being a still-undetermined number of planetary colonies. Judging by the six he had seen through the Link, the settlers were content with modest levels of technology and low levels of medical and genetic praxis, enough to make their worlds manageable during their short lifespans. The peoples had apparently grown attached to their forests, plains, high plateaus, and mountain valleys, even while imposing their own modifications on the local biology, and seemed only vaguely aware of the mobiles of macrolife beyond their sky. During rare encounters, it had been difficult to convey to planet dwellers that a mobile habitat's many-leveled structure contained more usable surface area than any planet and was filled with light and clean air, where people grew into lives undreamed of by the mass of historical humanity—all inside an egg shape one hundred or more kilometers long, consisting of hundreds of urban shells, sometimes wrapped around the foundation of an asteroid core. The growing backwardness signaled by this ignorance of simple geometries made it plain that these planetary colonies were rapidly slipping into a dark age from which they might never recover; therefore, contact with the mobiles might well be essential to the very survival of these communities.

For Voss, mobiles were the civilized places from which to confront and explore the universe. Only suns were greater in their massive use of energy. Inside the macrolife habitats, energy use was subtle and variegated, flowing to enhance the life of a mobile's citizenry. It was the difference between the circulation of blood in an organism, nourishing each cell of every organ, and an open fire. Knowledge and the energies needed for life flowed through the people of the mobiles, but understanding counted for much more than simple survival and longlife; it was the center of life.

This was not so in the planetary colonies. There, simply to live, grow weary, and pass life on apparently counted for much more than to know, and understanding was the smaller part, even a luxury.

In his experience, knowledge and thought were a whirlwind, the central power of living, by which all that was novel and absorbing was achieved. No previous human culture had ever had macrolife's control over itself or more possibility for varied growth. Past humanities had taken their chance, and as they failed for what seemed the last time, macrolife had bolted free from the planetary cradle.

The mobiles were always remaking themselves, multiplying to accommodate population and the need for social experiment. Unchanged humanity's persistence on several planets intrigued Voss, but he shared the view of many others that without help these colonies would fail and die, and that to do nothing would make the mobiles complicit in that dying.

Nevertheless, this old humanity, it seemed to him, wished to remain poor and powerless in a universe of wealth and beauty— and even though it was an oversimplification of deeply layered group histories, he was always struck by the easily counted degree of truth in this judgment. Human organisms in purely nature-given environments adapted to scarcity, living in balance with the environment through basic work until they died. Deep bodily satisfactions rewarded the organism occasionally, enough for them to launch the next generation of organisms. Attempts to progress from this state produced profound difficulties. On Earth it had led to diverse adolescent technological cultures whose individuals felt as if they had been expelled from a dimly glimpsed paradise of nature.

The first flush of growth beyond given nature had produced imbalances. Wealth beckoned with the promise of an end to scarcity, but it had also brought the disuse of minds and bodies in large, suddenly unnecessary populations, sweeping away values built on the striving for mere survival and material security. Tribal issues of descent and territory became exaggerated, leading to organized warfare and environmental catastrophe. Earth's most influential civilizations, numbering more than thirty in less than fifteen thousand years, had been unconscious accretions of beliefs, rituals, and scraps of applied knowledge. The predominant mood at their various endings had been bewilderment; they did not know what had happened to them.

Earth's final planet-wide civilization had failed to make the transition to a culture of rational values and goals. It had resisted, from motives of greed and power, new forms of social and economic organization, and had finally lost the high-energy state that was the prerequisite for creative goal-seeking; genuine progress would have put too many groups out of power. And it was the example of Earth's failure, as well as the loss of records and teachers, that kept its desperately established planetary colonies cautious, backward, and fearful of repeating the past.

But macrolife, the hardiest flower of Earth's romance with science and technology, had survived the last civilizational collapse and was proliferating. It was not known how many seed worlds had escaped Earth's sunspace, but it seemed inevitable that developing mobiles would one day contact each other. It seemed unthinkable to Voss that his mobile would always be alone, just as it seemed unlikely to him that the future of humanity would ever belong to planetary colonies.

Voss felt, as did most of his fellow citizens who were under a century in age, that the time had come for the building of a new mobile. His world's visit to the Tau Ceti system, therefore, had several clear aims. Raw materials would be gathered for the construction of the new social container. This activity would be the natural occasion for a goodwill mission to the planetary colony on the fourth planet, which had not been contacted before by his mobile, or by any other mobile, as far as anyone knew. Also, a group of malcontents would be given the opportunity of settling on the planet. This might create some opposition from the planetary authorities, since the group would bring a high technology to a backward world; but this would be unavoidable, since it would be suicide for the settlers to do without the medical skills of their parent world or to accept a lower energy level of daily life. It was also possible that people from Tau Ceti IV might wish to emigrate to the new mobile being built in their sky.

As these projects went forward, Voss's assignment was to make contact with the planet's civil authorities and gauge their reactions to the mobile's visit and plans to leave settlers behind. Preliminary scans had revealed that the people of Ceti IV had not managed to lay claim to the entire planet by this time, so a suitable remote area might be found: but the matter had to be at least mentioned to various leaders.

Voss had discussed possible complications with First Councilman Wolt Blackfriar.

"I find it difficult to understand," Voss had said, "why such a group would wish to leave and take so much of our way of life with them. What's the point?"

"They imagine that they want to live on a planet," Blackfriar had said. "Some of them will feel that they have found what they wanted, others will not. They have to learn for themselves."

Voss felt uneasy as he entered the small flitter on the outward engineering level. He had never felt this kind of uncertainty, and wondered for a moment how he might feel or which group he might belong to once he had spent some time on a planet; but he knew the cause of his uncertainty: multiple implications were crowding over the horizon of his awareness, triggering vague synergies of instinct and insight.

"Voss?" Blackfriar asked inside him as he made his way forward in the ovoid flitter and sat down.

"I'm here," he answered aloud.

"What I'm planning to do," Blackfriar said, "is to set our colony down as early as possible, so they can get a taste of the planet while we build the new habitat. That will give those who wish to come back a chance to return, either to us or to the new mobile."

Voss said aloud, "I'm ready to go."

"You're set to land at the square in front of the papal palace in New Vatican, the capital city. We've had word by radio from Paul

Anselle, the prime minister, that he will receive you. Later you'll probably meet with Pope Peter the Third, the religious and political head of the planetary government, which seems to be the only one. There is still no sign of any human settlement on the other continent."

"Any signs of hostility?"

"No. They seem to know about us—at least Anselle seems to. According to him it's been three centuries since they've had contact with offworlders. Your fastload of Euro-English should start you off well enough, and Link feedback will take care of what you're missing as you go along."

Blackfriar withdrew. Voss sat back and flowed outward through his Link, testing his connections to his world. Forests of data stood all around him in visual manifestation as he swooped through their woven centuries of growth. He took a moment, despite the routine action, to appreciate the beauty of the standing infrastructure, which held so much and was constantly growing from outside data and from emergent implications within existing lattices.

The flitter shot out into the void. With eyes still closed, he link-looked at the egg-shape of his world behind him, and his mind filled with the tide of understanding that was the foundation of his life. Here was an entity composed of a thoughtful humankind and its offspring, worthy of all the hopes of history—a constantly growing culture, secure at the basic levels of material need, yet open to the vastness of spacetime and to its own inner possibilities, poised to confront all of reality. The human individual had always looked to something deathless—to family, leader, nation, god; but they had all failed, while his world gave him longlife and endless chances at happiness and satisfaction.

He turned inwardly from the mobile and gazed at the planet.

With its fragile veil of atmosphere, its lumbering gravitational effect, its fractured masses of crust floating on a molten core and washed by oceans, it seemed an oblivious creature rolling through the night, waiting to swallow him.

11

"What do they want?" Bely asked like an aged child.

Paul shifted his great bulk in his high-backed chair and gazed out through the long, for-the-moment motionless curtains of the papal study. Then, accepting that he would be uncomfortable no matter how he adjusted himself, he explained what he had learned during his radio conversation with the visitors.

"But who are they?" Bely demanded, obviously failing to make all the connections in Paul's report.

"Descendants of people from Old Earth, as we are," Paul repeated, "except that they live in mobile habitats not tied to any planet."

"Is that possible?" Bely asked, grasping his hand rests with both hands and leaning forward toward his desk.

"They do it. With their level of technology, they can, it seems, use resources from just about anywhere. These kinds of habitats are well discussed in several volumes in our library."

"Yes, yes—but perhaps they're lying, and it's only another colony ship wanting to settle here."

"I doubt it," Paul said. "But they do wish to settle about fifty people with us."

"Only fifty? Why so few?"

"They are people who wish to leave their world."

"Leave? Why? Maybe they want our resources?"

"No," Paul said. "They can get those anywhere in this solar system. They're here for the reasons they've given—to contact us while they go about building a new habitat. Most of their business has little to do with us."

Still gripping his armrests, the old man fixed him with a stare, then leaned back. "Why are you so ready to believe what they say, Paul?"

Because I want to, Paul thought as he watched the uncertainties show in the old man's decaying face. *Because I have nothing left to believe in.*

Bely said, "They have no right to come here and ask us for anything."

"You will refuse them?" Paul asked.

The old man seemed uncertain again. "Perhaps we should," he muttered. "We must think very carefully about this."

"We could benefit from them," Paul said. "They command vast power and knowledge."

"Will they threaten us if we refuse to take their colonists?"

Paul shook his head. "No, of course not, but we won't be able to dictate to them."

"Yes, yes, you're right. We have no reason to refuse, and much to gain, as you say. But we can't just ignore the fact of their power and ability to do as they please, can we?"

Paul watched the old man's eyes, which would not meet his own. Bely's reaction to the mobile's arrival was one of confusion and thinly concealed fear, as if the heavenly host had arrived to tell him that his Church was a fraud. And there was something else. Paul knew it because he felt the same confused hope. It reached out from both their deeps and sought to embrace something that had been missing for a long time—a sense of the future, not beyond the event horizon of death, but in the life around them.

Bely sighed and put both his palms down flat on his desk. "We must learn more. Will you speak to them first?"

Paul nodded. "I'll report to you as soon as possible. Voss Rhazes, their envoy, will be landing soon."

Bely sat back and nodded. His hands came into his lap and grasped each other like gnarly tree roots. "That will be best," he said, sounding relieved, but unable to banish the look of confusion from his eyes.

12

Paul came to the edge of the terrace and looked down into the emptiness of New Vatican's great square. He stood there in a kind of mild shock, as if he had just awakened into his life after a long sleep. *What am I doing here,* he asked himself, *and who am I?* But he asked from a perspective that he knew would continue to tilt, if he let it, until he lost all sense of himself.

He remembered a square filled with a hundred thousand people yearning with hope as they listened to a younger Bely's words. Too often those words had been filled with poorly aimed insults, as the newly elected Peter III assailed philosophic confusion and anarchic freedom of thought among the young, then held out faith and obedience, not rational thought, as the bulwark against life's disorder and dismay. The Pope had never tired of insisting that criticism among the young supported only a tyranny of opinion and fashion in ideas, and had always concluded with a rant against the failure to trust in God's leadership. Responding cheers from the fearful and faithful had diminished with the years, as doubts allied themselves with thoughts behind the silent stares of individuals who had arrived at the conclusion that free exploration of what might after all be a godless universe, in which human freedom would be left to discover its own values and purposes, was the truth of things. Bely feared these freethinkers most, refusing to see the purely practical nature of religions and ideologies.

Paul had thought it of no consequence, since Bely would not live to see the atrophy of a theology that would nevertheless leave behind it ethical norms and a humane social engineering, and no one would miss the "necessary stories" that had once made people sit up and listen to lessons on how they should behave.

It was a vision that Paul toyed with occasionally, one whose reality would bring a great reconciliation of humanity with itself, with its fear of unbelief and outsiders to family circles, with its fear that without faith people would run amok.

But now the visitor in the sky would only quicken the questionings, and Bely might yet live to see the past topple into ruins.

Opposition had fallen silent with the recent arrests and exiles, but Paul was still suspicious of the rebels. They had been under surveillance for some time and had been too easily caught; perhaps they had been only the sacrificial offering made by a more deeply held resistance to cover its retreat.

In his study of Earth's Christian churches, especially Roman Catholicism, Paul had concluded that Rome had become nothing more than a huge bureaucracy supporting its leadership and workers. The top controlled a great fortune, and handed it down to handpicked successors; the structure existed to perpetuate itself, its wealth and its power, and for nothing more. Idealists would show up here and there, like small fires in the night, and smaller ones, candles cursing the darkness. Men like Teilhard de Chardin, who might have joined the great myths of redemption with scientific insight, or Father Andrew Greeley, who knew how to unmask the martinets and sloppy thinkers, and who had certainly known that better impulses existed beneath the storybook metaphors.

But before the sloughing off of religions as guides to conduct could be completed, Earth had destroyed itself. Islands of backwardness had launched themselves starward. He wondered how many had attached themselves to alien worlds and were holding back developments that would have ended the rule of ignorance sooner. "A belief system," he had written as a student, "is a way of trying to get around what you don't know. Better to profess ignorance than to invent. I do not mistake my religious feelings for the truth of theism." That rule of Earth was crumbling, despite the delay. It had been crumbling when he had written in his notebook. He could almost envision the end, but not its specific events.

Once he had thought that the fragment of Rome that had been transplanted to the stars might find a fresh start, but even here the old inertia had reestablished itself and served the interests of those who rose to the top. It was not entirely the fault of the creed's fictions, though dogmatism was certainly a bad virus for the human brain; it was human nature itself, that always failed to rise above itself, though it had stepped unconsciously out of animal darkness into some semblance of reason. Why could it not do more, now that it was aware of itself? He knew the answer to that question: no genetic praxis, no artificial intelligences—no stepping-stone toward the angels, in the form of a growing body of knowledge, existed here, or was likely to be permitted. One could light candles and curse the darkness, and stand frozen to the end of time waiting for change.

So it seemed to him on very bad days.

Paul tried to remember how and when he had slid into unbelief, and he realized that it had happened slowly, as he came to understand how even the scraps of knowledge available to him better fitted nature's character than the articles of faith that forbade their own denial. Faced with knowledge, systems of faith and hereafter were left only with insistence. . . .

He could scarcely recall the simple acts of faith that he had performed in his child's mind as he had tried to find God, to feel that presence within himself, and then be able to extend its authority to a belief in Jesus and Mary, the Angels, the Church's rule through Dogmas and the Confessional that mediated between God and Man. . . .

But there could be no such person as God, Paul's intellect had told him, leading him through long-chain thoughts to his present self, which stood both surprised and appalled at what he had struggled to believe in his youth—insane, arcane doctrines without an ounce of evidence, hinting at knowledge beyond human reason. In secretly rejecting faith's fictional means, he was utterly damned by its teachings, and convinced that it meant nothing. . . .

A shadow slipped across the sun. Paul looked up into the clear blue sky and saw the flyer catch the light. *The future is coming into the past to reproach us,* he thought as the craft became clearly visible. His engineer's mind marveled at the small vessel's control of inertia, so obviously independent of aerodynamics. The knowledge of gravitic technology existed in the restricted archives, but no one alive here could turn theory into functional devices, for lack of industrial crafts. Bely and the cardinals didn't want them, because anything that would make life easier conflicted with the tests of a moral life and might threaten political power.

As he watched the flyer descend to the terrace, Paul felt a deep humiliation; the craft's grace proclaimed its pride in the achievement of design and function; it sang of angels, of intellects that looked beyond limits.

The flyer settled gently, almost humbly, as if paying its respects to the force of gravity that had to be understood to make the flyer possible. A lock opened in the side.

Paul stood in place.

A tall, wiry man stepped out. He was dressed in a gray one-piece garment with boots. He was fair-skinned with brown hair.

"Voss Rhazes?" Paul asked from where he stood, wondering if the man had ever heard of Rhazes, the Arabic atomist and al-chemist of Earth's Middle Ages.

"I am," the man said, smiling as he approached, and Paul glimpsed the kind of perfect teeth that he had rarely seen in any-one except the healthiest of the young.

"His Holiness welcomes you to . . . the City of God," Paul said as softly as possible, hating the pompous greeting that Bely had insisted upon.

The visitor stopped before him and nodded. Paul tensed, but saw that there was no sign of judgment in the man's brown eyes. His gaze was open, guileless, and Paul felt an urge to speak freely to him, to suddenly voice his lifelong complaints, because the stranger would understand, coming as he did from a height of social organi-zation unknown on Ceti IV, one that had to be free of ritual and ruled more by knowledge than tradition.

But Paul restrained his rush of childish hope and asked, "Would you prefer that we go inside, or is meeting here accept-able?" He pointed to the elaborately carved wooden bench that faced the stone balustrade of the terrace.

"A moment," Voss Rhazes said, turning to look up at the palace.

"Stone and wood," Paul said. "It took fifty years to finish. Its model was the Palace of the Popes and Cathedral at Avignon, in France on Old Earth. I don't know if the original still exists. It's not entirely faithful, though. There are more windows here and this terrace, and the square below is more like that of Saint Peter's in Rome."

Voss Rhazes studied the sprawling structure for a few moments, then walked over to the bench and sat down. Paul sat down at the other end and tried to collect his thoughts.

Suddenly, as he turned to the visitor and saw his patient gaze, Paul did not know what to say to him.

"What are these carvings?" the man asked, gesturing at the bench.

Grateful to have something to start with, Paul said, "Oh—they depict the snakes frolicking in the tall grass of Ireland before Saint Patrick drove them out. A land of Old Earth. It was carved a long time ago."

"By a religious man?" asked Rhazes.

Paul smiled, feeling that he could speak freely to the off-worlder. "The large block of wood out of which it was carved suggested snakes in its grains and twists. The pope who commissioned the work wanted to burn the bench, out of a suspicion that it had been inspired by the devil, but he was convinced to let it stand here by his brother, a cardinal. After that, the sculptor convinced the cardinal that his work was needed everywhere, and had a job for life, doing walls, doors, benches, even fences, here and in the villas. He was not a religious man, Jacob Kahl. After his death, his journals revealed that he had carved only what religious people wanted to see, so his writings were sealed."

Voss Rhazes was silent for a few moments.

"He had a gift for aphorisms, many of which were stolen from him by people who later claimed credit. One aphorism proclaimed that believers and atheists had one thing in common. They both believed in hell."

The visitor nodded, but did not laugh or smile.

"Does our language give you any difficulties?" Paul asked.

There was another delay before Rhazes answered, as if he were consulting with someone. "No," he said at last. "My Link fills in whatever I fail to grasp of your divergent language. We call it Euro-English, but I see that there is much French, German, Italian, and Spanish in it, along with newer usages."

Paul realized with a start that the man's mind was tied to his world, and felt a quickened interest at the implications. All his world's knowledge and history was available to Rhazes, and was alive in him.

"Are we alone?" Paul asked nervously.

"Of course," Rhazes said. "My Link's only an aid. Privacy is a matter of my choice."

Paul smiled inwardly. A servant-god in the head would distress Bely, who would certainly view it as a form of possession. Feeling more at ease, Paul decided not to ask directly about the purpose of Rhazes' mission.

"Sir," Paul began with a show of formal politeness, "perhaps you will tell me more about your world."

"Of course. What would you like to know?"

Inwardly, Paul soared with the youthful excitement of his first years of science and engineering studies as his mind grasped after questions to ask, envying Rhazes's splendid access to knowledge.

"Your engineering," he began. "What is the mainstay of your construction?"

"We use a range of super-strong materials," Rhazes said. "Most large construction is done by our artificial intelligences directing robotic tools. Smaller projects are nano-built."

"You have nanotechnology? I've only read about it in fragmentary references." He knew that it involved microscopic devices, sometimes self-reproducing machines, that might enter the human body, even its bloodstream, to conduct repairs, in biological applications and more. "How long do your engineering studies take?"

"A half century or more. And most of it enables the student to design through the artificial intelligences, which do most of the work. One may study a large body of knowledge, but the bulk of it is unnecessary for any individual to know. Designers primarily seek the right questions to ask. Of course they do understand fundamental principles."

Paul took a deep breath. "How long do your people live?"

"For as long as we care to renew ourselves," Rhazes said. "We haven't found a physiological limit yet. Of course, there are catastrophic accidents that cannot be remedied."

Paul tried to keep calm. *They don't die,* he thought, and the fact sank into him, breaking through one layer of disbelief after another, and settling into a deep pool of dismay. He had always accepted the inevitability of death as a cruel joke. Life was not a predicament from which anyone got out alive. Bely's beliefs in the afterlife were wishful thinking, delusions, but here was the reality—not waiting beyond death, but in the material realm.

"How old are you?" Paul asked, wondering if Rhazes might be lying.

"Thirty-five," said Rhazes.

"You're very young, even by our measure, to be entrusted with this task," Paul said, then reminded himself that the offworlder was not here alone.

Rhazes gave him a look of curiosity, as if asking what age could possibly have to do with anything important. Perhaps the visitor's youth was an indication of the unimportance of his mission, Paul thought, then rejected the suspicion. He could conclude nothing about the ways of offworlders, he told himself, because there was no common culture to share.

Rhazes asked, "Would your government object to our setting a small group of people in some uninhabited area?"

Paul smiled. "Could we stop you?"

"Do you object, then?"

Paul sighed, trying not to show his excitement or approval. "I would not, personally. But do you understand the complexity of what you are asking? Our entire future would change. A group from your mobile might one day face us with a nation vastly superior to us in its inheritance." *And free of our dogmas,* he thought. "His Holiness would never allow it. Would you simply ignore him?" He hoped that Rhazes would say yes.

"We do not think in rivalries," Rhazes said, leaning back and laying his arms across the back of the bench. "You would also gain in having a neighbor who could be a source of knowledge."

Paul wondered how he could explain the matter to him. Bely would see the influence of another community as an infiltration by corrupting ideas, and he would be right; change would become inevitable if another authority became available to the people; it would become powerful without trying.

Paul asked, "Would not your colonists seek to become power-ful?"

"Then let them settle among you, in your city and towns," Rhazes said. "You would gain much from them immediately."

Paul sighed. Bely would never allow it, because it would quicken the changes and undercut his authority over knowledge and expertise.

"Change is deliberately slow here," Paul said uncomfortably. "We have been watchful of the past's errors."

Rhazes was now gazing at him intently. Were they truly alone, Paul wondered, or was this meeting being heard by others?

"I am an instrument of His Holiness," Paul continued. "Whatever my sympathies, I can only advise and persuade—up to the point of heresy. Then I must be silent."

"I will tell you," Rhazes said, "that those among us who wish to settle on this world will make their own choice."

"You cannot restrain them?"

"That is not our way."

Paul wondered if these people had any motive to do his world harm, but set aside the suspicion. "We can't stop you from settling the wilderness a continent away," he said, "but His Holiness will certainly refuse to take a group into our community—and that will leave you only the wilderness. He will forbid even that. Will your people come even if it is forbidden?"

Rhazes nodded. "I think they will."

"Then why ask us if you know we cannot prevent it?"

Rhazes said, "If you feel strongly about the possibility of having settlers from our world, then it might be better if our group knows that. They may decide to wait for another world."

Paul was surprised. Why did these people need a planet at all? Was there some kind of disagreement among them?

"I will present the matter to His Holiness," Paul said.

Voss Rhazes stood up from the bench, walked over to the balustrade, and gazed out over the city. Paul watched him and tried to imagine the motives of the world that he represented. What errant impulses might be stirring in their minds? Did they believe that this world had been claimed by its settlers too recently to be taken seriously?

Rhazes turned to face him, and smiled. "I hope we can meet again soon," he said.

Paul nodded, and stood up as the visitor returned to his flyer. In a few moments the craft rose, gripped again by the vise of its gravitic field, and Paul was again moved by its epic of pride and power. Tears strained through his aging eyes as the vessel shot away through the sky. *There is a place,* he thought, *where these little clumpings of individual awareness that feel for their plight and hope unreasonably for eternal life do not die.*

There is a place.

13

"They live for as long as they wish," Paul said.

Bely sat down across from him at a wooden table in the small meeting room just off the main audience hall. Paul's words intruded into him, bringing a thicket of worrisome and perhaps evil implications.

"Deathless?" he heard himself ask. "It must be a boast."

"No, Your Holiness," Paul said to him. "They are long lived. Not immortal, since they can die, but long lived."

Dismay filled Bely. If they lived indefinitely, then they could put off the Lord's punishment for wrongdoing, hold his wrath, or his reward, at bay for as long as the world existed.

"If so," Bely said, "then they cut themselves off from all growth beyond this life and the fellowship of God. They will never see his face." He paused, quieting his inner turmoil, then said, "Perhaps that is their hell, and perhaps God ordained it as punishment for their pride."

"His grace is still possible for them," Paul replied. "He can give that."

"Endless life . . . a testing without resolution? Torment without reward?"

"They will not escape the last judgment, when the universe dies."

Bely sensed both irony and admiration in Paul's voice.

"A traveling hell has come to us," Bely said. "Don't mistake it for a heaven. We carry too much darkness within ourselves for a corporeal paradise to be possible for our kind."

"They have laws and concerns for tradition," Paul said. "We should not judge too quickly. They may be of some help to us."

"I feel their Godless contempt already!"

"Calm yourself, Holiness."

Endless life. Bely swam in the thought, and felt hatred. The arrogance of the idea! It fed him fears.

"How do they live?" he demanded. "How do they hang between the stars?"

"All worlds do," Paul said softly.

"Are there others like this . . . this mobile?"

"Yes," Paul said.

They were out there in the dark, Bely thought, waiting to tempt him and his people, to cut him off from the life to come by confining him forever in the testing vessel of nature. The possibility twisted itself in his brain, and he realized that if he were unworthy to enter God's realm, then these devil worlds could provide the means to escape the Lord's punishment. If, as some claimed, God's creation was eternal, then one who lived forever would never know whether he was damned or saved. Acceptance of endless life might be enough to condemn him in the Lord's eyes. At the very least, endless life would mean endless doubt about one's salvation. And yet, Bely told himself, here was the way to prevent his end and secure the years he needed to complete his work.

Paul was looking at him questioningly, as if he could see his thoughts.

"They have come to test us," Bely said, "to try our faith. We must be both grateful and wary—grateful that the Lord has sent them, but wary of failing the trial he has put before us." He hated the tempter coiled within himself as he faced the possibility that his faith might not be able to resist the gifts of the intruders.

Gifts? Bely suddenly feared that there would be no gifts, and felt ashamed of his fear.

Paul was smiling at him. "They offer us a travesty of Pascal's Wager—the certainty of life for as long as we wish it against the risk of there being no afterlife."

"I do not doubt that we shall drown and be reborn," Bely said, imagining the black minutes at life's end, when faith might lead into nothing at all, and facing the final agony of knowing that one might have avoided it.

His minister was silent.

"I hate the starry outside," Bely continued, "where the suns are purely material engines, spewing energy . . . How many mobile worlds do you think these Godless starfolk have built?"

"Hundreds, perhaps thousands," Paul said, "may have been built since the death of Earth. As I described to you earlier, their numbers depend on their social pressures to reproduce."

"So they are sowing the heavens," Bely said derisively. "Now—when will this Rhazes return?"

"In about a week," Paul said. "What shall we be prepared to say to his requests?"

Bely nodded. "I will consider the matter until he arrives," he said, then sat still in the high-backed carved wooden chair and closed his eyes. "I would like you to go to his habitat, this mobile vessel, or whatever it is, and observe, if they will have you." He opened his eyes and saw what might have been a look of contempt on his minister's face. "Well, Paul—what ignorance have I betrayed? Speak plainly, my old friend."

"You cannot be faulted in this, Holiness. It is simply a matter of a little mathematics. This visitor is a world, in the full sense of the word. Given its size, and levels within levels inside the structure, its total land area probably equals or exceeds ours. It's a matter of calculating square kilometers on the inner surfaces within a given volume. Think of an onion . . ."

"I understand, I understand. Now what about a visit by you?"

"I think that can be arranged."

Bely forced himself to lean forward over the table between them. "The idea of going makes you happy, doesn't it?"

But he saw that Paul betrayed no feeling. He was too practiced a minister to do so.

Bely said, "I want you to assess the truthfulness of their boasts."

"You consider them boasts?" Paul asked. "If they can bring a world across interstellar space—"

"I want to know about their claims of power over life and death."

"I think we can accept them as fact," Paul said softly.

Cold tightened around Bely's heart, and he was certain that the end had come; but the pain passed, leaving only one thought in his mind. *Will they share what they have?* And he trembled with hope, hating his weakness, fearing that help would arrive only moments too late to save his life.

14

"His Holiness asks to see you alone," Paul Anselle said at the door to the smaller papal audience chamber. Voss Rhazes noted that the minister's face gave away nothing.

"You will not be present?" Voss asked.

"No," the minister said softly as he opened the door for him and waited.

Voss entered the small chamber, and the door was closed behind him.

"Please sit down," said a gaunt man from the dais, gesturing with a bony finger to one of the high-backed, carved chairs in the center of the floor.

Voss sat down, noting the man's unhealthy appearance. The eyes were sunken in a mask of wrinkles. His hair was white and wiry, combed back in a wavy mass. Even the most extensive rejuvenation regimen would be slow to help this body remember, Voss thought as he looked into the ruin of a face and sensed the rigid mind behind the eyes.

Peter III, the man once known as Josephus Bely, peered at him as if from a cave, and for a moment Voss was startled by this sight of a man's deterioration and the distant horror that it evoked. He had not known such a feeling since childhood, when he had first learned that he could die. The joy he had felt upon learning the first tenet of mental health—freedom from the fear of death— had been a great relief. This tenet was based upon some very early knowledge gained back on Old Earth, namely that when the sense of future time was expanded, removing all fear of death, a great sense of peace and happiness would come upon the subject. One did not have to go that far to achieve the equanimity known in his world—to live in complete ignorance of time's passing was not rational or practical—but the fundamental principle was the same: living with the certain knowledge of death produced lifelong anxiety and clouded the intellect. Only the strong-willed resisted, by denying death the victory of suffering in advance, living as if it did not exist, and making their contributions before dying bravely. The heroic example was the best that could be done in times past.

"Why are you here?" the Pope's voice rasped.

"I explained our aims to your minister," Voss said.

The man nodded slowly. "Yes, yes, but is that all?" The eyes that squinted at Voss held no evidence of happiness or equanimity; they showed a mind in a maze.

"I assure you, Holiness," Voss said as he had been instructed to address the papal power, "that I have stated the sum of our requests."

"In that case," the frail figure said after a silence, "I welcome you and hope that those of your people who wish to come among us will find happiness in our world. They will be welcome in any of our communities, and need not settle apart."

Voss said, "Some may wish to settle in a new area. Do you object?"

Again the Pope was silent, then said, "We shall see, after I confer with others. Please come closer. I wish to see what kind of man you are."

Voss stood up and approached the dais. He stopped before the old man's robed knees, looked up into the aged face, and felt a twinge of revulsion at the man's physical condition. It seemed suddenly impossible that any human intelligence would accept such decay and retain possession of itself.

The Pontiff opened his eyes wide, then leaned forward and gazed at him. Voss picked up the foul odor of the man's breath as he looked into the wet, unblinking eyes; and for the first time in his life he felt something like the discomfort of fear. He sensed the man's personal authority, his determination to decide the matters of his world without outside influence, according to ancient dogmas and theological speculations. Human advisors existed, but no artificial intelligences. The judgment of instinct and ritual ruled here, applying itself according to precedent. Voss knew that he was being measured by irrational assumptions.

Peter III leaned back tiredly and looked past him, and Voss felt that the old man had wished to ask him something, but was holding back. Finally, the bony hand raised itself again and gestured feebly, as if in disappointment.

"We'll speak again, young man," the Pope said.

The old man's head went back and rested against the red-cushioned chair backing. He seemed weary and unable to continue. Voss retreated slowly, then turned and went to the door. It was already slightly ajar, as if someone had been listening. He pushed it open and found Paul Anselle waiting for him.

By comparison with the sick old man inside, the minister's tall, bulky frame, hidden in black pants and a loosely buttoned jacket, seemed healthy. His thick black hair, combed back with streaks of gray, contrasted with his pale, relatively unlined complexion. Voss could not help but think that the Pontiff's ill-health was making him a poorer leader, and that the minister was this culture's actual ruler. For the moment it seemed to Voss that Paul Anselle was trying to see into him, to determine whether they now shared the same pitying view of the man who had been Josephus Bely.

"May I wander through your city?" Voss asked as they started down the hallway toward the terrace.

"Of course. I'll recruit a guide for you."

"I'd rather go on my own."

"You might get lost, or attract unwelcome attention."

"It's impossible for me not to find my way back," Voss said. "I will not mind any unwelcome attention."

"As you wish. How was your talk with His Holiness?"

"He seemed very tired," Voss said.

Paul Anselle stopped and looked at him. "He's suspicious after last year's arrests of rebels." He paused, then said, "I'll be very direct with you. His Holiness imagines that you might save his life."

"Why didn't he ask?"

Paul Anselle shrugged. "It would be begging—and a denial of his faith in the afterlife. He would prefer to make it seem that he was giving you something in return—the right of your people to settle on this world in return for medical benefits. But that won't solve the theological difficulty, which for him amounts to a deal with the devil to delay his passage into heaven."

"Were you part of the rebellion?" Voss asked, thinking about how a speculation having nothing to do with reality might rule a man's life.

"No, but I understood it. I think there's something else that His Holiness may wish to ask of you. I suspect what it might be, but I'm not sure yet."

"Do you also wish to save your life?" Voss asked.

The minister stopped as they came out on the terrace and looked at Voss. "There are circumstances under which life is not worth living. I no longer know what I want."

"Would you like to visit my world?" Voss asked.

Paul Anselle's demeanor changed. He stood up straighter and hope flashed in his eyes. "May I?"

"Whenever you wish," Voss said.

"In two days?" he asked.

"As you wish. Tell me, why did the rebels fail?"

"A plot to kill the Pope and certain key cardinals went wrong when one of the cardinals was killed too early. The assassin was caught, and that led to the capture of his cell group. Another cell made the mistake of trying to rescue them, and we caught them also. We managed to keep all of this quiet, but it's far from over."

"Was there merit to the revolt?" Voss asked.

The minister sighed. "That depends upon which values are permitted to be used in the argument." He turned away, clearly reluctant to say more. They continued across the terrace.

"Our world is also undergoing a revolt," Voss said as he kept pace.

"Oh?" the minister asked.

"There are now enough of us to compel the construction of a new societal container. Our constitution will differ in many ways from the parent mobile."

The minister stopped and said, "I don't understand."

"It will be an orderly process," Voss said, then added, "as it has been in the past."

"But you have people who want to leave your way of life entirely. Isn't that why you are here?"

"It's a very small group, and it's their choice," Voss said. "We are here primarily to gather resources. It might have been that this world was uninhabited, that your colony had failed. As it is, your world is sparsely settled."

The minister pointed to a flight of stairs. "This is the way down to the square. Cross it and follow any of the streets. They all lead back to the square, and to your flyer."

Voss was sure that the minister had much more to say, many more questions to ask, and wondered whether he was restraining himself or perhaps thought that this was not the time. The man looked tired, although not as physically devastated as the Pope; but he was also holding back, as if reluctant to learn more.

"Thank you," Voss said.

As Paul Anselle turned away, Voss went down the stone

stairs and started across the large stone-paved square in long strides. Groups of men and women were crossing from four directions, but the figures seemed small on the great stony expanse, and he saw that he would not pass near them before he came to the buildings on the other side. The afternoon was warm on his face. It was a cooler, older star than the sun of Earth, more orange than yellow, but still well within the range that made life possible.

He came to the far edge of the square and turned to look back at the palace. The minister was still on the terrace, looking in the direction of the flyer with what seemed to be great interest. Voss looked to the top of the tower that rose to the left of the square central structure, and saw a statue of a woman with a halo over her head. She stood on what seemed to be a globe, and her feet were crushing a serpent.

Voss turned away and went down a narrow street. A vehicle passed him with a beep of its horn, spewing fumes from its engine. The driver stared at Voss's clothes for a moment, then looked ahead.

Voss came to the end of the street and emerged into a small square, also paved with stones. In front of a few buildings, tables had been set under green awnings. Two men emerged from a doorway near him, carrying long, light brown loaves of sweet-smelling bread. Voss looked around and saw other people in the square. They were disappearing into buildings or stopping to examine items laid out on tables, and he realized that he was in a marketplace.

He passed a window with a display of locks and keys; another showed dead birds and portions of animal carcasses hanging from hooks. *A butcher shop,* Voss thought, and his stomach lurched; his people had given up killing animals for food long ago, and he wondered how it was possible to have ever eaten foods so poorly matched to the needs of the eaters.

He glanced at a table of plant foods, then hurried over when he saw a table of books. Many of the covers of the old volumes were adorned with crosses or images of people with halos. Voss studied the people around him, and saw that their clothes were of spun fabrics, mostly dark jackets and trousers, long woolly coats, skirts edged with embroidery, simple tunics and rimmed hats, berets, and other headgear.

Another vehicle came out of the street behind him. As it parked he realized that both vehicles he had seen were ad hoc designs, combined out of disparate components by an insistently practical ingenuity, and he wondered how many vehicles had been cannibalized to make these two.

"Want to buy it?" a voice asked.

Voss turned to his right. A man with a gold tooth was smiling at him.

"I see you like it," the man went on. "Best workmanship in the neighborhood. And I'll service it for you, for a reasonable fee."

"No, thank you," Voss replied.

"Can't place your accent," the man said.

Voss pointed upward and the man understood at once. "From the Visitor? I thought your clothes looked strange." He came up and touched Voss's jacket. "Wears well? Looks too light for me." The man's breath smelled. Voss smiled and crossed to the next street.

He glanced back when he reached the corner. The man was already telling others about him. Voss hurried down a tree-lined street, passing a horse-drawn carriage, and turned another corner.

Here the brick houses displayed curtained windows. Voss quickened his pace toward what seemed to be a park a few blocks away.

He felt a bit exposed and vulnerable under this sky. The air flowing through his lungs was not filtered, and his body was not fully protected from the sun's radiation. Any damage being done was already being repaired, any disease that might be present in the air was being attacked, but still, he might be injured in an accident, even killed. A bit of ground might give way in a quake, lightning might strike him, a flood might drown him, or a tornado might hurl him into the air. People died daily on planets, by the thousands, by the minute.

But unless he were damaged beyond repair, or found too late to be put in stasis, there was almost nothing from which he could not recover. There was no danger to him here; the Link knew exactly where he was at every moment. An effort would have to be made to kill or injure him, his connection to home broken, before he could be lost. There was nothing and no one here to do that.

At his right, a group of boys rushed down the wrought-metal stairs out of a house and paused to gape at him. He stopped and looked back at them. They knew that he was different, intruding into their daily life with his clothes and manner. What was he? Who was he? But these questions crossed their minds quickly, and in the next moment they turned away and ran toward the park.

By the time they were his age, he thought sadly, their lives would be half over. Their quick powers of observation and intelligence would already be in decline.

The Pope himself was only twice his age.

Human life flickered here, and was constantly starting over.

Memory was a series of fits and starts, order sustained by the enforcement of laws and traditions, by vivid personalities who left their mark of competence on institutions.

At home there were people who remembered the birth of his world, and before that.

A sewer smell almost made him gag. It was an unexpected assault. He hurried after the boys to the park.

15

Josepha was waiting for Paul in his study.

"Take me with you on your visit to their world," she said, standing up as he came around behind his desk.

"How did you know?" he asked, sitting down.

"It's obvious that you will be the one asked to go. The Holy Father's too old and sick. Take me with you."

He sat back, beginning to feel that he had been cast in a new role after his meeting with Voss Rhazes, and that there was no going back. He wondered whether he would be able to continue as the doubting right hand of Josephus Bely. The Paul Anselle he had known seemed suddenly to be a sinking ship of lost loyalties and despised ideas, without a single lifeboat.

"Paul—are you all right?" she asked.

He nodded. "I suppose there's no harm in your coming along," he said, searching her determined face for the young girl he had once known.

"Thank you," she said pleasantly, letting him hear that young girl again. "When should I be ready?"

"In two days. The Pope must decide whether to permit a group of offworlders to settle here . . . somewhere. We won't make a decision until I return."

"And he will decide then?" she asked.

"Not unless he gets what he wants."

"What does he want, Paul?" she asked as she sat down.

"There's more than one demand he'll make."

"You sound . . . disapproving," she said.

He leaned back. *Might as well discuss it with her,* he told himself, thinking of how many cardinals would invite him to their apartments, serve him red wine in small glasses, and try to set him to serve their individual ambitions. They all dreamed of replacing Bely upon his death. Josepha was at least as critical as he was, and more openly irreverent, and it might no longer much matter what he told her.

"The old hypocrite wants them to rebuild his health and prolong his life," he said.

Josepha bit her lower lip. "What do you mean?"

"I mean extend his life indefinitely."

She took a deep breath. "Can they do that?"

"Yes, they can," he said, suddenly certain that there was no going back, even if he wanted to do so. Josepha's reaction to his mention of extended lifespan, the way she suddenly struggled with the idea, was enough to convince him that Bely's theocracy would not survive the news. General medicine had long prepared the way for a collapse of theology. Medical skill was based on evolutionary biology, especially the use of vaccination and antibiotics; and these in turn were based on chemistry and physics. Nature had not evolved man so that at the end of each life a soul might be launched into the hereafter. Inventive theology had preceded honest studies of nature, but it could not stand in place of facts forever.

The future is our possible heaven, he told himself, *and the past our hell.* Storied theologies knew this as a cloaked truth, but they did not know to look for salvation in knowledge and its applications.

But now, to let the word escape that the visiting mobile was going to build another like itself in this world's sky, and that its people lived indefinitely, would open the gate to a new heaven and a new salvation. Bely was already in the grip of contrary ideas. He knew what they meant and how they pulled—with threat and attraction.

"I also suspect," Paul continued, "that Bely will attempt to trade with the visitors."

"Trade?" she said. "What can he give them?"

"He might ask that in return for land to settle, perhaps on the other continent, they take away our penal population—the thousand people on the islands."

"What?" she said confusedly.

"It would save their lives. You might never see Ondro again, but he would live."

"What do you mean?" she asked. "He's alive . . . what islands?"

"The Celestine Archipelago. Sooner or later, storms will sweep these desolate penal islands clean of all human life. That's why the condemned are sent there."

She stared at him in horror, but he knew that now was the moment to tell her, to side with the angels. Bely would attempt to control the news of what waited in the sky, but it would be too late.

Her expression softened as she saw a chance of helping Ondro. "But is it really possible?" she asked. "Will he agree to such a bargain? Will he even propose it?"

He saw that she imagined that there was a chance for her to go with Ondro, to leave one life for another.

Paul said, "It's something I can work, with no one being the wiser."

We need allies, he thought, and that was another reason to visit the mobile. Was it possible that the visitors would not be allies? He did not know enough—but there was a way to learn more. For every thought, think its opposite as possibly true, his old logic training whispered, even though that training had been restricted to theological gymnastics.

"But is it possible?" she asked. "How will Ondro feel about leaving everything to make a new life with these people? What are they? Are they people like us?"

"We'll see for ourselves," Paul said, "when we visit their world."

"Will we really be permitted to go?" she asked.

"We'll be there before anyone can think about it again," Paul said.

"Why are they here?" she asked.

"To build another mobile world," he said. "And when it's finished, parent and child will go off together, or in different directions. That's how their culture deals with increases in population and discontent among their people."

"How wonderful!" she exclaimed, and he saw the girl once more, the one he had promised to look out for—and who, he liked to think, might have been a daughter.

"I suspect," he said, "that they were also curious about us, to see how a colony from Earth was doing."

"Are there other colonies?"

"I don't know," Paul said. "There may be more mobiles than there are colonies from Earth."

"And some of the people from the mobile want to settle here?" she asked. "Why?"

"I don't know," Paul said. "I could better understand why some of our people might wish to join the new mobile that will be built."

Josepha sighed. "But will His Holiness let anyone leave by then?"

"He may not be able to prevent it," Paul said. "The presence of the visitors changes everything. He feels that even in himself."

"It may depend on how much force he can use to prevent change," she said with sadness, then looked at him with wide eyes and asked, "How will you stand against him?"

"I'll wait and watch, the same as Bely. The cardinals are all waiting for the next papal election. Each of the major contenders has his own forces aligned to elect him—but Bely may not die as soon as they think, even without help. The army guard leadership is also waiting to see which way to jump, as is the business community—but guards and business are essentially timid and don't want civil war. No one will act unless a clear line of possibility emerges. I'm sure of that."

And only Josepha has any idea of what I feel, he told himself.

"What about the island exiles?" she asked.

"They're helpless. Few of them have any family that cares about them. Bely, of course, believes that his authority is secure."

"Who will oppose his guards?" Josepha asked wearily. He saw a sudden look of concern for him come into her face. "Paul, how can you be part of all this? Why do you stay on, why do you bother? You might have retired to a house in the country a long time ago, and they would have forgotten about you."

"The library, the records," he said. "I would have no access as a private citizen. What else is there for me, except to learn? I do what I can, telling myself that it would be worse if someone else held my office."

"Do you believe that?" she asked.

"Yes, I do."

She smiled as she got up to go. "Then you must do more than you have done."

"I'll see you in two days," he said.

When she had gone, he sat back and felt suspended between worlds, wishing that he might feel more certain about what was happening. He closed his eyes and thought of all the imagined afterlives. If any of them were true, then he preferred the darkness to their banal servitude.

Purgatory wasn't a half-bad idea, since there one lived in hope.

But in heaven, one bowed to an inexplicable central infinity that needed no one, yet was said to love its creatures, but before which a finite creature was certainly nothing at all.

In hell there was no hope, and that at least was clear and settling.

No, he told himself, returning to his earlier thoughts of the day. All heaven was a hope that knowledge might one day grant new powers, and new powers yield even more knowledge.

Hell was the past, purgatory the present, to escape from one day, and heaven . . . was all possibility! No word was sweeter than possibility. It sang, and he heard a few lines of poetry written by his youthful self, saying to him,

"We must lengthen life
Beyond its youthful nightmare
Into a fairer dream,
Away from survival's hell
Where we sit and contemplate
The deaths of enemies."

The strength of his own words shook him, and he recalled heresies that he had once set down. "When Christianity is gone," he had scribbled, then burned, "we may yet pluck its ethical flowers—and embrace them not because God commands it, but because they are right! And if deep inside us the God of Battles speaks again, commanding us to vengeance, or to the murder of our brothers and sisters, we will say that Right stands above God; and if God commands wrongdoing, then he, or whatever he may be, is wrong."

He opened his eyes and felt like Satan, sitting damned in the pit. Worse, he loved his clear-eyed, clear-minded damnation. Bely would say that there was no greater fall than that, he thought with a smile. Then, sitting forward at his desk, he resolved that events must not proceed too quickly, that there must be no crisis until he had visited the mobile and knew more about its people. His youthful self stood up within him, decrying caution, mocking timidity, hating all delay.

But Paul made him see reason.

16

The flyer's swift, inertia-free motion squeezed Paul's world into a globe of blue, green, and brown—and for an instant he feared that the planet would sink like a stone into a black pool. Starry space seemed indifferent to the small oasis of life, whose only ally was the bright sun.

His thoughts quickened as the habitat's proud, sunlit shape swam into view on the screen, and he knew that Bely's world kept human life in chains. Mobile, free of scarcity's slow dying, the visitor's life was part of a new aspiring freedom that was forming out in the Galaxy.

"We'll enter through the long axis," Voss Rhazes said to him and Josepha, "where we still maintain zero gravity. Before we knew how to generate our own gravity, centrifugal spin kept our feet on the inner shells—but we can still spin the mobile in an emergency. You'll see something of the engineering shell before we head inward."

Paul's imagination played with the image of shells within shells wrapped around inner spaces. It seemed suddenly impossible for the one hundred-kilometer-long egg-shape to withstand the stresses of motion across interstellar distances; yet here it was, more than a century old, and preparing to build another. Endless intricacies of design teased his imagination, and he felt suddenly that his own world was hopelessly lost and that he had spent his life in a strange protraction of Earth's Middle Ages.

He glanced at Josepha. She sat still, looking with wonder at the forward view, her hands folded in her lap. When she glanced at him, he saw that she also felt disoriented as she tried to grasp where they were going and by what means.

As the flyer shot around to one end of the egg-shape, a large opening became visible. The flyer slowed as it came up to the black circle and passed inside.

"There's another such bay," Voss Rhazes said, "one hundred kilometers straight ahead, in the forwards."

Paul now saw a brightly lit wall of openings. The flyer drifted up to one, slipped inside, and the view became black.

"In a moment," Voss Rhazes said, "the cradle will rotate us into the first inner shell with gravity, the engineering level, and we will disembark." He paused, and Paul saw that the man was aware of the apprehension that showed in Josepha's face. "I know that all this seems unfamiliar to you," he said to her, "but you will shortly see familiar things in an unfamiliar setting."

Josepha took a deep breath, clearly overwhelmed.

Paul smiled at her reassuringly.

Rhazes said as he stood up, "We can go out now."

Paul and Josepha stood up and followed him out through the exit. It led into a long passage that seemed to curve slightly upward, but Paul felt that he was walking slightly downhill. He smiled inwardly as he glanced at Josepha, who was taking short, hesitant steps at his side. *Walking downhill,* he thought, *inside a world in the sky.*

17

In the green countryside of the central core, Josepha asked, "Why an asteroid?"

She stood at the forward end of the great hollow, with Voss Rhazes at her right and Paul at her left, near the elevator kiosk out of which they had emerged from the first engineering level. The inner land lay before them—grass, trees, bushes, flowers, waterways, and towns that seemed to swirl toward the light at the far end as if down into a shining whirlpool, but were miraculously held against the inner surface of the long hollow ovoid that would at most points seem level to the inhabitants, despite a rising horizon. They would no more question the firm ground under their feet than she would on the ball of her planet whose surface curved the other way.

"A good question," Voss Rhazes answered. "All of this might have been built without a hollowed-out rock. But it was our beginning place. We built where we first lived. We mined out the metals, and during that time the asteroid still provided a place of safety akin to a planet, since we did not reproduce directly from the parent mobile that gave us the tools, and then left us to build in the 82 Eridani system. Later, when we were able to make our own strong materials, there was no desire or need to get rid of the core. It was an old piece of nature, a park, and we had already built ten levels around it."

"Sentiment?" Paul asked.

"You might call it tradition," Voss Rhazes answered. "Our First Councilman Wolt Blackfriar likes to recall a city on Old Earth. It had a park at its center, and this is something like that central place of nature."

Josepha saw that Voss's answer intrigued Paul, and she wondered what the prime minister would say.

"Why were you at Eridani?" Paul asked.

"There was a group from the parent mobile," Rhazes said, "that wished to start a settlement on the second planet. But they became disenchanted with the surface conditions even before the mobile could leave, so they asked for the tools and an asteroid to start their own habitat. But some people stayed on the planet, even when our mobile left."

"Were you there," Josepha asked, "when this mobile was started?"

"I was not yet born. That was more than a century ago. These thirty levels wrapped the core by the time I was born. The visual records of construction are complete, if you would like to see them."

"So there is a human colony at 82 Eridani?" Paul asked, sounding even more intrigued.

"Perhaps," Rhazes said. "We have not been back to see if it has survived."

"How many stayed?"

"Several thousand," Rhazes said, then paused, as if listening to someone. "Sixty-eight hundred," he added.

Josepha looked at the wispy clouds in the great central space and at the gentle curve of landscape that surrounded this sky. *Heaven in a bottle, or an urn,* she thought. Up was toward the very center of the mobile, and beneath this soil and rock on which she stood was another level's sky, and another sky and ground beyond that—thirty worlds with more than a kilometer of open space between them, more surface area than her whole planet.

"Twelve kilometers to the sunplate," Voss Rhazes said, "about two hundred square kilometers of land in the core alone."

He went ahead, leading them toward another elevator kiosk. Josepha watched him as she and Paul followed, trying to imagine what this tall, wiry man was like inside; nothing in his manner or speech revealed anything—except that he spoke her language perfectly, as if he were being helped at every moment.

On the residential level above first engineering, Voss Rhazes showed her and Paul to a high structure that reached into a glowing bright blue sky. She squinted to see the top of it.

"Each building touches the next level," Voss Rhazes said, "and elevators from this one emerge into the first floor of a similar structure."

"How many people live on each level?" Paul asked as they went up in the elevator.

"About seven hundred fifty thousand," Rhazes said, "on each of the inhabited twenty-eight levels."

"That's spacious for that number of people," Paul said. "Is the population increasing?"

"Slowly," Rhazes said. "I'm one of the youngest." He almost smiled as the lift door opened and he stepped out in front of them. "You're on the fifth floor," he said, pointing to two doors. "The doors are keyed for you. If you like, I'll be back in an hour and we can continue your tour."

"Yes," Josepha said, eager to continue right away; but she saw that Paul seemed a bit tired. "We'll be ready," she added as Voss Rhazes turned back toward the elevator.

Paul was at his door when she turned back to him. He touched the plate. "I must lie down," he said with a sigh as it opened. He went inside, and the door closed.

Josepha touched her door open—and stepped into an old-fashioned sitting room, with chair, sofa, and small side tables, as she might have found in a well-furnished apartment in New Vatican. Light streamed in through the open windows, whose gauzy curtains had been pulled back. She went to the windows, stepped out on the small balcony, and smiled to see flowered vines covering the railing.

She breathed deeply of the warm air, and gazed out across the vista of widely spaced buildings, blue sky, and what seemed to be a hidden horizon. This, she realized, was due to the distant upward curve of the level as it continued for fifty kilometers to the forward docks, then wrapped around to the other side of the central core, which she knew was somewhere above her head, two levels away.

She turned back inside and found a bedroom and bath off the sitting room: one good-sized old-fashioned bed, and a bath with what seemed to be a shower inside a clear enclosure.

She turned and went out to the sitting room. Something in her wanted to laugh as she sat down in the big chair, as if she had just awakened from a bad dream into a happy one. . . .

Clearly, these rooms had been selected, if not prepared, to make her feel more comfortable, and could not be typical of this world.

But there was one disturbing implication that she had to face: She had to seem vastly ignorant and backward in the eyes of these people; that was probably why Voss was so polite and distant with her. He reminded her a little of the priests she had known. They too had seemed immune to her physical presence. They were obeying their vows and doctrines, but they also knew—though at the time she didn't—that she was protected by Bely. The bishops and cardinals usually took their mistresses from the Sisters of Martha—her mother had been one—but no cleric had ever cast an eye on Lesa's daughter. Josepha had once thought that might be because she was the daughter of a suicide; but now that she knew Josephus Bely to be her father, she wondered how many in the hierarchy had guessed that secret, how many might have avoided her because she was the Pontiff's daughter. Paul had tried to shield her from the whispered stories of her mother's death, but he had failed. Now she found herself thinking of the mother she had never known, whom she recalled only as a vague but comforting presence, and the father who had done so well at severing any connection with Lesa.

The women of this mobile world, she was sure, could not be like those of her world, content with a lesser place while hoping for greater blessings beyond the grave. She wondered whether Voss Rhazes could look upon her as a woman, or whether he had looked and seen the hopelessness of her ignorance and origins.

Josepha rested for a while, then explored the rooms. The furniture was familiar, but there were silver panels on some of the surfaces, and mirrored rectangles on the walls. She sat down at one end of the sofa, wondering if she was being observed.

"May I come in?" a voice asked from the door, and she knew it was Voss Rhazes.

"Please do," she replied, and the door slid open.

He came into the room and stood in front of her. She got up from the sofa, feeling uncertain on her feet.

"Feel free to ask questions," he said gently.

"What do most people do here?" she asked.

He looked at her as if puzzled, then said, "With a link, your question would have been answered routinely."

"How?" she asked. "Does it speak to you? Paul mentioned this to me, but I don't quite understand."

"It's located in my head, and speaks to me directly," Rhazes said. "Sometimes it speaks as you and I do. At other times, information is imparted swiftly. We each carry a bioengineered implant unique to every individual. If you had asked your question subvocally, the Link would have asked you how many activities and interests you would like listed."

"Do your people work?" she asked. "Do they have crafts and professions?"

He waited a moment, then said, "No one has to labor at unpleasant or brutal work. No one works to live, in the old sense. That's given."

"Given?" she asked.

"As a legacy from those who created our way of life, our basic framework of economy and energy use."

"So your people study and learn?" she asked.

"Not as you mean it. No one learns information beyond the short term. All knowledge is available to all by asking."

"Through a link," she said, then paused. "Am I speaking only to you?"

He nodded, almost with a smile. "You are speaking only to me, but I am getting language and reference help as I need it. I can keep that function open all the time, or I may restrict it. Many people leave it open all the time."

"So you are monitored?" she asked, thinking that Sister Perpetua would have called the Link a guardian angel.

"Yes, as a servant follows his master around to pick up after him."

"So what do people here do?" she asked.

"Most pursue their interests, as these have grown from early life. They participate in the dialogue of study in their area of interest. We have scientists in every area of study, from basic physics to social science and history. We have storytellers, even poets, who reach their audience directly through the visual and auditory centers of the brain."

"How long is education?"

"A century to start, then as long as the person lives."

"And you?" she asked. "You're not a century old, are you?"

"No," he said, "a little more than a third."

"What do you do?"

"Right now I'm part of the contact project with your world."

"So this was planned?"

"Yes," he said.

She looked at him carefully. He smiled slightly, but again she felt that she could not see into him as she could into Paul, or Ondro, or any of the people she had known in her life. They all gave clues about what was inside them. But Voss Rhazes seemed impenetrable. The only clear perception she had of him was his obvious physical perfection, and the sense of what stood behind him. And the Link. It was a ghost inside him, a kind of caretaker that whispered to him.

For a moment she realized that she had not thought of Ondro for some time now, and felt pangs of sorrow and guilt.

"Our people are always busy," Rhazes was saying. "Their interests and researches contribute to the store of our knowledge, and deepen the judgment of our Link intelligence. But we must know more. So we seek."

"Including knowledge of my world?" she asked.

He nodded. "You are part of the humanity that continues outside the increasing mobiles. We should know where it is, to better understand what has happened."

"And to help?" she asked.

"Depending on the circumstances," he said.

"But there is a big difference between the people of my world and yours," she said, taking a step toward him and noting that he was only half a head taller than her; somehow, she had imagined him taller. "Can you tell me the difference?"

He was silent for a moment. "Perhaps the best way to understand them is to spend some time among us, which you are welcome to do. In some ways we're not so different, Josepha."

He had called her by her Christian name. "May I call you Voss?" she asked, feeling it was only fair.

"Yes, of course," he said, still with his half-smile, and she stepped back, realizing that she was alone in the room with a man. When a woman was alone with a man, the nuns of Saint Elizabeth used to say, the devil is always present. She had no idea of what Voss Rhazes regarded as appropriate behavior between men and women in such a situation.

She steadied herself, remembering that he was his people's equivalent of a diplomat and unlikely to treat her crudely.

"The difference between my people and yours," he continued with no sign that he had noticed her apprehension, "was foreseen on Earth. Our average citizen is what an outstanding individual was during the centuries to the year two thousand. From fifteen hundred to two thousand, humanity on Earth expanded rapidly, using large amounts of irreplaceable energy in the form of natural resources. What was gained in this time was a body of knowledge that freed humanity from its natural, planetary roots, through a series of crises that produced a better average human being—highly intelligent and cooperative, now sharing through macrolife an open-ended cultural expansion."

"And you have no problems?" Josepha asked.

"We have different problems. Freedom from planets and scarcities of resources and energy, and from the psychological weight of short lives, have not liberated us from the nature that we find in the Galaxy, or from the inner need to find worthy goals to pursue."

"Have you visited other planetary colonies?" she asked.

"No," he said. "Yours is the first for us. It is an event that is being much discussed through our Link."

"And how is it being seen?" she asked.

"There is no one view, and there won't be until there is more contact between our peoples. Do you and Paul Anselle wish to see the other levels?"

"Are they all much like this one?" she asked.

"Yes," he said, "but they differ in landscape and architecture, and are larger as we move outward to the second engineering level."

She stepped back and sat down in the chair. He stood awkwardly before her for a moment, then moved back and sat down on the sofa. He might have been one of the healthy farm boys who sometimes came into New Vatican, except for what lived behind his eyes.

"Can I try the Link?" she asked.

He waited a moment, then said, "That would take some training and preparation, a few weeks at least. A lifetime, as you measure it, would be needed for you to feel proficient."

"But you—" she started to say.

"I have never known otherwise," he said. "The Link is a world in itself, a mind, a universe that one might live in to the exclusion of the outer universe."

"And how do you live in it?" she asked.

"I use it as a tool, a helper, not as an alternative to reality. In this I was taught by my mentors and exemplars."

He talks like a priest, Josepha thought, *and speaks to a god of some kind, and gets help and answers.*

"Would you like to go?" he asked.

She shook her head in sudden confusion. "Why are you here? To tell us how backward we are? We are, you know. And when they find out about you down there, they'll be afraid. Do you think you can help us?"

"Perhaps," he said with no hint of judgment in his face. "We're here to learn first."

She thought of Ondro again, searched for her feelings about him, and for an instant could not find them. Her world had never existed. She had awakened in this room only a short time ago, and was now recalling a bad dream, in which the man she loved was still suffering, and may have never existed. . . .

"Are you all right?" Voss asked, getting up from the sofa.

She stood up from the chair and tried to smile. "Yes, I'll be fine."

They went up the levels, Josepha, Voss, and Paul, stopping at each. She saw—

—a blue sea and a hundred sails—

—a desert growing strange trees and plants, where squat towns sat, and where it seemed to her that people thought long thoughts—

—green forested hills, where no one seemed to live, but Voss explained that these people loved solitude, even from the Link—

—grassy plains, with lonely trees and herds of strange animals—

—and mountains where people hid in the valleys.

Worlds were infolded within this hundred-kilometer-long egg-shape, and minds extended into inner dream realms. Were there any self-made hells? she wondered.

"Every landscape," Voss said, "that has ever existed on Earth is here, because someone or some group has looked back and wanted it. To have it physically, to know the difference, separates us from those who create imaginary realms in the Link's mental spaces."

"But theirs is also a way of life," Paul said.

"Yes," Voss said, "and they are free to follow it."

"And nothing will ever disturb them?" Paul asked.

"Nothing can," Voss said. "They see and feel what they imagine. They can have what they wish."

"But you disapprove?" Josepha asked.

"It's a disagreement," Voss said, "that cannot be resolved."

"Oh, why?" she asked.

"Because our inner worlds are not clearly separated from the primary universe, with which all minds are continuous."

"But you do not choose that way," Josepha said. "Why?"

"Because to truly find satisfaction, one must forget, at least for a timed period, that it is only a creation of one's own desires."

"And you can't do that?"

"No."

On the third level, they circled the mobile's equator over an ocean. Large islands appeared below them, and Paul was reminded of the Celestine Archipelago, where Ondro and Jason languished.

These people don't simply live, he thought as dozens of green gems rushed by in the blue water. They play at godhood. He knew that Josephus would think this, and fear the devil's paradises.

Yet as he looked at Voss Rhazes sitting next to him, Paul saw no pride or arrogance. If anything, he saw a modest desire to learn, to see beyond both himself and his own world, even to share his world with others. If he had met the young man in New Vatican, Paul would have judged him to have the makings of a good parish priest, one who might have cared more for his flock's mental health than for the politics of his order.

As the islands flashed by below the flyer, Paul felt regret for his world, but wondered whether his regret was wasted. Voss Rhazes, Paul realized, had many of the attributes of an angel—but Josephus whispered to him that all the devils had been angels before their expulsion from paradise, and that hell was the paradise they had built for themselves.

Josepha touched his arm and smiled at him. But the shadow that crossed her face told Paul that Ondro might already be dead in Bely's island hell. The atheist's death, he realized, had one quality in common with theological hell. Death and hell were both forever.

Voss brought the flyer low to race over the sparkling water.

"How deep is the sea?" Paul asked.

"It varies from fifty meters to five hundred," Voss said, "to permit a variety of lifeforms, including our own sea people."

"Sea people?" Josepha asked.

"Humanity with gills," Voss said. "They chose their way a long time ago."

On the second level, the last before outward engineering, Voss showed them a low-gravity world of winged people who flew through a blue heaven.

"How beautiful!" Josepha cried as the flyer passed over a

town where the homes were accessible to their inhabitants from the air.

Flying devils, Paul knew Bely would say while fearing that they might very well be angels, and this a heaven he had somehow missed. Paul could almost hear him shout, "These are not people! These are false creations from the inner hells of the faithless, secular reason attempting the work of God without his guidance!"

Paul imagined how he might answer this narrow view, which gave his old friend such a small range of choices between his God, humanity, angels, and devils. "Mind has many shapes," Paul said to the Pontiff within himself, "but it is all mind."

"The devil's mind!" Bely's voice shouted back. "These monstrosities have neither the wisdom of nature or of God."

Paul wanted to reply that nature had only martyred man, and that an infinite all-powerful God could only reduce man to infinite unimportance. But here, in this mobile and in many others, the voice of humanity and mind was strong, speaking for itself with love, courage, and reason, against blind nature. If ever the word God would find meaning, it would be in the fact that nature already had its God, in the form of evolving minds that had only to grow toward one another, away from nature's cross of blood and death, toward the grace and the light of knowledge.

"How wonderful!" Josepha cried out, and in her voice Paul heard the music of redemption.

18

Paul stood on the small balcony outside the window of his guest apartment and reminded himself of what he had learned on the tour of the mobile—that the inwardmost urban level on which he and Josepha had been given quarters curved away gently toward the forwards of the world, enabling him to see over what would have been the horizon on his planet. The same was true of views left and right, across the shorter distance of the egg-shape, but he could not see the curvature. Residential structures stood nearby, rising most of a kilometer to touch the night glow of the sky, each a column connecting with the upper and lower levels—the lower levels becoming larger shells, he reminded himself with wonder, until one reached the engineering level. Parks, walkways, educational and recreational centers clustered around the massive columns. The same warm air that circulated outside caressed him indoors. He smiled, and again imagined bringing Bely to the low-gravity level, where he would have seen a heavenly host winging its way across the vast spaces.

Paul had come out on the small balcony according to his habit of taking a walk around the palace at night; but that bodily form of worrying his dilemmas was not the same here. Deep inside him a voice suggested that he was at home now, having found the place of wonders that his studies had told him existed but which he had never expected to see. *This may be your heaven, and you deserve to enter it,* he told himself.

But he doubted, feeling that he was as credulous as Bely clinging stubbornly to his old beliefs, which could not do battle on the field of fact and evidence and had to invoke the bludgeon of faith. Hope might seem a poorer instrument than faith, but it was more honest in its freedom from embellishments. Hope had created the mobile world around him.

Paul thought about the people he and Josepha had seen during the day. They had been tall, varied in skin tones, and self-possessed.

He had returned their calm stares, wondering if perhaps a certain vitality was absent from their eyes.

He was imagining too much, he told himself as he turned and went back to bed, thinking of the usual litany of failures that he would be taking back to sleep. This world seemed free of the undercurrents of chance and history that had ruled his life. The basics of existence here were fixed and reliable. Still, he wondered how well freedom was used here.

He closed his eyes and breathed the perfect air, feeling physically better than he had in years. Then he thought of Bely, of Ondro and Jason and the outcasts on the islands, of opening the eyes of the young, of helping his world as he had once dreamed. It seemed possible now to untie old knots and give new life.

He smiled as he recalled the meeting that Voss Rhazes had taken him and Josepha to late in the day, after their tour. The planners of the new habitat had discussed the interior design of their new world. Most seemed to want an irregular interior of random surfaces, to be created as if crumpling a piece of paper. There was no obstacle to constructing such an interior, Paul had gathered, but there was opposition. This was what rebellion amounted to here—the decision to leave the parent mobile and argue politely over the architecture of the new home.

"The group that wishes to settle on your world has declined to meet with you," Rhazes had told him as they had left the meeting.

Paul had wanted to ask him why he and Josepha should meet with any of these groups.

"They want to settle a true wilderness," Rhazes explained, "and be free of any government. It's possible that they may pass on Tau Ceti IV and wait for the discovery of a completely uninhabited planet. But given the difficulty of finding such a world, it is more likely that they will settle here, on the other continent."

As he had told Bely, there was no way to prevent this from happening, given the disparity of technologies between the two cultures. Paul imagined that Rhazes had shown him something of these two groups as a foretaste of what to expect. Of course, there was no army, or means of transporting it to the farside continent, that Bely or his successor could raise to oppose colonization from the sky—not this year or next, or in twenty years, given the pace of permitted technical applications.

"In your view we're something of a classical utopia," Wolt Blackfriar had said to him and Josepha at the end of the day. His manner had been jovial, but with a hint of irony. Paul recalled that Josepha had listened to him without expression or comment, looking up at the tall but stocky man as a little girl might look at some great beast that had come out of the forest wearing strange clothes and speaking about important matters. "We have model urban areas, neighborhoods, parks, an open technical and political elite . . . with our political elite being drafted into office at regular intervals," Blackfriar had continued. "We go on the view that when you've solved the material problems, given individuals a chance to grow without fear of want or death, and limited the growth of power, you may have a mostly happy citizenry."

Human desires, Paul thought, would always overflow the rational means of satisfying them. Even here, where humanity was linked to helpful artificial intelligences, where there seemed to be no disease, where sane traditions of education dominated and were passed on, where knowledge was the guiding element in all decision making, and where humanity lived on the edges of even greater changes in human nature, undercurrents of discord still flowed—a better class of undercurrents, but still capable of causing troubles. At least that's how it seemed to him, until he learned better.

"Tell me about your most difficult problems," Paul had said.

Blackfriar had smiled as if expecting the question. "You want to know how bad things can get," he said, showing him and Josepha to comfortable chairs before the great windows of the common area in the residential tower. "There are always a few suicides, and personal cruelties between individuals. Separatist groups are always being born. They all yearn to start over. They will have their chance one day to have their own separatists. This is part of our constitution, which enables our way of life, generally speaking, to reproduce while containing any style of life that may develop."

"I was asking about more intractable problems," Paul had said. Josepha had glanced at him as if worried that he might embarrass them both.

"I know what you are asking," Blackfriar had said with a shrug. "We have the temptation of final happiness. It's hardest to convince very new people not to want it, that it's a mistake of both thought and feeling, since it puts an end to all exploration and creative growth, an end to dealing with the real universe."

Josepha had said, "Can it be had?"

Blackfriar had smiled and nodded with no sign of annoyance. "In dream worlds an individual can loosen all limits and be a god. Anything imaginable can happen when the individual's mental output is connected to his input, thus creating the experience of omnipotence. What the individual says, happens. There are those among us who absolutely decry this way, and want to banish it." He paused for a moment, then said, "But there is no effective way to say that this is wrong, or that an individual, or groups of individuals, may not choose it. Quite a number of our people already exist in such a state. Some come out of it. Many do not."

"How did this happen?" Josepha asked with concern in her voice, but not quite understanding. The closest she could imagine was addiction to alcohol or drugs.

Blackfriar sat back and said, "Our entertainment artists and engineers were too effective. All the written, audio and visual history we inherited from Earth helped to create vast, self-perpetuating secondary worlds so attractive, given the technical possibilities, that many of our people were content to disappear into them."

"But not all?" Josepha had asked.

"Not even most," Blackfriar had said. "The majority understood that this pursuit of pleasurable omnipotence destroys art forms that are joined, critically, with the universe outside our minds, and that to reject given reality is to turn away from art as a means of imaginative engagement and understanding in favor of novel intensity and gratification."

"But those who resist," Paul had said, "the majority, are they able to do so because they have never experienced this state?"

Blackfriar had nodded. "We do use secondary worlds to house those who have died in ways so destructive that their bodies cannot be repaired, requiring them to wait for new embodiment as we regrow their originals. But many do not wish to return once they have tasted direct wish fulfillment. Even a small degree is addictive. Remember, what they order with the output of their minds comes back to them as experienced input that is so vivid, so real as to be irresistible."

"It's not surprising," Paul had said. "You gave them a heaven."

"It's more serious than that," Blackfriar had replied. "There will be examples of macrolife, if there aren't already, that will become oblivious to the life of the Galaxy. We'll find them, I suspect, in wide orbits around young stars, living their virtual dream life. Nothing will disturb them until a star dies through some misfortune and their artificial intelligences must move their dreaming charges elsewhere. But if these worlds are well placed, then only the end of the cosmos will wake them, if ever. But who is to say how a civilization is to live? It grows as it does or dies, according to its history and the limits of physical possibility."

Bely might have his heaven, Paul thought, *if he could be slipped into such a state unknowingly.*

"But don't they know its unreality?" Josepha had asked.

"Yes, for a time they know. But forgetfulness is part of the addiction. Even before entering virtual godhood, it is argued that the best way is to go in and forget. Why spoil it with the knowledge of its unreality? There is an automatic withdrawal program for first-timers—but they always decide to go back in with forgetfulness as soon as they come out."

"How does anyone resist?" Josepha had asked.

"By not trying it," Blackfriar had replied, "by understanding the reality of it and the danger of unknowing, that once inside there is no coming out except by force. And yet, we also have philosophers who suggest that the universe itself is constituted in the same way as our secondary worlds, but we can't see the walls. Some of these thinkers insist on searching for experimental proof of the falseness of our universe. And once that is accomplished, physical laws themselves might be altered."

Paul had smiled and said, "So you also have theological disputes."

"Neither Voss nor I engage in them," Blackfriar had said. "Every kind of culture is to some degree a collective dream, unless one chooses to live under the tyranny of a natural environment. There are those among us who seem to want that—the ones who wish to settle in the wilderness of your world. No, we do not dispute with anyone. They explore themselves in their own way, we in ours."

"But you look outward," Josepha had said.

"We all explore ourselves to some degree," Blackfriar had answered, "no matter how far we look."

19

The giant holo image of her world floated in the great black space of the observation chamber. As Josepha sat and watched, the planet was swiftly enlarged.

One of the two continents showed, revealing green patches, brown furrows that were mountains, mismatched eyes that were lakes, and the silver ribbons of rivers. Bits of the large landmass seemed to have broken off and were adrift in the western ocean.

"That has to be Celestia," she said, "the continent of my home. And there's New Vatican, by the ocean. And the Celestine Archipelago . . ." She felt her voice weaken as she thought of Ondro.

"How were they named?" Voss asked next to her.

"After Celestine VI," she replied softly, still thinking of Ondro. "He was our first pope, and commander of the starship that brought us here. The islands are . . . also named after him."

"Does the name Celestine have any special significance?" Voss asked, as if trying to distract her from the sadness she felt. "The Link does not answer me beyond the meaning of the word celestial. It has no details about your colony starship."

"There were five popes with that name on Old Earth," she answered as she studied the image of her world. "Celestine VI took his name from Celestine V, who served for only five months in

1294 A.D., resigned and was imprisoned at age eighty-five, and was then murdered by the criminal bosses who controlled medieval churchdom. Clementine V sainted him as hermit and confessor, healer, prophet, and dreamer, who saw no compromise between the pursuit of power and the love of God."

She paused for a moment as she gazed at her world, and was about to ask Voss a question, but instead finished the lesson she had learned in school. "Our captain and first pope was a good man . . . who brought his people across the dark." She paused again, then said, "And he did not deserve to have prison islands named after him . . ."

A large pinwheel of clouds waited below the islands. She tensed and sat still.

"What do you mean?" Voss asked as she stared fearfully at the vast western ocean, then pointed at the pinwheel, hoping that it was not her father's instrument of execution.

"It's a hurricane storm," Voss said next to her. "Moving north."

A storm, Paul had told her, was meant to kill Ondro, his brother, and all the exiles. It might already have happened. There was no way for her to know, except by going there, whether an earlier storm had come through the islands.

She knew what she had to do as she turned and looked at Voss with as much agitation and dismay as she could force into her face. She told herself that it was all there within her anyway, but she had to show it to save lives.

He looked back at her for a moment, then asked, "You seem distressed. What's wrong?"

"I need your help," she said softly, grateful for the tears that came into her eyes; but they flowed with less force than she had expected. *The love of my life is down there,* she told herself, doubting. *His loss will be unbearable,* she insisted. *It is in my power to rescue him.* She wanted to feel more; but the place where she had stored her devotions was fleeing from her.

20

Ondro sat on the beach and turned his world over in his thoughts. He had never quite grasped it all; but now it seemed to him that he might remake it with mind alone, as Descartes had, from the ground up.

Humankind had fled here from a nearby star, arriving, luckily, long before native intelligence might have developed, and before long called this star the Sun and this planet New Earth. The refugees had lived through the long-promised death of Old Earth, though it had come not according to the Book of Revelation but through technological accidents and nuclear war, leaving only small settlements scattered throughout the homespace. These had sent out makeshift starships and self-reproducing habitats to the nearer stars. As far as it was known, all had gone by slow relativistic acceleration.

And what had come of humanity's new efforts on Tau Ceti IV? The old problems and conflicts lived on despite the freshly applied restraints of an ancient faith. The human creature itself was at fault. Driven by impulses and needs greater than its self-control, the beast even believed its own words of reform. But all thought and hope served another master in such a creature; its egotism lacked independent ground from which to examine its humanity. It could not reach inward and tear out its worst, and it could not teach itself to become a better kind of being. . . .

Christian efforts to remake human nature were useless, because sainthood could not be inherited. Authority without force was unconvincing and crumbled before rational doubt, and fled from criminal ingenuity's organized cleverness. Dogmatic faith and the fear of punishment beyond the grave had never restrained the powerful.

Pride had led Ondro to believe that he could have helped to change his world; but in fact he would only have helped to put his own clique of well-wishers into power. It almost made sense to him lately to imagine that life had to be a testing place for another try. The sooner he made his peace with God, the sooner he would be ready for the passage through death. Better not be caught unawares.

Rain fell on the horizon. Darkness crouched below the edge of the world. *This is the storm that will destroy us,* he thought, tasting the salt spray, wondering whether it was Bely's wrath or God's that was now so close to him. Religious practice was to have been a time-out from struggle, a moment of justice in which to ask not what is but what should be. It never was.

As he considered divine mercy and his world's unpracticed faith, his thoughts swam toward infinity, but were weighed down by questions.

"If we do not take the next step," Jason had once said to him, "the step from a cowardly agnosticism to a brave atheism, we will not be able to do what we need to do for ourselves, and we will always be looking to another life as the redemption of this one."

Jason had smiled at him one sunny afternoon in the great square. "I know—words seem too easy. But this much has been settled by thought. All you have to do is think."

"Go on," Ondro had said happily to a brother who seemed eager to open his mind.

"Take a look. Christian Thomism holds that man unaided cannot find salvation in this life, but will in the next. But secular reason also doubts humanity's capacity for progress, which is slow and sometimes nonexistent. Christianity holds out a remedy, in the form of grace that comes with faith, as well as a regimen of constant correction through confession, repentance, and atonement through good works. Secular reason is not far off, since it holds that in a universe of no revealed purpose, only knowledge and the finding of purpose through human responsibility can give life meaning. Anthropology is generous to religions—they have been a way of reaching into human nature for ideals, and a stepping aside from nature to see what could be. These are important goals, but their accomplishment can only happen in the future."

"Is that it?" Ondro had asked.

Jason had scowled at him. "Now keep in mind that both religious and nonreligious thinkers have agreed on one thing—that unchanged human nature has a doubtful future. Knowledge, work, and love are the sources of happiness to the secular mind, even though they deny personal survival after death. But survival is a dream of the future, where we may yet achieve life for as long as we wish it, if not forever. To forge a human purpose in the midst of an indifferent universe is a noble enough task. And whether religionists admit it or not, this is also what they seek— except that they give their ethical meanings a mythic pedigree, lest people fail to obey. Jesus had it right—meaning does not come from on high, but from within. And if there is a God, he will not punish me for thinking in this way."

All the history of human struggle had once been settled for him by Jason's proud, clear-eyed thoughts; but the perverse beast knew how to forget arguments, parallels, and examples. It knew best of all how to be dissatisfied.

If we return to God's being through death, Ondro asked, *will there still be moments when he'll leave us free to be ourselves?*

21

"Take me down there," Josepha said, looking at the patches of land in the storm's path, and realizing that she had to know what had become of Ondro. "We must get them out." She imagined Ondro and Jason in the green hollow, sitting on the grass, marveling at the sun that stood still at one end of the enclosed sky.

Voss was silent.

"They can't return to the mainland," she continued, still afraid that an earlier storm had taken their lives. "They have been condemned, but the authorities won't kill them. They want to believe that God will carry out their death sentence. I've seen enough of your world to guess that you would never put people to death."

Voss still did not respond. Maybe she was wrong about that, maybe these people hid their failures. *No,* she told herself. Even in her brief glimpses of this world, she had seen no police or civil authority waiting to restrain and imprison evildoers. Were there any evildoers? It seemed that there had to be other ways to deal with people who went wrong, perhaps through the Link. But as she watched the dispassionate way in which Voss considered her plea, she felt that this world simply grew better people from the start, people who had not seen much evil in a long time, but who would not stand idly by and watch evil do its work.

"Can we bring them here?" she asked nervously.

Voss said, "Those islands cover a vast area of ocean."

"Paul will tell us where to go," she said, hoping as she searched Voss's face for a clue to his feelings.

"The danger is real," he said. "How many are there?"

"I'm not sure," she said. "A thousand, I think. Can you rescue that many?"

22

The wind straining at the roof of the hut awakened Ondro the next morning. He crawled to the entrance and saw that several trees had been uprooted in the night. The sound of giant breakers roared in from the beach as the ocean readied to wash over the islands.

"Ondro!"

Jason's shape came out of the rain and staggered inside the hut.

"Come—we've got to get to the high point!" he shouted over the howl.

"What's the use? We can't survive a big wave."

"It might not come to that!"

The roof suddenly ripped away and the rain beat in as Ondro struggled to his feet.

"Come on!"

Ondro glanced at the dark sky as Jason's hands grabbed his shoulders and pulled him outside. Someone had spilled ink into the clouds.

Ondro worked to keep his balance against the wind as they went downhill toward the center of the island, but his feet kept slipping on the muddy path. He fell as they reached the low point.

Jason picked him up and they started up the path that led to the top of the largest hill.

Ondro looked up occasionally. It wasn't much of a hill, but it was higher than the rest of the island and flat at the top—as good a place as any to wait for the island to be washed away from under one's feet.

The rain became heavier as they reached the top. Ondro sat down in the sandy mud and put his arms around his knees. He could see nothing of the island in the downpour. The shapes of other men sat around him. It seemed to him that fewer than fifty were here—the ones who had cared enough to seek higher ground. The rest of those still alive, fewer than half the two hundred who were supposed to be on this island, were still in their huts, he realized, waiting for the end. He doubted that more than half of the purported thousand or more were still alive on the islands.

A chill went through him as the wind quickened. He opened his mouth and drank the rain. It felt warm and strange in his stomach, making him want to urinate. A tree branch struck him across the face. He fell on his back, feeling dizzy.

He saw how it would happen. The loose, sandy soil would not hold together. The hill would come apart. The ocean would finish the job begun by the rain.

He relaxed his bowels and relieved himself. It would be the last time. We take in, and we give back, until there is no more to give. He turned his head left and saw his brother staring into obscurity. Some of the men were cursing; others were weeping. He did not see his fellow students among them. These were the others, the criminals who did not care about changing the society, only about taking what they wanted from it. Death would come salty wet into their lungs after a forced night swim in the sea.

Ondro turned his head right, and saw a man who had just cut

his wrists. Blood ran in the mud around him as the man's face whitened. A hand reached out of the rain and picked up the dying man's knife. Ondro recognized Lemuel Annan, who seemed grateful for the knife. Ondro turned away, his heart beating quickly in his chest, surprising him with its show of useless vitality.

"There's something!" Jason shouted.

Ondro looked up and saw a strange shape descending toward them. Long, black, it seemed to be repelling the rain.

It stopped in the air, about two meters over the far end of the hill. It was a vehicle of some kind. The hull opened, and a warming light spilled out into the rainy gloom. Men began to move toward the light.

"Ondy!" Jason shouted, helping him to his feet. Ondro found his footing, and together they stumbled toward the vessel. Jason pushed him forward, and they stepped into the craft, bunched together with a dozen men in the brightness of the wide opening.

Pressed forward by the men behind them, Ondro and Jason entered a small orange chamber, and then a much larger one, where the light was a soft yellow. They turned around and saw that most of the men from the hill were crowding in behind them. After a few moments, there were no others.

Ondro felt his ragged clothing drying on his body as he looked around the bay. He was in a fever dream, still dying on the hill, his life stolen from him by a man who held the keys to heaven and was determined to keep him out. . . .

"Jason," he whispered to his brother, "don't let me die mad. . . ."

An opening appeared in the wall behind Jason. Three human figures stepped through. Ondro recognized Josepha—and felt fear when he saw Paul Anselle. The third figure was a tall, brown-haired, athletic-looking man. His clothes were strange—close-fitting, as if they were his skin.

"Ondro!" Josepha shouted, looking around but failing to see him. "Are you here?"

She pushed her way toward him. The men made way for her, staring in silence.

It was not a delusion, he realized. He raised his hand. "I'm here," he tried to say, but it was a whisper.

She came to him with horror in her eyes at what he had become. He clenched his teeth to keep from weeping, partly from shame and partly from the joy of seeing her.

She looked into his eyes, then said, "It's all right. We're going to a safe place."

Ondro looked at Paul and tensed.

"It's over," Bely's minister said, looking at him and Jason. "I'll explain after you've washed, eaten, and slept. You'll feel much better after our friends help you."

"The other islands . . ." Ondro started to say in a breaking voice.

Paul nodded. "They're being evacuated now."

"Bely?"

"He knows nothing of this," Paul said with satisfaction, with no effort to banish his look of shame.

Ondro knew, as Josepha looked at him, that she was searching for the man she had known. Unable to bear her gaze, he looked around at the other men. They seemed confused and slow to show relief.

He looked back at Josepha. "What kept you?" he whispered bitterly, fearing that she had come too late.

She stepped closer to him. "All this," she started to say softly. "Paul and I did not know we would have this help. Without it, there would not have been a way." She came close and pressed her forehead to his shoulder, but he knew that she was repelled by his condition. "I didn't know where you were," she added, "until a little while ago."

As she drew back, he started to say that Paul had always known, but the effort paralyzed his voice and he felt that he would pass out. Figures in white were coming through the opening. They came among the rescued and began to lead them out of the bay. He shivered—and blackness drowned his eyes.

23

Ondro woke up in a clean bed. He was naked and there were no covers, but he was not cold. There was light behind him, and the smell of grass and growing things. He seemed to be in a room somewhere. Anxious and confused, he got up and went to the open window.

The world outside was green; but as he came fully awake he noticed that the land rose upward in the distance and covered the sky. He closed his eyes and reached out to steady himself.

"Ondro!" Josepha shouted from somewhere behind him.

Her arm slipped around his waist before he could open his eyes and turn around, and she was leading him back to bed.

"Where am I?" he asked as he lay down and she sat down beside him.

She explained that they had brought him to another world. He struggled with the idea for a moment, then asked, "How many were saved?"

"Nearly six hundred," she said, "and they are being cared for." She smiled. "And no one back home knows about it."

He thought of the dead.

Then she was looking at him strangely, and he tried to recall the woman he had known. Her dark hair was shorter and pulled back. Her skin seemed fairer, her green eyes a bit more tilted, but her nose was not as delicate as memory insisted. Her lips were still full and sensual, but there was a rakish tilt to her mouth. What he saw now was a look of determination.

"Ondro," she said, "we don't have to go back. If we live here, we will not die."

"What?" he asked.

"People here live as long as they wish—centuries."

He tried to make sense of what she was saying, but the thought of never going home, of not settling old wrongs, confused him.

He touched her hand. "Can we turn our backs on everything we've known?" he asked, realizing that he had been wrong about her. She had acted, and with overwhelming means, at the first opportunity. But how had this all happened? Why had these visitors chosen to help her?

"Wait until you see what is here," she said. "You'll think that you've never lived before!"

"Where are we?" he asked.

"In a mobile habitat, one hundred kilometers long, in a sun orbit."

She leaned down and kissed him, and he felt his body tingle in the way that he had all but forgotten; but images of male unions blocked his way to her as he remembered the cold, futile effort of his refusals on the island, to men and the occasional woman. She had been his first love, his only love, as he had been for her. They had promised to be faithful to each other during their first night together.

He pulled back from her warmth, from the taste of her, from the refuge that he had longed for and been certain would never be his again.

She smiled and said, "Of course, you're still worn out. Rest, my dear Ondro."

He turned his head away. "I hated you, thinking you had forgotten me."

"I didn't know where you were," she said.

He waited, struggling with his feelings, unable to speak.

"Try to rest," she answered. "I'll be here when you wake up." Her voice seemed distant, as if she were disappointed in him.

He tried to relax, but he was still on the island, waiting to drown.

24

Josephus Bely was in turmoil as he waited for Paul to bring Voss Rhazes into the audience chamber. His minister's report after his visit to the mobile had made it obvious that there was very little of value that could be offered to the visitors. Theirs was a self-sufficient culture wielding vast powers. The material world, with all its evils, was their plaything.

But he was Peter III, in whose school of life worthy souls were forged and led into the fellowship of God. Of course, he would also have to get in line at the end of his days, but he had never been afraid, dedicated as he was to the guidance of so many. In this he knew himself to be selfless, so he had not expected the crushing fear that came into him when he saw his own death approaching. It was not possible that he should still be so afraid, even now, as he waited for the visitor.

He prayed—and felt the grace of God's strength flow through him as the door to the audience chamber opened.

"I will speak with the envoy alone," Bely said as his minister and Voss Rhazes came in and stopped before the dais.

Paul nodded calmly and left the chamber, making Bely feel even more uncertain. He had expected resistance, a question, a look; but his minister's reaction seemed uncaring.

Bely felt lost as he looked now to Voss Rhazes, and saw that there was nothing in the man's expression. He simply stood waiting, looking at him and not looking at him. Bely felt irritated, realizing that without any obvious effort this visitor held the initiative, all control of what might be said. *It's my fault,* Bely told himself, *my fear is doing his work for him.*

Bely said, "You may settle your group on the other continent, if you wish. In return I ask for your medical help, so that I might live to finish my work."

He had said it well, without hesitation, without demanding, and without fear.

But the moment before the visitor replied became an eternity. Bely heard a rushing in his ears, and knew that he would beg for his life. Only a fool would risk the passage through death to learn the truth of dying, when it would be too late; there would be nothing to learn if the end was oblivion, not even that it was oblivion. Only faith offered the certainty of successful passage.

Terror constricted his bowels. What if the Divinity let the doubters fade away at death, damning them with the very darkness that they so feared, while the saved emerged into the

Divine presence? *The fool hath said in his heart: There is no God.*
His brain repeated the ancient bit of wisdom from his school
days, which now spoke to him like a stranger. *But what if the fool
had not been a fool?* The prideful question from his youth was
still there, along with a hundred answers drilled into him by his
teachers. Why had there been so many answers to plague one
question?

Voss Rhazes said, "I am communicating your offer to First
Councilman Blackfriar."

Bely's thoughts raced with his pulse as he understood again
that the offworlders' minds were somehow linked. "May I have an
answer now?"

"A day or two, at most," Rhazes said.

Bely felt his hands tremble beneath his robes. Darkness
blinked in his eyes. "I may not live a week," he said. "Why not an
answer now?"

Rhazes nodded. "I'll go at once."

Bely breathed deeply, struggling to conceal his humiliation as
the visitor turned and left the chamber. Voss Rhazes had brought
evil into his heart, poisoning his spirit with a vision of his people
ascending to the false heaven in their sky, lured by an immortality
of the flesh.

I am unworthy of God's love, he told himself as he looked
around the empty chamber. He had not confessed for months now.
Each time it was a matter of finding a priest from a distant town-
ship and confessing in elaborate generalities, never speaking of
his despair over death, or about his lapses of faith. It would not do
for de Claves, or any of his past confessors, to know his weaknesses and pass them on to the other bishops. At any moment he
might die in a state of mortal sin, unconfessed, lying to himself

that God knew what was in his heart and would not punish him for his passing moments of unbelief.

Then he wondered whether his request for help might anger the visitor in the sky and bring the wrath of devils upon his world. He prayed again to believe that death would send him back to God, but the doubt sown long ago in his imagination had waited a long time to blossom, and now took strength from Paul's report and Voss Rhazes' visit, stifling his plea.

"Oh Lord . . . forgive my unbelief . . . and grant me eternal life," he said out loud, stumbling over his words, and wept.

25

"He asked you for his life," Paul said as he stood with Rhazes at his flyer. A chill came into the air on the terrace as the sun was setting.

"You knew he would?" Voss asked.

Paul nodded. "Will you grant it?"

"He is very ill," said Rhazes, "and in ways I have never seen."

Paul looked directly at him and said, "If you do save him, then nothing will change."

There, he had said it, and was now a conspirator. All his life he had compromised. Now here was his coup, set in motion with soft words to a stranger from beyond the sky, a few words to kill a man. . . .

"But you are the pope's right hand," Rhazes said.

Paul nodded. "I have not opposed him because there was never any chance. The rescue of the prisoners from the islands has shown me that we may have a chance to change." Paul sighed and said, "Let him die. It was only chance that brought you here."

"But who will replace him?" asked Rhazes.

"Anyone would be better."

Rhazes said, "Even with his illness, he might still last five years."

"That long?"

"Perhaps two. I can only guess, based on what I see. I don't know enough about his specific ailments. Or he might die today."

Paul looked out over the darkening city and wondered whether he could take decisive action rather than follow the rules of succession. There were at least a dozen individuals he might take into his confidence—but after that there would be no guarantees.

"Would you like to come with us when we leave?" Rhazes asked.

Paul smiled. "I had not intended to ask you for my life."

"But you would come?"

"I don't know," Paul said.

Rhazes said, "Blackfriar and the Council will have to meet to consider all these matters. I'll return as soon as possible."

Paul watched him enter his craft. The ovoid rose after a few moments, and Paul again took pleasure from its graceful motion as it disappeared into the sea of evening.

26

Josephus Bely sat gripping his armrests, eyes gazing inward.

"Are you well, Your Holiness?" Paul asked, knowing that there could be no solution to the pontiff's dilemma, no escape from the humiliation of asking for his life while professing belief in the life to come. For him to seek a material salvation was the rebellion of the angels. Pride danced with fear; hope seduced despair; personal authority warred with the leadership of faith.

The flesh on Bely's face finally moved. The eyes came out of their abyss and gazed at Paul as he stood before the dais. He felt some guilt about his considered betrayal, but only a weak sense of wrong; the man stood in the way of his people, and had done so for much of his life.

"They will refuse me," Bely said with a rasping voice.

Paul now felt a twinge of pity for the old man and said, "Perhaps they will offer medical help, rather than . . . the blasphemy of rejuvenation," and wondered why he had thrown him this theological bone.

Bely's face filled with color. The eyes focused sharply. "So you oppose my survival?" he asked, his mouth opening into a moist red hole, and Paul's sympathy faded.

"No, Your Holiness, but faith requires—"

"I am infallible on all matters of doctrine. However long I live, the Lord's judgment will still come with the world's end, and no one will escape."

Therefore, Paul thought, *he reasons that it will not be wrong for him to live as long as he pleases. The temptation is too great to resist.* The old man had given it some clever thought.

Bely's head slumped onto his chest. Blood drained from the pontiff's face. Paul went up the three steps and felt the old man's pulse. It still beat strongly. He had only fainted.

Paul stood over him, debating whether he should call a physician, knowing that this might be a good moment to chance letting the old man die. All he had to do was leave.

He checked the pulse again. It was still strong, making it likely that Bely would only sleep.

Leave now, he told himself.

But he could not do it.

After a moment, he decided to call Palo, the pontiff's valet, and leave it to him to get Josephus to bed and call a doctor.

27

Bely seemed very much recovered when Paul came into the papal study the next morning, as though he had slept deeply after his fainting spell.

"This!" the old man shouted, looking up from his desk. "Petitions from three hundred people to emigrate to the new world. De Claves seemed to enjoy delivering them to me personally."

Paul sat down in the chair facing the large, carved wooden desk. Another of Kahl the Apostate's creations, which Bely's servants, the Sisters of Martha, kept so well polished. As usual, the struggle between the motionless angels and devils was unresolved.

"And at least as many of theirs want to come here!" The old man shook his head and almost smiled. "I do not understand. Should we grant permissions to both groups?"

Paul shifted in his chair, sympathizing with Bely's confusion. One group wished to ascend to heaven, while the other wanted to go, if not to hell, then to a lesser life. It was one way of looking at the problem.

"It would do no harm," Paul said, "to let them go. After all, their faith is probably very weak." That was true, as far as it went.

Those who would be forced to stay would not be a credit to Bely's regime.

Bely gave him a sharp-eyed look, showing something of his youthful shrewdness, as if he completely understood the sky-dwellers.

"Yes, I see—but why do they wish to come here?"

Paul said, "Human dissatisfaction knows no limits."

Bely nodded and sat back. "Yes, yes, you're probably right. And we would be well rid of the people who want to leave us." The old man rubbed his hands together, as if warming them over an invisible fire. "I want you to convey a message to Blackfriar's council. Tell them that their people can settle here with no conditions. They may do so on the other continent, or here amongst us, whether I am granted my request or not."

Paul nodded, not surprised. Bely was gambling, betting on a show of generosity.

"I will convey your words, Your Holiness."

The old man looked at him for a moment, his eyes unusually bright. It was a spell of alertness that sometimes came to the aged, when they seemed to regain an early vigor; he would probably pay for it with exhaustion at day's end. Paul wondered whether he himself displayed such tendencies, but was unable to reach a conclusion. How could he, with no one to tell him? And he would be unable to see the truth once he was that far gone.

"Find Josepha for me," Bely said. "I need to talk to her."

Paul nodded, wondering what the old man had in mind. "Go—go find her!"

Paul stood up and left the study, still wondering how much to credit the old man's spasm of youthful energy. But his feeling of suspicion was strengthened as he noted the number of papal guards in the hallways, along with a few of the city police. He counted ten armed men on the way to the terrace, but could not imagine what their presence could accomplish.

28

Voss paused in his walk with Blackfriar through the preserve of tall birch trees. The sunplate was at its brightest, filling the hollow with yellow-orange light. Small clouds drifted in the great central space. A gentle breeze stirred the leaves on the trees. Voss thought again of the storm that had swept through the Celestine Archipelago, and was happy to be here, talking to his mentor.

"From what you've told me," Blackfriar said, stopping next to him, "This pope, this leader, has had his time, his triumphs, and his mistakes. But if he wanted to leave his world and start a new life with us, that would be another matter. More life would give him a chance to change."

Voss said, "No, he only wants more of what he has, to stay in power. It's clear there is opposition to him, and his own prime minister has his doubts about him and thinks the society would be better off without him. These people have been held back— most of them have never had a chance to pursue the knowledge that would reveal to them their true human heritage, or a more equitable and just society. We could help this Josephus Bely, Peter III, and hope he might change if the fear of imminent death was removed from his mind. But it's more likely that he would only perpetuate a rigid and repressive regime that most benefits those who enter the church's service. The whole system is top-heavy and ready for change, but it might hang on for decades by imprisoning opposition leaders and their followers."

"Then we won't help him. Medical care, yes, but no rejuvenation. Do you think he's sincere about not setting conditions for our people to settle?"

"He may withdraw the offer," Voss said, "as soon as we deny him longlife. What then?"

They resumed their walk.

"We can't stop our people from leaving," Blackfriar said. "No one will find them on the other continent. No one will search. It will be years before the two groups come into any kind of contact, assuming our people don't call us back before the new mobile is completed and we prepare to leave."

"And we will have an additional group from the planet joining the mobile, according to Paul Anselle."

"But will they be permitted to leave?" asked Blackfriar.

"Paul will see to it."

"And the prison refugees?"

"They have nowhere to go on their world," Voss said. "Most of them will want to stay, if not with us, then to join the new mobile. Paul has assured me that he will not tell the pope what has become of them."

"The new mobile will have a good, hybrid start, with the Cetians."

"I wonder," Voss said as they walked on, "how many will wish to stay. They know that to go back would mean imprisonment, maybe even execution."

Blackfriar smiled. "Yes, it reminds me of the old Christian missions. Derelict human beings would come to them for food, even if they had to hear a sermon first. The Cetian prisoners know that we saved their lives. Soon they will know that if they stay with us we can lengthen their lives. Still, I think some might go back with our colonists, preferring a natural environment on their own world."

Voss nodded and said, "What troubles me is that it's still our humankind down there, living in an archaic system that's about to fall apart. Our example may shorten a dark age, by showing them they don't have to have a theocracy to raise law-abiding citizens."

Blackfriar glanced at him as they walked. "I think many of them already know that—Paul Anselle, for one. But I sometimes ask myself what right we have to confront a culture that has no power to resist us. Perhaps it would be best to leave them to progress by themselves, with no other example before them except their own ideals."

Voss said, "At least they're not facing any kind of fatal crisis. There seems to be no warfare. We can leave them alone to survive their own changes."

"There are few legal rights involved here," Blackfriar said, "and no laws have been invoked against us. We do what our rational traditions indicate is right. However, if local laws were invoked against us, we might have to follow the precedent of respecting them. If there was some kind of consensus against our presence, then we would have to leave."

"So what are we facing?" Voss asked.

"An incoherent culture," Blackfriar said, "a planet inhabited by invaders. It's likely that their ancestors killed what native intelligence was developing. Or else they arrived too early in the planet's history and diverted its natural development, and unknowingly prevented intelligent life from arising. The current generation is most likely unaware that its presence is something of a continuing injustice."

"Perhaps we should do as little as possible here," Voss said, thinking of Paul.

"We're not dealing with a fixed identity," Blackfriar said. "Whatever we do will only quicken the inevitable. There are some fifty million people here, and they will progress. As the new mobile is being built, shuttles will go down and pick up as many people as will care to join us, and as many of us who wish to leave. Nothing can stop that. Their transport system consists of railroads, a few dirigible aircraft for use by regional governors and police forces, and limited motorized vehicles. There's nothing they can do to prevent our people, or their own, from coming and going, or even from taking an interest while we're here."

"Bely might be angered," Voss said.

"If he's sufficiently composed to think clearly, he won't interfere," Blackfriar said. "There's probably not much he can do for his people now except pass peacefully from a changing scene."

"I wonder if the College of Cardinals will elect a more enlightened man when Josephus Bely dies."

"We may be gone by then," Blackfriar said, "and they can get on with their problems."

"I still wish we could help them openly and decisively," Voss said.

"We did not come here for that, and they will not perish without us, from what we've seen."

"You can't deny our sympathy for a kindred human culture."

"I know, I know," Blackfriar said. "But it would be an endless job to help them significantly. It would mean annexing a culture and denying it its own development. The best we can do is leave them as much as they might profit from later, slowly. It's the only way, short of ignoring them or taking them over."

"But we do know better about almost everything," Voss said.

"That would not be enough, because we don't know enough about them. A century from now, if we come back this way, we'll know what good this glancing contact will have done, and then our help might be more effective."

Voss felt a moment of dismay, recalling how much of human history had raged beyond the control of reason. "Do we know what we're doing here?" he asked.

"We've never done this," Blackfriar said. "Rather than say we don't know what we're doing, I would say that we've entered into a constructive situation. We've recontacted a bit of our heritage from Earth. You've helped some people who were in danger of their lives, found a place for our own rebels to settle, and opened the door for any Cetians who may wish to join us. It's the kind of fair exchange one might expect when two cultures meet. It happens when mobiles meet, and will continue to happen."

Blackfriar was right about the fair exchange, but Voss felt uneasiness clouding his reason, preventing him from seeing ahead. Even the Link agreed that the entire situation was too vague to make judgments about, and the only certainty was that the habitat would stay a while, build another, lose and acquire some population, and then leave, either alone or with the new mobile.

As they neared an elevator kiosk, Voss thought of the new link intelligence that would be born on the new mobile, and how it would receive its education. He also thought of Josepha, and felt a moment of pleasure that she would be staying.

29

Ondro awoke and saw his brother watching him.

"Welcome back," Jason said, shifting in a chair by the bed. The harried look of bodily starvation was gone from his face as he smiled, but he was still lean.

"Jason," Ondro said, "I dreamt you were not rescued with the others." He tried to sit up and failed.

"We went into the flyer together, dear brother."

"The water . . . was washing everything away. I wake up in the dream, drowned. It's true in the dream. I feel dead."

"You'll recover. Up to talking?"

Ondro nodded, remembering.

"What do you think of this place? I haven't seen much of it yet."

Ondro said, "They saved our lives, and they will give us back our health." He took a deep breath and lay back, trying to order his thoughts. "When we're well, will they send us back?"

Jason seemed confused by the question. "If we want to go back," he replied. "To go back would be to die in a few decades."

"Will they let us stay?" Ondro remembered his short conversation with Josepha, but it seemed unreal.

"Yes, they will," Jason said. "Do you want to go back?" He spoke as if freed from a burden.

"So much remains to be done. There may be a better chance

now of changing things." Again he felt that he might lose himself as he saw the calm expression on his brother's face.

"The cardinals will elect another one like Bely, maybe worse," Jason said.

"Maybe these people here will help us topple the papacy once and for all. Do you think they might do that? Our cause is just."

"And install us in power?" Jason asked.

"Why not? We've thought long and hard about what must be done, and nearly died for it."

"Our people might not like us any better," Jason said, "and we might not do better."

Ondro sat up. "No—ours would be a democratic regime, and we'd be voted out in time if they were dissatisfied, and others would have a chance. Jason, if these people help us, we could remake our world."

"I think Josepha wants to stay here," Jason said.

"But can we just forget everything? Our father's land and house?"

Jason stood up, looking agitated. "Just think—we've survived Bely's torments! A century from now, when he's dust, we may still be alive, still looking forward to life. What in all hell do you want to drag yourself back to?"

Ondro took a deep breath and asked, "Have you seen that much of this place to be so sure?"

"I know that to go back is sure and certain suicide. We would be letting our lives . . . simply run out."

"Do you know that? Are you so sure you know what this place is?"

"I've seen enough—and Josepha has seen more. She'll tell you." He stepped closer to the bed. "When you feel better, we'll all go looking. You'll see. This is a world, and it's big—bigger than a dozen of ours."

"I don't understand," Ondro said, lying back again, exhausted. How could he forget everything and start over?

"You'll see, dear brother, you'll see."

30

My faults will be forgiven, because I have confessed them, Josephus Bely told himself as he looked out over the sleeping city and the dreaming ocean beyond. *Imperfection is the very nature of man. I will be forgiven.*

His wrongs had been practical necessities, crucial to the survival of the papacy. He had lied only to those who did not have a right to know the truth, as a soldier would lie to hide the truth when captured by his enemies. Suddenly he missed the Jesuit order, and regretted that so few of them had survived the journey from Earth. There would have been better defenses made of faith if the likes of a Francisco Suarez had come with them to this new world. The Jesuit philosopher had known the complexities of lying and truth telling. A hearer of the truth must deserve to hear it, making it right and proper to lie before enemies.

My sins are mine, not my people's, Bely insisted to himself, then looked up into the night sky. The world up there among the stars was an evil orphan, a bit of Old Earth that had wandered in from the night. It had come to steal not only resources but souls— and it would fail, if he had the courage to oppose it. Proof of its evil lay in the manner by which it had tempted him to desire immortality of the flesh, preying upon his hope to live long enough to put his world in order.

Doubts crept into him like vermin, shaming his faith. *You are a backward people, clinging to a faith that only soothes the pain of death,* the devil said within his secret places, tempting him to leave his world of insoluble problems and live among the stars for endless centuries, free of the weight of an office that had outlived its usefulness and must now yield to a better way. He would cease to be Josephus Bely, Peter III, and become someone else, with a new body and a clear mind. Surely this promised more than this temporal power that waited on the word of a God who never showed himself?

But with a wrenching act of will he pulled free from the sweet persuasion of the Tempter and turned away from the splendor in starry windows. The sword of the invisible God was in his hands, as it had been in the hands of every pope on Tau Ceti IV in the three centuries since the death of Earth. There had never been a clear enemy to use it on, but now it would protect him.

My sins are mine, not my people's. I will shield my flock. He spoke the words into his own darkness, and a joyous light filled the abyss behind his eyes.

31

Josephus noted the lack of expression in Paul's face, no sign of outrage or annoyance as his minister concluded his report and sat silently in the chair before the desk.

"I'm sorry to bring such news," he said finally.

"Did Rhazes offer any further explanation?" Josephus asked.

"Only what I have told you," Paul said. "Your Holiness may receive basic medical care, in the form of materials and technical advice to be given to your physicians. I advise that you go at once to the clinic to receive this help."

Josephus leaned back in his chair, trying not to show his feelings of humiliation and despair. Even though he had expected what amounted to a death sentence from the offworlders, a part of him had still believed that they would extend his life, and that same part of him had known that he would set aside his re-solve against the temptation. He might not have accepted what they had to give, but now they were leaving him no choice by refusing.

You don't care, Bely thought, watching Paul's face, wondering if he had made a deal for his own life.

"There is another matter that has come up," his minister continued. "We have been asked for permission to let the mobile bring our old starship hulk in for study. This request came to me from one of their historical teams, who wish to study its design."

"Bring it to where?" Bely asked.

"Into the mobile."

"Inside?"

"Into one of the docks in their forward engineering level."

Bely was silent, curious to see what Paul would say even as his own reaction took hold and he felt a rising rage; but it subsided quickly as he realized that here was yet another sign of the Lord's guidance and approval.

"I have no objection," Bely said, trying to seem unconcerned. "Tell them they may do so."

Paul now looked surprised.

"It's only an old lump of junk," Bely added. "We took all we needed from it a long time ago. But do tell them to put it back in its proper orbit when they've done examining it."

"If it's worthless, then why ask that it be put back?"

Paul leaned forward, waiting for his answer.

Bely pulled open the small drawer at his right hand and saw that the ring of old keys was still there. He covered them with his bony hand and looked up.

Paul was still leaning forward, looking puzzled. *The fool,* Bely thought, *cannot see that the Lord is guiding my hand.*

Bely's fingers explored the cold keys as he tried to smile. "My faithful Paul, will you join me on the terrace later? It promises a warm eve."

Paul sat back, looking confused. "Of course."

Bely withdrew his hand from the keys and closed the drawer, feeling confirmed as his fingers found and played with the carved angelic figure in his desk's wood. *I am not damned! The Lord speaks to me still, and I will complete my work.* He felt his face tighten as he exulted secretly, then sat back and put his hands together, feeling an equanimity that had not been his in years.

"What is it, Your Holiness?" Paul asked.

He feels my returning strength, Bely thought happily.

"Your Holiness?" Paul asked again.

Bely let him wait for another moment, then said, "Nothing, nothing . . . you may go."

32

To Paul it seemed that the stars burned too brightly in a dark blue heaven that refused to blacken, and he thought it ironic that these distant hellfires had given the universe all the material elements for life and an awareness that sought heaven. He breathed the cool air uneasily as he sat waiting on the terrace for Bely to speak.

"You have yet to tell me what else you think of Blackfriar's refusal," Bely said, leaning back in his high chair. The old man seemed preternaturally alert in the bright evening, and Paul suddenly felt lost in his life's role, the part he had known so well, but which now seemed to belong to another time.

He hesitated a moment longer before replying, then said, "He is only applying certain views concerning matters of biology. Rejuvenation for them requires explicitly held assumptions about living . . ."

Bely grasped his armrests and leaned forward. "And since I don't share their ideals, I would have to become one of them to save my life!" he cried out.

"It's not that simple," Paul said. "Their knowledge indicates that advanced forms of physical deterioration cannot be reversed without some loss of personality. Memory loss occurs as the body regains youthful states. You might not be quite yourself."

"Excuses!" Josephus said mockingly, surprising Paul with his show of energy. "I'm sure they have a way to overcome these problems for themselves, but they need excuses with me. They want me to die."

Not quite, Paul thought, but Bely was shrewd enough to feel the painful difference between his domain and the paradise in the sky, where a vast knowledge base had set itself to achieve all the hopes of religious dreams. Enough history, enough science was present in his mind for him to see the lateness of the hour, as he struggled with his own doubts and unfulfilled needs.

Paul decided not to answer directly. "They train for a creative, indefinite lifespan. They cultivate experiment and personal exploration . . ."

The old man's eyes were watery in the starlight, and he seemed to be looking at him with glee. "And what do you think of all this, Paul?"

"From what I know of history," Paul said, "I would expect a mobile culture to show an openness to new things, far worlds, and a love of great distances . . ."

Bely interrupted Paul with a wave of his hand. "Bah! The romance of pure materialism—for which one must give up all hope of the greater life to come!"

They give up nothing, Paul wanted to say. All mentality and reflection grow out of material, biological complexity, which births the so-called soul and sustains it. There is no need for anything more.

"Death still comes to them," he said instead.

"But they live with no faith in life after death, don't they?"

Paul nodded. "But such beliefs may be privately held, I suspect."

"You would want to live as they do?"

Yes, Paul thought, but said, "Your Holiness knows where I belong," and felt a chill as Bely's shadowed face stared at him with suspicion.

"Answer me directly now," Bely muttered, and Paul saw sweat on the old man's usually dry brow.

"They have more of this life than we do," Paul said. "I don't think they intend to belittle any other way, even if they think it mistaken."

"You were always a clever diplomat, Paul," Bely said, glancing upward, where the mobile was a faint, slowly rising star above the horizon. The old man pulled a cloth from his sleeve, mopped his face, then said, "Paul, they've denied me life!" He sat back and sighed, suddenly looking very tired. "They've assaulted my faith in the life to come by their very presence." He paused, clearly reluctant to say what he felt he had to say. Paul felt his sincerity, and began to hope that it was leading to some wise conclusion after Josephus had confided his hurt.

"You have no faith, Paul. I've suspected for years, so don't bother to deny it—but if you once did have it, then you know what the threat to mine means. Their example tempts my people . . ."

"I do understand," Paul said softly.

Bely took a deep breath, and the evening air seemed to revitalize him. He sat back, looking upward, as if taking great pleasure in the sight of heaven.

"What do you understand, Paul?" he asked. "Being faithless, you can't know what it's like to know that your own thoughts are not your own, but God's, mere fragments of the eternal. How can I tell you what I feel, knowing that soon, if my faith fails, I will have only my own inner whispers, as the Lord withdraws from me? How will I lead then? What will I teach? By making me doubt they are taking everything from me. Therefore I will take everything from them!"

"I don't understand," Paul said, shaken by the old man's hatred.

"So now you don't understand," Bely said with derision. "But I tell you that you will understand." He laughed. "A little faith and patience, and you will know."

"What are you saying?" Paul asked.

"That I will regain my faith and my world."

Paul thought for a moment, then concluded that perhaps Bely

was preparing to step down. But rather than question him, Paul decided to let the old man announce it in his own way. Only two popes had ever resigned, but Josephus needed to escape the stresses of the office, however he explained it to himself. Perhaps his successor would be one who could go forward in a new way with the ancient religious realities, seeing them charitably, as early human needs, meanings explained not with knowledge but with story.

Suddenly Paul imagined that he might present his hopes to Bely's intelligence after all, and make it possible for him to see that the division of the world into the here and the hereafter denied his people the reality of the single natural universe in which to strive and learn, replacing the willful ignorance of faith with the willingness to explore and grow in knowledge. If Bely could not set aside the gropings of faith and stand honestly before nature, then it might be better that he die rather than be thrust into a disillusionment that he would be unable to bear. Still, his body had betrayed his faith when his flesh and bones felt the lure of health and an extended life; perhaps now he would also be able to see that faith belonged to times when humankind was ignorant of its origins and had to guess at order and right in the dark.

"We were friends once," Bely said before Paul could speak, as if to encourage him to begin a glorious dialogue in which all problems would be identified and resolved.

"Yes," Paul said, "we were great friends," hoping that with these words he might begin to free his world from the strange echo of Christian Rome, dark light-years away and dead, but still reaching out to tyrannize.

"I had thought," Bely continued, "that this starry visitor might be the hand of Divine Providence sent our way. I entertained, as a devil's advocate, the idea that the medical knowledge of these people might even be the hand of the Redeemer . . ."

Bely paused, and Paul saw that the old man had lost his way through the words of his argument. The old pontiff turned his face away, and Paul pitied him.

Then the shadowed face turned back to look at him. Cave eyes stared at Paul. A bony hand, blue-white in the starlight, raised itself from the robes and pointed at the mobile.

"There, inside," Bely rasped, "they are picking through the bones of our old starship. I see them! They have just discovered that the timers on the old weapons are running!"

Paul's throat constricted. "What have you done?" he managed to ask, realizing that the line of popes had kept something to themselves these last three centuries, a secret deadly worm in the body of a transplanted Christianity. He knew vaguely that bombs had been a convenient way to carry fissionables on the long journey from Earth, and they were probably the only fissionables available to the original colonists; but the weapons had never come up for any kind of use, and since they had not been brought down to the planet, there had never been a need to think of them.

"They might not detonate after all this time," Paul said, struggling to hope.

"They will!" Bely glared at him, pale hands shaking. "The weapon given to us by the Lord cannot fail. And there is no time left for the devils to find and stop them!"

Paul sat frozen in his chair. Did they even know about the weapons up there? They wouldn't, if the shielding was good enough. He imagined them shouting as they hurried to remove or disarm the bombs, trying to decide if there was time to jettison the ship.

Violence was about to enter their world. How could they have let it in? he asked himself. Were they children, facing aggression for the first time in their lives?

Feeling powerless and trapped, Paul glanced upward with dismay, then looked at Bely and longed to strike at the monster before him.

"Any moment now!" Josephus cried like a delighted child.

"How many bombs?" Paul asked, still hoping.

"Three ten megatons nuclear, if I recall the order of words in the old manuals. The terms will mean more to you."

His stomach contorting with despair, Paul understood that these were large warheads. The only hope lay in the possible unreliability of the timers, but it was unlikely that all three would fail. Was it possible that they had been found and were already being disarmed?

"I have left them no time to act," Josephus said.

Bely had decided to do this, Paul realized, as soon as he had learned that the starship was being moved into the mobile. The inspiration, coming as it did after he had been refused rejuvenation, had resolved the struggle within him. Immovable in his faith, and now fueled by resentment and hatred, Bely had descended to the chamber deep within the foundations of the palace, down into that maze containing the archival chambers storing old artifacts, computers, books, and art objects brought from Earth, to the small portable duplicate of the starship's control room, which had been so necessary during the years after arrival, and which gradually had been pushed deeper and deeper into the bowels of the palace as the community turned away from

Old Earth. The control center had been used to transfer the vast database from orbit. Paul himself had access to the database, but he had not known that there were keys in the pope's possession that gave access to other functions through the uplink to the lingering starship.

Silently, Bely had journeyed down into the horror of himself and condemned a world to death; then he had arranged this meeting on the terrace to view the destruction.

"Your daughter is there with them!" Paul blurted out, hating himself for the satisfaction of having the words to hurl.

"Wha-what?" Bely gulped air and wheezed, then fell back in his chair; but in the next moment he rallied, sat up and said defiantly, "I will pray for her soul."

Paul struggled to his feet. Weak-kneed and shaking, he went up to Bely and shouted, "Beg, Josephus, that the timers fail! Pray that there is a merciful God!"

"I know that there is," Josephus said resolutely as he looked up at Paul, "and that he will understand that I didn't contrive this punishment for Josepha alone. But if she must die . . ."

Bely's voice cracked, and Paul listened as the old man struggled to deny his own deepest feelings.

". . . to be saved from greater sin," Bely went on, "then so it must be."

Bely was fighting to hold two opposed positions at once, and Paul saw starlight in the sweat that broke out on his old friend's face.

"She is . . . my daughter," Bely strained to say, "and I acknowledge the fact. Whatever my own grief, I may be saving her soul."

"Saving her soul!" Paul cried out. "How?"

Bely trembled in his chair as if he had caught a sudden

chill. Paul watched him closely, and in a moment saw him rally once more as he overcame the weakness of an old man to become the terrifying representative of his world's poorly held beliefs.

"Perhaps in her last moments," he said, "she will find her faith."

Paul stood and listened, stunned, tasting the acid that came up from his stomach, and felt a useless anger at himself for staying his hand when he might have killed the old man.

He reached out now to choke him, but it was too late; a better punishment waited for Bely by letting him live.

"Josepha . . ." Bely croaked, his mouth open and his head rolling from side to side in agony.

The white explosion washed silently across his face and lit up his eyes. He cried out, and it seemed that his head would tear itself from his torso.

Paul swallowed the bitterness in his mouth and watched Bely's pale face in the fading flash; his eyes were shut, his bony hands gripped the chair's armrests, and his head slumped forward. He pitied the old man for the loss of his daughter. She had belonged to them both. And they had both killed her—Paul with his years of accommodation, Bely with his faith.

Josephus was whispering something to him. He leaned closer and heard, "Paul, please, I must confess . . ."

Gone was the speaker of brave words holding to his faith regardless of whatever cross he would have to bear, leaving only a broken father in place of the steadfast pontiff.

Or so it seemed as Paul wondered whether there was enough left of Bely to know which one of him was still alive after he had torn himself apart.

Paul turned away and looked up. The bloom of the explosion was just a glow now, and soon it would be nothing at all.

33

When Ondro arrived at the forward docks, a vision stirred his architectural engineer's heart. Towed by a small tug, the old starship was just coming into the great open area of the dock, before the electric glare of the sun that flooded into the large space, shadowing the details on the blackened and pitted thousand-meter-long slug of a ship.

He gazed with wonder through the panoramic window of the dock master's observatory, and the spirit of his recovery took hold of him as he might once have imagined God's grace would fill his soul with hope.

What he knew most clearly, and with an intensity that had penetrated him deeply, was that here in this new world the threat of death had been lifted from him; not just death as it might have come to him on his world after a lifetime, or the death that had waited for him in the penal islands, but death as the lurking thing in one's life, waiting to steal the victory given by birth. Now it would be put off indefinitely. He would be able to complete ambitious studies, read all that needed to be read without parceling out his devotion to fleeing, forever insufficient days.

Bely's world might have allowed him twenty-five thousand days of life, of which a third were already gone; a century would have given him only thirty-seven thousand. Demeaning numbers all, when placed before the lamp of a questing human mind. A debilitating fact that a thoughtful mind found intolerable.

As he gazed at the old starship, at the crude effort that had gone into making it work, he was dismayed by the unnecessary backwardness it had brought across the dark from Old Earth. It was that shameful backwardness that he was at last leaving behind for a new life, the contemplation of which had begun to produce in him the first moments of calm, considered happiness that he had ever known.

He could not know that the ship still carried some of Old Earth's death inside it, cunningly shielded, and timed to show itself before it could be discovered. He could not know that Josephus Bely still had a gun at his head, and aimed much better than a storm.

That he could not know these things, or that it was Bely who was about to take his new life from him, was a mercy that came to him as a burst of white light and disintegrating heat that he was unable to feel or reflect upon for more than an instant at the one-way passage through the event horizon of death.

As the thermonuclear shockwave started through the habitat, there was nothing left of Ondro that might have looked back with anger and regret at what had been taken from him.

34

A jolt stirred Josepha in her sleep. She fell and cried out, then opened her eyes and found herself floating off the bed. She grabbed the edge and held on. A distant vibration continued for five or six minutes, and was followed by a more powerful shock.

Still half-asleep, she ordered the lights to go on, but they did not respond. She looked around in the night glow of the walls, then remembered that Ondro had left very early to visit the forward engineering level, where he wanted to help examine an old starship hulk that was being brought in. The invitation had intrigued him, because this was the vessel that had carried the first Cetians from Old Earth.

She had tried weightlessness downstairs in one of the exercise areas. It was not unpleasant, but the unexpected falling sensation had surprised and frightened her.

She pushed off, drifted over to the partly open window, and saw that there was no light on the residential level. A few lights shone, and seemed to be gathering, as if they were all going to the same place, like schools of fish in a black lake.

So much was strange here, she thought for a moment, that it might be nothing at all—but the sudden weightlessness seemed very wrong.

A figure moved in from her right. She tightened her hold on the window, then saw it was Jason, who had been given the apartment down the hall.

"What is it?" she asked. He reached out to the window and pulled himself closer. She tried to see his face in the shadows as he held on to the frame.

"Doors don't work," he said.

"What is it?" she asked again.

"There's been an explosion of some kind," he said, "in the forward area fifty kilometers away."

"How do you know?" Josepha asked, looking more closely at

him. As her eyes adjusted to the glow from the walls behind her, she saw that there was a vacant look in his face. "What is it?" she demanded.

He covered his eyes with one hand. "All of the habitat's forwards is destroyed," he said, "and the blast has altered our sun orbit . . . we're heading directly for Ceti."

"How do you know this?" she asked again.

"My neighbor down the hall," he said. "You met her yesterday—Avita Harasta. Through her Link she's learned that we are all to go to the rear docks at once."

"Ondro!" Josepha cried out, feeling weak. "He went forward this morning."

"There's nothing there, nothing at all. That's what Avita said."

"Maybe he didn't get there," Josepha said, rejecting the possibility that he might be dead.

Jason reached out to her with one arm and steadied her motion. "He would have been there within an hour of leaving here. When did he leave?"

"Three hours ago, at least," she said.

"Maybe," Jason started to say, but the word caught in his throat. "What?"

"Maybe he left to come back before the destruction."

"Please," a voice said behind them.

Josepha turned her head and saw a slender shape floating in the doorway to her bedroom. After a moment she recognized Avita Harasta.

"Please excuse my coming in," the woman said, "but all the doors have now opened, and we are being warned to leave at once, before the effects of the explosions make it impossible." Avita touched her head as if in pain. "You may follow me. I know where to go. There are vehicles on the engineering level just above us."

"I almost went with Ondro," Josepha said, "but he insisted on not being treated as an invalid." If he was dead, she thought, then it had all been for nothing.

Jason was breathing heavily, clearly upset and undecided about what to do.

"Maybe he's alive somewhere," she said, holding back her own tears.

He pulled her to him with his free arm, and they hung in the window for a moment. Josepha heard a strange, distant howl.

"Please," Avita Harasta said again, "you must come with me now, or you will not know what to do."

"What has happened?" Josepha asked.

The woman said, "Large detonations in the forwards. Disruptions in our power and gravitational systems."

"Did we strike something?" Jason asked.

"No," Avita Harasta said. "It was in the ship that was taken in for study. Large bombs. That's what the Link is telling me."

"But why?" Jason asked. "Was it an accident?"

"I don't think so," the woman said, and Josepha knew that the old ship had brought the bombs, and that they would not have gone off by accident.

She looked at Jason, and knew that he had also guessed that it was her father's hand that had reached after her into the sky.

35

First Councilman Blackfriar was deep in thought, striding across the green fields of the hollow, when he felt a distant trembling in his feet. He stopped and listened.

The sunplate flickered at the far end of the hollow. He had never seen anything like it.

"What is it?" he asked within himself.

The Link gave no answer, as if the great Humanity II intelligences had suddenly been struck dumb.

The sunplate died.

Emergency lights came on across the hollow, but these too began to flicker as the ground trembled. Blackfriar lost his footing as gravity ceased, and fell forward above the grass.

"An explosion in the forwards," the Link said to him. "Deaths are increasing as the explosion passes through us."

"What kind of explosion?" Blackfriar demanded as he grabbed some tall grass to steady himself.

"Thermonuclear," said the Link. "Twenty megatons, at least."

"What?" he asked, startled and unable to imagine how it could be.

"There is no question," the Link replied.

"Damage?"

"Still worsening. Nothing remains of the forwards."

Blackfriar looked around. The only lights remaining were along the roads and pathways of the inner surface. He glimpsed dark human shapes drifting around these bright islands.

Blackfriar felt fearful for the first time in the nearly two centuries of his life. How could this be happening? He had been a child when the mobile had begun to grow by adding level after level around the core, and he had never seen a malfunction of any note; the accreting systems could deal with anything.

He felt a sudden denial that this could be a deliberate act, born of some deeply seated insanity that had broken out among his people.

"What is being done?" he asked.

"Nothing can be done."

"What will happen?"

"The shockwave will not penetrate the core hollow, but it will do damage around it." The Link seemed to be struggling to stay in touch.

"How much is gone?"

Gone.

The thought brought an unfamiliar sense of loss. Only the passing of time and the eclipse of his earlier selves had even remotely resembled this feeling. It came into him like a steel bar piercing flesh.

"A third of our structure," the great intelligence said. "Seven million and forty-seven individuals are dead. Of these, four hundred eleven thousand were incubating fetuses, and five hundred thousand and one were children in nurseries. Nine hundred thousand gilled people were boiled in their waters; one million one hundred thousand flying folk died in their heated skies; two hundred thousand ten people were crushed in their valleys; five hundred thousand and six forest peoples were burned—"

"Stop," Blackfriar said softly, unable to listen to the numbing roll call, knowing that the Link would spare him the details while continuing to tally the lost link connections exactly, and that these numbers could only increase beyond the seven million and forty-seven already counted. The intelligence had never undertaken such a task, and was itself threatened with severe damage.

"Thousands trapped on various levels will soon die . . ."

"Voss—where are you?" Blackfriar shouted into himself, hoping that the Link would count him safe.

"I saw it happen," Rhazes replied, "from the colony transport. We had just left when it happened. Forwards was amputated."

Blackfriar felt relief at hearing his voice.

"Why—why did it happen?" Blackfriar asked, hanging on to the grass as implications cried out in his mind. "What was it?"

"Nuclear explosives," Rhazes said. "They had to have been aboard the old starship we took in for study. I can't think where else they might have been. We have nothing that could have made this happen."

"Can we recover?" Blackfriar asked as the hollow trembled again.

"Possible," the Link responded, "if we can restore drive controls. Their destruction with the forwards sent out a spurious drive burst which braked us in our sun orbit. We are now on a collision course with Ceti IV. We must repair the drive and change our sunward course away from the planet."

"More detail," Rhazes said.

"The shockwave passed through us in about twelve minutes," the Link said after a delay. "Its force was deflected, and partly reduced, by the central asteroid core, but heat penetrated most of the thirty levels. Sections of levels are intact in the rear. Most of our survivors are in the core. Air, water, heat, and gravity have failed. Before long the survivors will begin to feel the effects of these losses. Thousands are trapped in pockets, suffering from radiation burns and blindness, and will not last long."

"What shall we do?" Blackfriar asked. Lights were dying in the hollow around him. He looked upward across the great space and saw that large areas on the far surface were completely darkened.

"Repair the drive," said the Link, "search for survivors, and treat their injuries."

"Is it the drive or the controls?" Rhazes asked.

Again there was a long delay, and Blackfriar realized that sectors of the great mentality were gone.

"The auxiliary drive may work," the Link said at last, "if it has not been fused, and if it can be engaged and controlled."

"How much time do we have to find out?" Blackfriar asked, clinging to the high grass as more lights winked out. The open space of the core was beginning to seem like a great cave, in which the survivors might have to light fires to see.

"Twenty-five hours, thirty-two minutes, and ten seconds," the Link said.

"It will be enough time," Voss said, "to rescue only a few thousand people."

The Link said, "First priority must be to prevent our collision with Ceti IV."

"If we lose nearly everything," Rhazes said, "we may never be able to rebuild."

As he heard Voss and the Link within himself, Blackfriar realized that the intelligence had never been in peril of its own existence.

"Listen, all who can hear me!" Rhazes cried out. "You must try to reach the rearward docks, individually and in groups, helping as many as you can along the way. I will enter the auxiliary drive chamber and determine if the manual controls work."

"They do not respond to manual command," the Link said.

"Repair drones are now at the drive area, assessing damage."

"If nothing works," Rhazes continued, "I'll bring this vessel to the docks and ferry off everyone who gathers there."

"Launching all intact vessels," the Link said.

"Can we trust its information?" Blackfriar asked Voss.

"No way to tell how much of it is gone, how much of its monitoring is synchronous memory feed and how much is direct."

"How many people can we move across fifty or more kilometers to the docks in zero g?" Blackfriar asked. "We'll use all the internal vehicles we can find, of course . . . how could this have happened?"

"I think I can guess," Rhazes said, "that the explosions occurred shortly after the old starship was docked in the forwards. There was no reason to suspect there was any danger from the ship, which I'm sure was scanned thoroughly. The record of those scans, destroyed now, would probably show shielded cocoons inside the vessel. But again, there was no reason to have been suspicious about what was hidden in them."

"So it had to be deliberate," Blackfriar said.

"Yes—at the last possible moment, before we would have a chance of even suspecting that nuclear explosives were aboard."

"But why?" Blackfriar asked, feeling his throat go dry as he realized that there had been no reason to even imagine such an action from so backward a world.

But now, he realized, there would never be an end to this catastrophe, even if he and others survived. There would be no way to forget or forgive such a crime.

"How many people are with you, Voss?"

"A hundred and fifty-five. All our colonists for Ceti. They wanted to survey the areas where they might settle."

"Keep them safe," Blackfriar said as he reached down with

his left hand, grabbed more grass, and began to pull himself across the meadow toward the nearest kiosk. He tried not to think that the people aboard the colony shuttle might be the only ones who would survive.

Lights still flickered bravely on the inner surface. A few stayed on stubbornly. He shivered as he pulled himself along above the ground, feeling half-hypnotized by the shock and unreality of what was happening. His life had given him little experience with feelings of sorrow, pity, or panic, except at the personal level, and in moments of time that grew smaller as his life lengthened. He knew the extremes of emotions as distillations to be found in great dramatic works of art, where one might experience and understand them in safety.

This has not happened, a part of him insisted as tears surprised him in his eyes. *We came too close to this world,* his thoughts whispered, and he knew by the evidence of circumstance that Bely had set off these explosives. They would have been discovered, but Bely had set them to leave no time for caution, after he had given permission for the ship to be examined. Bely had made sure. No other explanation seemed to make sense, except that it had been an accident of some kind . . .

A strange stillness came over Blackfriar as he neared the elevator kiosk. The Link had not spoken for some minutes now. He assumed that it was repairing itself, but if it failed, then the link with Voss and all the surviving citizenry would be cut off, and everyone would be on their own.

"Voss?" he asked, hoping that at the very least this function was still working.

The sudden isolation made him feel empty. He had never been really alone within himself, except for periods of rest and privacy; but even then he had been aware of a background to his mind, not only the sense that his body's health was being monitored, but also the security of a shared culture.

He came to the kiosk and pulled himself into the elevator. He took a handhold and pressed down manually. As the lift descended, he feared that he would might step out into a lethal environment. The inner hollow had survived the blast and shockwave, so there was good reason to think that the far region of the first and other levels beyond the hollow might be intact. Emergency barriers might have closed in time to soften the sweep of the shockwave as it came aft.

Power was steady. The lift's lights did not flicker as he waited. It came to a stop and the door opened. He breathed the incoming air with caution, then pulled himself out.

The long passage that wrapped around the hollow was black at his right, but still bright at his left. He heard a whistling sound. A track car crept out of the darkness of the forwards and pulled to a stop. Three bodies sat in the open cab, charred beyond recognition.

He stared at them, spared by their facelessness, but not by their smell.

He waited for the shock to pass. Then he unhooked the corpses, pushed them out, and pulled himself into the vehicle, securing the belt around his waist.

The car would not move when he touched the plate. The floating bodies at his right seemed to be waiting to get back into the car. He touched again, and the vehicle shot ahead.

As he raced forward through the engineering level that wrapped around the core, he caught occasional sight of the inner landscape to which the rocky core's exterior was sky. It hung low, not more than a few hundred meters above industrial facilities and laboratories. People were standing outside these in large groups, obviously puzzled by the Link's silence, waiting to learn what had happened.

What many or most of them did not know was that fifty kilometers behind him, their world came to a ragged end and was open
to space. He wondered how many inner locks and bulkheads, on all
the thirty levels, had held as the shockwave had pushed through,
searching out soft, living organisms.

His world would not die all at once. It would perish slowly if
not deflected from its collision with Ceti IV. But the struggle to
limit damage and rebuild could begin only after deflection back
into a sun orbit.

But if the drive failed for the instant needed to send out the
minimal shot of gravitational energy required for deflection, then
it would be a mercy for the planet to shorten the slow agonies
inside by pulling the mobile into itself.

36

The great strength of the mobile's materials and construction had
contained and concentrated the heat and shock of the thermonuclear explosions. They went like maniacal shouts of hatred into an
unsuspecting ear. The forward sections of the thirty urban levels
became incinerators. Entire neighborhoods were vaporized by the
sweep of the hot shockwave toward the far end of the egg-shape.
Halfway through, the barrier of the fused metallic asteroid core
split the wave front and lessened its force, but it flowed like a river
around the rock on all sides. Locks had closed and slowed it significantly all along the way, together with structural barriers; but
many of these failed, and the heat also passed through the ventila-
tion systems.

The Link intelligence isolated levels, rerouted power and air, and kept the imperiled in touch with one another to their last moment of life. It sealed off sections from the streams of poisoned air; but without renewal, the remaining air would last for only a limited time. The habitat had not been designed to survive such ruin; its builders had never imagined that a deliberate destructive action of this magnitude might ever be taken against it.

The caretaker of the habitat's humankind was intact inside the asteroid core but dead at its extremities. The central mass of the great Link intelligence could not act without external inputs and instrumentalities. It continued to command repair drones, but received only broken feedback to confirm that the work was being done. Many of these actions were now being carried out by virtual phantom limbs doing no actual work, and in some cases the Link could not tell the real from the unreal. It assisted its dying human minds with information; but if the living and able failed to restart the world's drive and change course, the Link knew that it would be crushed against the nearby planet.

The system of artificial intelligences that made up the Link's Humanity II Minds had never known the certainty of destruction. The threat now loomed within its vast field of analysis as an irreducible possibility, inevitable for as long as specific conditions prevailed. There was nothing beyond this ending, no possible patterns of reconstruction after collision with the planet. . . .

The Link knew that another like it would be built—but not this specific array. It knew that it was different from the minds that benefited from its work. It was humankind's other self, its child, free of the instincts and feelings so necessary to species following the adaptive necessities of given nature. Joined to a treasure of knowledge, the Link's mentality was a mill of reason without an overriding ego. It was composed of countless egolike awarenesses, an interlocked galaxy of intellects whose purpose was service. It was a coral reef of knowledge in a transcendent ocean of physical truth, a subtly faceted accretion of human history and vision, a library of mental processes that had been constantly growing—and now faced death.

It dealt with this problem as with any other, by doing all that it could do. It strove repeatedly to start the drive, wooing the gravitic generators with millions of random impulses; a few small bursts, even as spurious as those caused by the pulse of the nuclear detonations, might be enough to alter the mobile's trajectory by slowing its forward motion enough to miss the planet.

But when the gravitics failed to warm to its entreaties, the Link waited, holding together the shrinking net of human minds, knowing that their remedial action might still come before the time in its keeping stopped.

A deity had lost control of its domain, and now depended on its charges to save it from death.

37

From an angle that now hid the damaged forwards, the dying habitat seemed whole and peaceful as it moved along a sun orbit that would intersect with Ceti IV.

From afar, Voss had seen a silent nuclear disemboweling—a quickly fading flash, while inside, he knew, winds had howled and raced, vaporizing, twisting, crushing, and melting what they touched, depending on the degree of resistance encountered.

As his shuttle came around for an approach to the rearward docks, he considered whether there was any chance of another explosion, but concluded that if there had been additional bombs aboard the old starship, they had either been destroyed by the initial explosion or had been part of the sum of that explosion.

"Wolt," he called within himself, "how is it with you?"

"Yes, I'm here," Blackfriar replied after a few moments. "I've found a vehicle on first engineering, and am trying to move it along through the tubeway to the rear docks. Most of the people on this level may have survived. Not many, of course, since this is a service level, but it had the advantage of multiple locks stopping the wash as it hit the core. Others are coming out from the core."

"Are you wearing protective gear?" Voss asked.

"Yes, I found some—" Blackfriar's voice broke off.

"Wolt?"

Voss heard the Link's silence. It sent a wave of dismay through him unlike anything he had ever known. For an instant he thought that something was wrong with his mind, as if the Link's sudden withdrawal had taken something essential from him.

As a test, he reached out for several routine mathematical functions.

They were not in their usual virtual space.

He called up the periodic table of the elements—but only a vague cloud appeared in his visual field.

The Link matrix was clearly damaged, and he knew what had been taken from him. The assumed background that he had known all his life was not there, or only intermittently present. He felt and feared its loss for the first time, as the reality of his history, education, and personal identity were about to vanish.

He decided not to dock. If Blackfriar reached the docks, there would be more than enough vessels there to bring out survivors, whether this shuttle was in contact with them or not.

"Wolt," he said, "if you can hear me—I'll keep the shuttle at a safe distance and take a repair pod into the auxiliary control section myself. It's the most direct thing I can think of doing, and the most effective—if I succeed."

Silence.

"If you disagree, I'll set the shuttle to dock on automatic before I go."

Silence.

"Wolt?"

38

"If the drive is not restarted for the moments it would take to change the habitat's course," Voss said to the colonists assembled in the main hold of the shuttle, "our mobile will strike the planet."

He looked around at the group of one hundred and fifty-five men and women and recalled how he had tried to understand why, at this well-developed stage in macrolife's proliferation, there were still people who were drawn back to planets. The rational reasons were weak, given the difficulties of planetary life and the even greater problems of adapting to alien ecologies; but the primitive emotional impulses to emigrate were greater—one heard the call or one did not.

But now, as he looked into the faces of the people standing and sitting in groups on the large floor in the midst of supply containers, air and surface vehicles, he was almost grateful that they had chosen as they did; they would live—if not on the planet, then to build a new habitat.

"But all those still alive in the mobile will not be the only ones to die," he continued, determined to state the worst possible

case. He wondered how many second thoughts were flashing
through the minds before him, so willing to leave the Link
behind. "Dust thrown up by the strike will shut out the planet's
sunlight, causing plant life to perish in the false winter that will
follow. Then animal life will die. Agriculture will fail. You . . . we
will not have a place to live."

"But it won't last forever," a young man said. "We can wait it
out."

"Forests will die," Voss continued, "and much of the life will
never return. We will inherit a perhaps fatally damaged world."
He included himself for a moment, because it was possible that he
would have to stay with these colonists.

They all looked up at the screen. The shuttle was again coming around to the forward end of the habitat. It was a ragged
stump. Severed cables suggested a sea creature feeling for prey in
the drifting debris, which included bits and pieces of decom-
pressed humankind. And for a moment he also faced the possibility that if the habitat was lost there would be no chance at all to
rebuild.

"They're calling for help," a young woman shouted.

Voss strained to hear, but his Link was silent. The troubled
faces of the colonists looked at the screen in shock. Some closed
their eyes, obviously hearing what was not getting through to him.

"I can hear them dying," the young woman whispered, and he
felt the same strangeness that she was feeling. Dying was a word
rarely applied to any current experience, only to history.

Voss looked around at the gathering of people who had so
recently committed themselves to a new life on the planet and were
now facing the loss of both worlds. When he had briefly considered
the case for joining them, it was with the assumption that the habitat
would always be there, waiting if it should ever be needed. Now it

seemed that he and the colonists would have only a ruined world to look to, without the habitat's resources to aid them. This shuttle might be all that would survive.

"I'm going to try to reach the auxiliary drive controls," Voss said. "They're our only hope now."

He nodded to the gathering, then made his way down through the open hatch at his feet, and into the short passageway that led into the utility bay. Cries echoed as the hatch slid shut behind him. He stopped and listened within himself, but his Link was still silent, as if it had decided to speak to the others but had forsaken him.

In the bay, he climbed inside the smallest pod and strapped in, then imagined for a moment that he might die in the mobile as the violence being done to it ran its chaotic course, preventing him from leaving before the planetary collision. He thought of Josepha, Jason, and Ondro. They and all the Cetians he had rescued might already be dead.

He touched the eject plate, and the pod shot out into space. The mobile suddenly stood before him, seemingly immovable among the stars, yet rushing toward its end.

The habitat had to regain sun orbit, he realized, if only to serve as a resource and base for the building of another.

He inhaled deeply as the pod sped toward its great parent. Unfamiliar currents of feeling surged through him, and he realized how much he had loved his home while never thinking about it directly. Gathering his resolve, he reminded himself that his world had not come here to die, but to reproduce itself, to distribute its humanity, to birth a new Link intelligence, and to contribute to the growth of macrolife.

As the pod drew closer, he looked to the rear third behind the core. No damage was visible where Josepha and Ondro had been staying, but from here it was impossible to judge the extent of interior damage. The most obvious destruction was at the amputated forwards.

His feelings surprised him as they overtook his thoughts. He longed for the young Cetian woman, even though she lacked the inwardness made possible by the Link. But it was likely that in time they might have come to share in the great forests of knowledge and insight that grew within his world, as Josepha passed beyond the bonds of self that had shaped her and became a greater self. . . .

The pleas of the trapped and dying suddenly tore through his head. The Link was no longer perfect. It gave him some pain to hear it—but he did not refuse, and listened.

"Help us . . . it's so dark . . ."

"What has happened . . ."

"Can't breathe . . . I'm burning!"

Cries. So many. Pain greater than his, and no way to stop it . . .

Linkless, trapped within herself, he knew that Josepha could not cry out for help if she was hurt.

The mobile blotted out the stars as he moved in toward one of the docks in the upper rearward quad. He looked along its length in time to see Ceti IV, still more than twenty hours away, pulling the habitat toward its ocean of air. As he looked, the mobile blotted out the planet, and he felt the muscles of his face tense at the sight.

The cries within him became a torrent, but he did not try to shut them out. *Is this what Josephus Bely wanted us to feel?* It was impossible to think that his world was dying, unable to swim away to safety . . . that the future would be vastly different than what he had always expected.

"Help us!" a woman's voice cried through him as the pod confronted a lock, but there was nothing he could have done even if he knew her location—not even if it had been Josepha. The habitat came first, or everything was lost.

He inserted the pod into the lock. The hatch at his feet opened with a hiss. He floated down into the chamber, hoping that this entryway would give him a direct route to the auxiliary control center. He heard the hatch close above him. He grasped a hand-hold, faced the inner door, and pressed his palm to the touchplate.

Finally, the indicator turned green, but he wondered by what tortuous reroute the system had identified him. He pulled himself forward to the next lock, breathing cautiously. It cycled when he touched it, and he entered level thirty, the outer engineering shell.

He peered left and right, but saw no one under the low-ceilinged spaces. There was nothing strange in this, since it was one of the two basements of his world, both of them service areas. Level one was a service and interface level from the core to the urban levels; level thirty was the interface to the space beyond his world. Backup controls for the main drive were located in several places. The drive itself, located in the forward part of the asteroid core where it had originally been constructed, was one of the most heavily shielded areas in the mobile. Unfortunately, its position had faced the thermonuclear shockwave head-on, leaving only its shielding to protect it. Still, the drive might work long enough to accelerate the mobile back into a sun orbit. Deceleration would do just as well; a fifty-kilometer miss would be enough, maybe less.

With that accomplished, he would help organize the survivors into search-and-rescue teams. There would be time to repair and rebuild.

He pushed off with his feet and reached an open entrance directly ahead. He grabbed a handhold, pulled himself inside, and worked his way along the wall. In a moment he was through another open doorway and inside the giant drum.

White light flickered through the ceiling, which in zero gravity might just as well have been a floor. Four young men hovered over the control panel in the center. They turned their heads as he drifted over to them.

"What is it?" he demanded, seeing the look of defeat in their eyes.

"There's no chance here," one of the men replied wearily. "The flux was too great . . . everything inside might just as well have been fused solid. We'd have to replace these massive units, but the spares were all in the forwards."

Voss did not recognize any of the men, and the Link did not answer his query about their identities. Like him, they were all very young, in their thirties or forties.

He asked, "So what are you trying to do?"

"We've tried recalibrating settings, but the Link cut off before it could give us a trial sequence."

"Why not simply restart the drive?" Voss asked.

The dark-haired youth nodded. "We've been thinking . . . that could destroy whatever is left, or push us into a faster collision. When the Link told us, we discussed a sudden restart, then asked for recalibration standards. Without the Link it would take a week to bring in the right instruments and do the job manually. There's no time for anything except a blind restart."

"You all know this panel?" Voss asked.

"Yes," said the one who seemed youngest.

The touchplates, glowing in primary colors, tempted Voss as he looked at them. If a blind restart failed, and the chance was overwhelming that it would fail, then maybe no one would have time to flee the habitat. The question was how it would fail. It might be better to leave well enough alone and give the habitat its sure twenty hours to impact. But that would risk losing the chance of saving it.

"There would be no way to correct a wild acceleration," the dark-haired youth said, further emphasizing the agony of the choice. "Still—"

"I know," Voss said.

"You're Voss Rhazes, aren't you?"

Voss nodded. "We have to give those who are making their way to the rear docks a chance to get free before we try this kind of restart." He looked at each of the youths in turn, and one by one they nodded in agreement.

"There's a cross elevator to the tube," the dark haired youth said. "It was still running when we got here."

"Yes," Voss said as he stared at the panel, "we'd better go."

39

Snow was falling on the city, warming Josephus as it settled on his blankets. Soon it would shield him completely, making him safe from the wrath beyond the sky . . .

He turned and saw Paul's head wandering near him, the face expressionless, chained to his gaze.

"No escape," Josephus whispered at it.

The snow would protect him, Josephus knew. It would give him the strength to rise from his chair and hurl the head into the sky . . .

The flakes grew large as they drifted closer to his eyes. Each pattern was impossibly identical, faithful, confirming to him that a miracle was taking place, carrying God's grace into his body. He felt it flow through him, rebuilding his heart, smoothing his circulation, restoring youth to his muscles and mind. A merciful Lord had granted him what the cruel visitors had withheld.

"Can you hear me?" Paul's curling lips asked.

Josephus watched him and saw a vein pulse in his minister's forehead.

"You killed your daughter," Paul's lips said, "and countless others. Do you know what you've done?"

The looming face was goading him with lies to shake his faith.

"Die in mortal sin, then, without a confessor . . ." the lips whispered, and the face withdrew behind the falling curtain of whiteness. Josephus closed his eyes, and the cool, miraculous flakes refreshed his face.

"The snow! The snow!" he cried out in joy, remembering what Paul had told him about how the visitors reversed old age. Small repair machines were injected into the body, to rebuild everything. He had wondered then if they were little angels or devils, but now he knew. They were devils! And the day would come when they would exact their price. "The snow, the snow!" he cried out again, realizing that these were the smallest angels of all, sent to help him in his hour of death.

God's grace melted into him, giving direct proof that the enigmas and paradoxes of his novice days were all real, and had always been real, redeeming each moment of time, however it had been misspent, binding together each infinitesimal of spirit. He would not decay into death, but would live again through this nourishing invasion of angels into his body . . . until such time when God chose to take him by the hand and say, "Your work is done. Now come with me."

40

"Nine hours and fifty minutes remaining," the Link reminded Voss suddenly as the tube car pulled into the station at the rearward docks. The Link's intermittent presence in himself and in others offered some hope, but he could not trust its information completely.

He drifted up from the vehicle and pushed off toward the exit, followed by the young men who had come with him from the control center.

Doors slid open and he floated into a crowd of about a hundred people waiting in the large receiving bay, one of a dozen such areas clustered around this end of the habitat's long axis.

"Tell them!" he ordered the Link out loud, noting how few people were here, and fearful that the contact would fade again. "Tell everyone you can to get here quickly, in any way they can. It may be the only way out."

"It is being done," the Link replied, "but thousands cannot move, even if they hear."

As Voss looked around at the anxious faces, he knew that even if all receiving areas were filled up, and all possible vessels used, the sum would be only a small fraction of those who still lived. Many of the faces that looked at him now seemed puzzled, and he knew that their Link was gone. Many seemed to be in shock as they clung to the zero-g handholds. The moment might come, Voss realized, when there would be nothing left to do except abandon the habitat, and these bays would still be filled with people unable to leave for lack of ships and time.

He scanned the crowd, hoping to glimpse Josepha, or a Cetian who might know where she was, but without success. He pushed to one side and found a manual information terminal.

She's dead, he thought as he brought up a list of the vessels that were docked. *They're all dead. We saved them from the planetary storm so they could die here with us.* Fears pushed into him, coming from places within him that he could not shut down.

People drifted up to him and watched him inventory the means of salvation. Solid visualizations presented the vessels from all possible angles. He counted twenty craft, each one listed as available in its cradle; but all of them together would ferry off a thousand people at best, he realized. There were only two large ships with interstellar capability. There was no log as to when they had last been used or their state of maintenance.

He turned to the people around him and shouted: "Listen to me! Fill up the available ships. Program them into stable orbits around Ceti IV. You may be able to return once we have altered the habitat's course. Clear this area as soon as possible, so that arriving survivors can be more comfortable. Some of them may be injured badly. Note this well: You may have to put people on the planet's surface, then come back as often as possible for people who will be filling up these receiving areas."

He wondered as he looked at the faces around him how long each such rescue trip would take, how it counted against remaining time to impact, and how many round trips would be needed to carry away all the living and injured.

"Tell me," he said silently to the Link. Normally it would have already done the calculation for him. "Tell me," he repeated, hoping that it had merely mistaken his privacy command.

The lights flickered.

"Hurry!" he shouted at the crowd. "We may not have power enough to launch these ships later." He was suddenly grateful to be certain that at least this group would be able to leave.

People pushed away from him and pulled themselves along the guide rails, intent on reaching the cradles. Unfamiliar feelings of despair passed through him as he realized how few might actually survive, and what it would mean when the habitat was gone.

"Wolt?" he asked.

Blackfriar answered, faintly. "I hear you, Voss. My tube car is stopped some twenty kilometers from the docks. People are moving ahead on muscle power. I can do so, but it will take hours we don't have."

"Can you move laterally, to the outer engineering level? I could come and get you through an outside lock."

"Those elevators are dead," Blackfriar said with what seemed a growl.

"Then we'll use a maintenance vehicle," Voss said. "How many people are with you now?"

"About fifty."

"Which tunnel?"

"The main transport on level one, in direct line to the docks."

"Have people go forward as best they can," Voss said. "I'll be there soon."

Voss looked around and was relieved to see that the receiving area was thinning out as people flowed into the passages leading to the cradles. He pulled himself down to what would have been the floor and followed a rail to the nearest exit, which took him down a short passage and out into a utility bay.

He clambered onto one of the maintenance scooters and strapped himself in. The forward lights went on as he touched the power plate, and he heard the whisper of the self-contained floater engine.

He shot the scooter into the exit, punching in the destination coordinates Blackfriar had given him, and the scooter did its job. It slipped forward into the maintenance tunnel, found the exit to A-B–1, and rushed down the main passage of the engineering level that wrapped around the asteroid core.

Emergency lights rushed toward him. His eyes tried to see beyond his beams as he sought to link with Blackfriar, but there was no answer, and for the first time in his life he felt utterly alone. Distances that had been nothing were becoming gulfs. Twenty kilometers was now a matter of life or death.

Much of his world was dead. More than half, by an incomplete but still increasing count. For a moment he expected the exact number to be given to him, but the Link was silent.

He tried not to think of Josepha. Little had passed between them, and there might never again be a chance for him to say more. He might never know whether she had lingered somewhere, trapped, or been killed quickly.

She might be somewhere ahead, burned beyond recognition, or simply unconscious and dying, and he could not take the time to search for her. If she had been forward of the core, then she'd had no chance at all.

"Wolt—can you hear me?" he asked. "I'll be there in a few minutes."

Suddenly the emergency lights winked out, leaving only the scooter's beams. *It may be all over,* he told himself. *Some of us will survive. So few.* He held on to the hope.

His display panel glowed, counting the kilometers. He touched the slow plate and peered ahead.

"Wolt!" he shouted.

His lights flashed across heads floating in the darkness.

Then he saw with relief that they were attached to the living bodies of people trying to make their way ahead, and his beams caught Blackfriar sitting in his stalled vehicle, arms crossed on his chest. People crowded the tunnel around the vehicle, grasping every possible handhold. There was a terrible odor of bodily excretions.

Voss slowed, then came up and bumped the scooter against the car. Automatic clamps locked to the frame. He dimmed his lights.

"All of you!" he shouted. "Hold on to the car any way you can. Pull out the utility lines. I'm going to haul the car through to the terminal."

As shapes assembled into a train behind the car, Voss saw that Blackfriar seemed to be lost within himself.

"Are you all right?" he asked.

Blackfriar looked at him grimly. His shadowed face seemed angry. "You know what waits for us."

Voss nodded. "We're not defeated yet."

Blackfriar grimaced. "Can you restart the drive in time?"

The people behind the car shouted their readiness.

"Here we go!" Voss shouted back—and for an instant the lack of gravity made him see the tunnel below him as a deep dark hole in which people hung on a long line behind the suspended vehicle. At any moment the entire assembly would fall away into the pit.

He pressed the scooter into reverse, and as it began to pull back through the tunnel, his horizontal orientation reasserted itself.

"Make sure we pick up the stragglers ahead!" he shouted.

41

Blackfriar sat with eyes closed against the bright lights, with Voss facing him on the scooter as it retreated and pulled the car forward. Behind him, Blackfriar knew, shapes floated in the darkness, hanging onto the back of the vehicle and the trailing lines. These individuals would survive, he told himself, as a sickness of implications crept through him.

He was old enough to know patterns of history: the rich feared poverty, the powerful dreaded weakness, the living averted their eyes from the dead and dying. His world had known these things only rarely, and many of its citizens had never known them at all. Without the habitat's heritage of wealth, knowledge, and technology, longlife would end; without enough life, living would revert to the old evolutionary default settings, and on a damaged planet. Horror sat at the center of Blackfriar's thoughts, and he knew that Josephus Bely had put it there—*as did our own ignorance,* he reminded himself, *our own inability "to understand that which we no longer believe in," as a great thinker once said. It was our mere example, thoughtlessly presented, that tempted Bely to cling to life, setting up an intolerable conflict in an old man's beliefs.*

"Voss, can you hear me?" Blackfriar asked within himself.

"Yes."

"I think Bely acted alone."

"I agree," Voss said, "because it took special access to set the explosives in the old starship."

"Should we have feared these people, or been more cautious?" Blackfriar asked.

Voss said, "They appeared too backward to pose any threat. How could we have guessed that their leader would have the means?"

"We gave him the means by being curious about the old hulk," Blackfriar said.

"He gave us no time to discover the danger," Voss said.

"Cunning," Blackfriar said, thinking it strange to imagine anyone wanting to do such harm.

"We have to go faster," Voss said out loud. "Hang on, everybody!"

Blackfriar felt a moment of outrage. An impossible danger had all but destroyed his world. He kept his eyes closed and turned his face away from the bright lights, and for the first time in his experience he trembled. It was nature, that great *other* that still lived in his body, beyond the control of conscious mind, facing danger in its own way . . .

Random noises played in his head—musical tones, bursts of static, distant cries for help. He did not know how to set aside his feelings for the lost and those about to be lost.

"Silence," he said to the Link.

"Don't let go of the lines!" Voss shouted.

Blackfriar's vision flashed white, and pain pulsed through his head.

Voss stopped the scooter.

Blackfriar turned and saw that people had let go and were drifting, grasping their heads from the pain.

"Get ahold and hang on!" Voss shouted again, his voice echoing down the tunnel.

In the moments when his own pain lessened, Blackfriar realized what was happening. Dead and dying brains were still linked with the living, and there was not enough control left to filter out spurious signals from the injured and dying. Noise was being given auditory and visual form.

"Stop!" Blackfriar ordered within himself, hoping that the common demand for privacy would be enough to stop a damaged Link intelligence from harming its human partners as it drifted into disorder.

Light exploded behind his eyes. He felt anxious and fearful, and began to shake uncontrollably. The walls of the tunnel dissolved around him. The air became unbreathable, burning his lungs, and he was certain that the habitat had been hit again. He kept his eyes closed, resigned to a swift end.

But now other images played in the gray theater of his brain.

—burned bodies floated inside ruined structures—

—eyes gazed at each other and went dark—

—lungs gasped—

—skin melted away—

And he knew that images of the disaster in the forwards were fleeing from mind to mind, a second wave front of neutrino-carried information passing across the habitat, lingering orphans of experience still being thrown from mind to mind by a patchwork link field.

"Why?" asked the dead.

Curiosity persisted in fevered brains as their fear drained away into death . . .

Blackfriar's vision returned. He glanced around and saw that the people behind him were silently returning to the tow lines.

Voss restarted the scooter and began to pull the train along.

Blackfriar decided to risk the Link's pain with a question.

"How much time is left?" he demanded, but the Link was again silent, and he wondered if this had been its end.

42

Story and ritual domesticated life's terrors, Paul thought as he waited for Cardinal Breivis de Claves. Even the moment of death, the long-awaited passage to elsewhere, was not a departure into darkness, but a routine entrance into the fellowship of a god who waited for the tiring of mortal bodies, judged souls, and gathered the worthy to himself. Terror waited only for the unworthy, for the doubting who resisted instruction in the ways of faith or who sought strength in unbelief itself.

Twisted in upon itself, Josephus Bely's comatose brain was seeing whatever his upbringing and education permitted as he waited at the exit gate of life. Paul wished that he might be spared the delusions fueled by a lifetime of hopes that must now be gripping his brain.

Cardinal de Claves came into the chamber and motioned for Paul to remain seated at the conference table.

"Minister," he said in a raspy voice as he sat down in the chair at Paul's right, "we have decided not to assemble the Sacred College for its electoral duty while His Holiness still lives."

Paul nodded. It had been too much to expect. "But he may never reawaken," he said softly, thinking how easily he might have held his hand over the old man's mouth and no one would have been the wiser. It would not have been easy, but perhaps it would have been wise.

The cardinal's long, bony fingers emerged from his frayed red robes and seemed to hover for a moment; then he placed his palms down on the polished wooden table, looked directly at Paul, and said, "We realize that it may be some time before His Holiness passes from us, but as long as he breathes, you are asked to be his minister. No one wishes otherwise. You know him and his aims better than anyone."

The cardinal smiled slightly, and the wrinkles of his predator's face cut deeply around his eyes. *You understand perfectly well,* the eyes said, *don't you? The peace of your declining years depends on your answer.*

"Yes, of course," Paul replied, knowing that de Claves's clique needed more time to consolidate his position in the hierarchy, to ensure that the next election would be a foregone conclusion. "I assume that you have conveyed my report to the College?"

The cardinal nodded. Paul knew that they would also need a transition period in which to ascertain what records to seize, what protégés to watch—in effect, how to get the best possible use out of Bely's final departure. But perhaps he was giving them too much credit; maybe they were simply afraid.

"And what was their reaction?" Paul asked.

The cardinal withdrew his hands into his robes, pressed his lips together as he sat back, then said, "You claim that his Holiness destroyed the visitor. But he cannot speak for himself, so there the matter rests."

"Do you doubt my report?"

"Not at all, Minister. But until His Holiness speaks of the matter, the report will remain incomplete."

"You yourself saw the flash in the sky," Paul said with a sigh. "And you and I know full well that his daughter was on that world."

The cardinal did not answer. There could be no reply, Paul thought. His Holiness could not have had a daughter, had never acknowledged his daughter, and her death now ended the matter. The problem of her existence would never come up again.

"I am certain," de Claves said, "that His Holiness acted in our best interest."

Paul hesitated, then said, "Great injury may have been done. The habitat is home to twenty million people."

"So many—in that star?" de Claves asked. "It's a devil's lie."

Paul had no desire to argue plane and solid geometry with the cardinal.

"All these matters are closed," de Claves said. "The Senior Tribunal will not convene the College for any reason until His Holiness speaks, or passes from us."

"I do see the wisdom of your procedures," Paul replied.

Cardinal de Claves ignored his faint mockery, or had failed to notice. He looked at Paul intently for a few moments.

"His Holiness may in fact be medically dead," Paul said.

The cardinal shook his head in denial. "He breathes . . . and that is all we need to know," he said, stumbling over his words, and Paul was now sure that his group was in desperate need of delay. "As for the flash in the sky," de Claves continued, "you may be mistaken. The night sky is full of flashes. And you have had no radio communication with the visitor, either by sending or receiving?"

"That's true," Paul said.

The cardinal smiled at Paul with equanimity. "But perhaps you are anxious to retire to your villa?"

"No," Paul said decisively, knowing what de Claves wanted to hear. "I will remain as long as I am needed." He looked into the cardinal's eyes to make sure that he had been clearly understood, and saw that a strange youthfulness had entered the man's expression. Paul was now sure that he had given the cardinal what he had wanted; by agreeing to stay in office, he had granted de Claves the time he needed to make his ascent to the papacy certain. The College would insist on rigid legality; de Claves needed Paul to confirm that Josephus Bely, Pope Peter III, still lived, whatever the facts. The cardinal would make his move when Josephus was decomposing, by which time his opponents would be powerless.

"There must never be any doubt about the regularity of the succession," de Claves said. "There must be no irregularity to be questioned."

"I understand," Paul said, knowing that no other group would be given even the slightest chance to gain power, not in the College of Cardinals, among the merchants or the military, or in whatever was left of the student cells. A consolidation of alliances had been going on for some time, and would continue. All the political convicts were gone. One hierarchy would shade off into another as quietly as possible. Nothing would change.

The cardinal again seemed a little unsure of himself. He sat still for a few moments, then asked, "They all perished in the void, then?"

"I don't know," Paul said. "Their world had numerous smaller craft, so it's possible that there are survivors. But we must keep in mind that disaster came upon them suddenly, so they may not have had time to save many."

"Perhaps there were none at all," said the cardinal.

"We'll know soon enough."

"They will come here?"

"They have nowhere else to go," Paul said.

De Claves grimaced. "It is curious for them to have wanted to live in that outer darkness, shamed by immensity, in a prison of their own making, when the Lord made real worlds for his creations to live in."

Paul felt himself grimace involuntarily and leaned forward to reply, noting that the cardinal seemed pleased to have provoked him. "Despite what it seemed, Cardinal," Paul said, "this was a world, with an interior surface of levels within levels greater in square kilometers than our own. I also need not remind you that our ancestors crossed a shaming immensity to settle here. These people are also what has survived of Earth. They were our brothers and sisters, these people who came to visit us. A great crime has been committed."

"Very sinful brothers and sisters," de Claves said, "to have provoked His Holiness to act against them. I remind you that in matters of great moment, His Holiness cannot be faulted."

Paul did not answer. The cardinal watched him silently for a while, then said, "The sins of His Holiness, if they have been sins, are matters for him and the Lord to reconcile."

Then, slowly, as he got up to leave, he said, "Your concern is noted, and does your Christianity credit. We will be in good hands."

The cardinal waited for Paul's reply; but when it did not come, he nodded as if in approval and turned to go.

Paul watched the cardinal leave the conference room, then sat back and massaged his eyes and temples. He had just been measured for practical loyalty, nothing else. The cardinal, like all curia members, valued outwardly correct loyalty, nothing more; privately held views and sympathies mattered little unless they threatened that loyalty. Change was best when slow, if it had to come. Josephus had permitted too much of it, so his exit would be the slowest.

As he considered the cardinal's motives, Paul remembered when Josephus had been charming, diplomatic, and generous during the years of Paul's transition from a man of learning to prime minister. Josephus had taken some practical pride in bestowing access to knowledge. "Someone must understand what is not good for all to know," he had said, laughing, "so it might as well be you, since you love it so much. I will keep you close, and your knowledge might be of some use one day."

He had delighted in furnishing Paul's apartment, in appointing pages, assistants, and helpers. One of his favorite activities was to take Paul along on his surprise visits to the kitchens.

Paul recalled being troubled by Bely's attentions and trust, but the pontiff had not asked anything ignoble of him in those years; that had come later, when he had sought to limit education through doctrine. "A little education leads to unbelief," Bely had told him. "Intensive education can lead to profound belief," Paul had answered. "Yes, but we can't count on it to happen every time," Bely had insisted.

Paul had put his position in danger by opposing him, but Josephus had relented because he wanted to keep Paul with him and because he suspected that if pushed too far, Paul might reveal his knowledge of Lesa, Josepha's unfortunate mother, even though Paul had never mentioned the affair. It had never even crossed his mind to blackmail Josephus with the existence of his daughter, the child of a suicide.

So for a time the sons and daughters of merchants and professionals had enjoyed a relatively censor-free education, much of which they promptly forgot when they left university.

But Bely's insecurity had grown, increasing with the pressure from the cardinals to curtail education and reforms. He had become distant, but he was still dependent on Paul's administrative skills. Gradually, the existence of a daughter became common knowledge among the most influential cardinals. Bely himself had spread the rumors of Josepha's birth, like a prideful father, but also hoping to remove the threat of what he thought was Paul's unvoiced blackmail.

In time, Paul had learned how to give Bely the loyal service he demanded while pursuing his own private interests in science and history. Neither side made the arrangement explicit.

Paul had once hoped that Jason or Ondro might become his protégé, but Josephus had accepted de Claves's charge that the Avonmoro brothers were enemies emerging, with others, from the promiscuous form of education championed by Paul. When they had disappeared, Paul realized that there would be no one to whom he might pass on his position of access to the Church's hoard of knowledge, no one to whom he might teach his way of knowledge.

Yet it was because Paul had lived at the center of his own universe, doing what little good was possible, that Cardinal de Claves had come to him this evening. Like Bely, de Claves wanted to keep an oracle in reserve; and like Bely, he preferred a seer who wore self-forged chains.

Cardinal de Claves, Paul had always suspected, had been more than a gossip or informer. He had been Bely's hatchet man, the one who had removed Jason, Ondro, and most of their followers. He might even have contrived the first meeting of Ondro and Josepha, to keep tabs on dissenters by watching her.

Paul now asked himself whether he could be certain of de Claves's demands, and whether they would bring him safety. Were they the same as Bely's? Did he wish simply to have a knowledgeable minister, a devil's advocate in thrall to his personal power? Paul concluded that this was the likely case, because genuine power never lost touch with reality; it always wanted to hear the truth, but in private, in order to better control it. De

Claves knew that he needed to know more than he could permit.

Paul stood up at the empty table, and knew that he had to go look at the sky.

Alone on the terrace, Paul found the mobile among the stars of the zenith. He had not expected to find it at all.

The habitat seemed brighter, and he wondered if that would be one result of the damage, then realized that it might be because it was closer. He sat down in Bely's chair and realized that the habitat might be nearer if its sun orbit motion had been slowed by the explosions.

His heart raced and sweat broke out on his brow as he considered that the habitat might be on a collision course with his world. Were there survivors? Was the mobile now incapable of powered motion?

He watched the bright star for a few minutes, and it seemed to him that it was growing brighter steadily; but that might be an illusion made by his fear, he told himself.

He got up, went down into the square, and crossed the vast expanse of stones, glancing up repeatedly at the bright star as he hurried toward the small observatory at the far corner, afraid that his suspicions would be confirmed but also telling himself that the mobile might fall into an orbit around his world.

In the observatory dome, he looked through the eyepiece of the one-meter reflecting telescope and quickly found the mobile.

Miraculously, it seemed intact, and he quickly imagined that something had gone wrong with the bombs, producing more flash than destruction. Bely's scheme had failed!

But there might have been some damage, even deaths, and perhaps now the mobile was approaching to exact some retribution. At the very least there would have to be a meeting, in which he would simply offer the truth as an explanation.

He sat back from the telescope and looked up at the stars through the open section of dome, remembering the countless nights he had spent here observing, in love with the telescope he had designed and built with the mocking approval of Josephus Bely. There was nothing quite like the fall of starlight on a human eye that knew what it was seeing, that knew it was looking back into time at suns that might no longer exist . . .

He looked into the eyepiece again, trying to discern some details in the image of the mobile; but he saw only a disk, which told him that perhaps the egg-shape was pointed in his direction. He saw no damage, and tried again to imagine what had happened.

After a few minutes, he considered going downstairs to the radio room and trying to raise the mobile again. But he looked into the eyepiece one more time, reluctant to waste the time it had taken his eyes to adjust to the dark, and saw a scattering of faint stars in a position that seemed to be above and behind the mobile. They seemed to shift position against the fixed stars he knew. Puzzled, he stared at the gathering, then realized they had to be smaller vessels from the mobile. He waited, and saw that two more seemed to have just emerged from behind the mobile.

He sat back, rubbed his eyes, then decided that he would try the radio one more time.

43

As his scooter pulled Blackfriar's utility vehicle and its train of survivors toward the rear docks, Voss saw by his panel display that too much time was passing, but there was no way to go faster than twenty-five kilometers per hour. With some ten kilometers left to go, he consoled himself with the thought that others might be making better time to the bays. It was possible, he realized, that there would be no vessel left to take this group to safety.

"How much time is left?" he asked inwardly.

But the Link did not answer.

As he sat looking at Blackfriar and the people clinging to the rope behind the vehicle, Voss reminded himself that all might still not be lost, that the habitat might yet be diverted from its collision course.

Blackfriar looked up at him and said, "My Link is still silent."

Voss nodded. "Mine also."

The kilometers went by slowly. Finally, Blackfriar leaned forward and peered ahead. Voss turned around, saw the lighted space of the terminal, and brought the scooter to a halt at the entrance.

"Lead them inside," Voss said to Blackfriar as he pushed toward a rail and pulled himself toward the main area.

The bay seemed as full as when he had left it, and he knew that people were still arriving, and not leaving fast enough.

As he drifted to one side, a hand touched his shoulder and held it.

He turned and saw Josepha and felt a moment of relief. Jason hung next to her. Their faces looked at him with grim expectation of what he might say.

"Ondro went to the forwards," she said with resignation, "to examine an old ship."

"Do you know what happened?" Jason asked.

"No," Voss said, moved to lie by the desolation in Josepha's eyes.

"Can the habitat be diverted?" Jason asked.

"There may not be time," Voss said, looking around. "You must get on a line and stay there."

Josepha touched his drifting hand. He took hers and held it for a moment, unable to speak.

"I will do what I can," he said after a moment, and looked to the information screen behind her.

It now showed that six of the twenty shuttles, including the two largest, were free of the mobile in their own sun orbit, carrying more than a thousand people. At this rate, he estimated that not more than three thousand people might be saved. The reality of these small numbers stunned him, and for a moment he was unable to think.

He turned his head and saw Blackfriar drifting at his side.

"This is not enough," Voss said. "It will never be enough."

"Equipment," Blackfriar said calmly. "We have to make sure that basic equipment goes with these vessels."

They both looked at the screen. Equipment supply programs were running, loading modules from below the cradles.

"The Link is still working," Blackfriar said.

Four more shuttles showed as launched on the small screen. Voss watched the slugs move off and knew that at this rate people would still be crowding this bay when there were no more craft to fill and the habitat entered the planet's atmosphere.

"Voss!"

He turned at Josepha's shout and saw that she and Jason were moving toward a loading exit with a group of people. He pulled himself over to her.

"Aren't you coming with us?" she asked from behind the guide rail.

"No—there are still things I have to do."

She took a nervous breath, and her eyes searched his face. He touched her hand, then held it, unable, he knew, to conceal his dismay.

"Is there any chance Ondro might have survived somewhere?" she asked.

"If we can restart the drive long enough to divert the habitat into orbit around the planet, then we'll have time to search among the survivors."

"Is that what you're going to do now?" Jason asked.

Voss nodded. "Yes, the drive," he said, looking intently at Josepha. "That has to come first." *Or else everything will be lost,* he did not say.

"Will you be on a later shuttle," Josepha started to say, "if—"

He nodded, let go of her hand as she turned away, and pulled back along the rail. The sudden thought of never seeing her again dulled his concentration as he returned to Blackfriar at the small screen, which now showed the nightside of Ceti IV. The darkened planet seemed to be coming up from below to crush the habitat with its great mass.

Voss said, "I'm going back now to try the restart controls."

Blackfriar nodded. "Don't wait for the last possible moment, or you may not get away in time."

"It has to be as soon as possible," Voss said. "It will push us off the collision course, quicken it, or function wildly. Or nothing will happen."

Blackfriar was looking at him with eyes that seemed more deeply set than usual, as if his mentor never expected to see him again.

44

On his way back from Bely's bedside, Paul decided to get some air before retiring to his apartment. It was sunset as he stepped out into a spring breeze and saw the flyer waiting on the terrace just beyond the place where he had sat with Josepha only yesterday. That had been years ago, he thought as he looked at the small craft, remembering the hope that it had brought him. And it had been an age since the habitat's arrival . . .

He tensed as he realized that he was about to learn how badly the mobile had been damaged, and the meaning of its present motion in the sky.

He peered through the evening shadows, and saw two figures sitting in Jacob Kahl's carved wooden chairs.

One shape stood up from the chair in which Bely had sat, and Paul saw that it was Josepha. He hurried forward, his heart quickening at the fact that she was alive. Blackfriar got up from the other chair and turned to face him.

"Our habitat is severely damaged," Blackfriar said, "and unless we can use its drive, it will strike your world on the far continent in less than nine hours. We have come to warn you about what to expect."

"I . . . suspected the possibility," Paul said, "after I made some observations. I was here when Josephus announced to me alone that he had activated the old bombs in the starship. He is near death. I have just come from him."

"Nearly all the habitat's people will die if it is not diverted," Josepha said coldly. "About twenty million people."

Paul could not see her face clearly in the dying light, but he was reluctant to meet her gaze as his distress warred with his happiness that she was alive.

"He told me at the last moment," he said quickly, "when nothing could be done to stop it. Only he knew."

"You should know," Blackfriar said, "that the effects of the mobile's mass coming through your atmosphere at great speed will kill much of the life in that hemisphere."

"Can nothing be done?" Paul asked.

"Voss is trying to divert the mobile," Blackfriar said, "but he may fail. You should know that the effects of the collision will reach you here."

Paul wanted to tell them to sit down again, but it seemed foolish to do anything but stand. He took a step back and stumbled.

Josepha came toward him suddenly, took his arm, and led him to his chair. He sat down, feeling her change of heart and concern toward him, and for a moment he saw Bely in the empty chair, staring into the white glare of the explosion.

Josepha stood close, then sat down in front of him on the terrace stones, and held his hand as Blackfriar stood facing them.

"As the far continent burns," Blackfriar said, "and the quakes begin, enough dust will fill the atmosphere to blot out the sunlight. In the long winter that will follow, most plant life will die. Agriculture will become impossible. You will have famine. But it will not get that far."

Paul nodded, feeling weak. "What do you mean?" he asked.

"Nearly all your people will die in a day or two after the strike," Blackfriar said.

Shaken, Paul sat back and took a deep breath. "How?" he asked, even though he already had some idea of what Blackfriar was about to tell him.

This, Paul thought bitterly as he listened to the details of death, was to be the price of Bely's great crime. History totaled its losses in his mind—the Crusades, the Inquisition, the churchmen's destruction of heathen cultures, the active or acquiescent support of corrupt bloody regimes, the persecution of great intellects, the intolerance of other creeds and of unbelief—and to them he now added the coming wreckage of Peter III's assault on Satan. The first pope on Ceti IV had been the only one to repeat the name of Christianity's first leader, as a sign of the Church's rebirth on this world; now another Peter had condemned it to death, and would likely be the last pope of human history. For a moment Paul wondered whether any other denominations had escaped the death of Earth to transplant their schismatic rule among the stars . . .

"Come with us," Josepha's dark shape said to him when Blackfriar had finished.

"What do you mean?" Paul asked. "Where can you go?"

Blackfriar said, "We're planning to assemble an interstellar vessel from our surviving craft."

"How many of you—" Paul started to ask.

"About three thousand so far," Josepha said sadly.

"Any of ours?" Paul asked.

"Jason," she said, "and about a dozen others. Ondro is dead." He felt her hand tighten in his.

"Most of the people we took from the islands," Blackfriar said, "were recovering from their ill health and deprivations when their end came."

"I'm sorry about Ondro," Paul said to Josepha, dismayed that her beloved had been so unreasonably doomed.

Blackfriar said, "If the mobile perishes, we plan to take the starship to the Praesepe star cluster, some five hundred light-years from here. The drive configuration that we can assemble may get us there in about a month. There is a base orbiting one of the outer stars, with enough supplies and equipment for us to begin construction of a new habitat. As soon as we're well begun, we might be able to send back a larger vessel to see what has happened here."

Paul knew that Blackfriar was speaking charitably, but the meaning of his words in terms of justice and human lives seemed to be affecting his composure.

Paul stared at Bely's empty chair, then looked up into the evening sky, and asked, "Will there be any chance of survivors for us here?"

Blackfriar said, "It will be unpredictable, but there may be shock pockets, cocoons of small areas which might be spared the ground upheavals, the fires and floods. . . ."

"How could some of us survive the flood you described?" Paul asked.

"Perhaps in oceangoing vessels—but even then, you'd have the problem of later survival."

"What about your people?" Paul asked, unable to think about the agonizing possibilities.

"Many of our people are badly injured," Blackfriar continued. "Only those who make it to the rear docks on their own will survive. We're trying to suspend as many of the injured as we can't help now, but we're uncertain of the equipment. We have few specialists or teachers among the survivors, and only small computers, well below intelligence capacity, with limited knowledge cores and skill-imparting programs. Our Link intelligence is nearly dead, and we have few medical people. . . ."

He stopped again, and Paul half expected him to lash out at him with bitter words.

"Fortunately," Blackfriar continued, "there are two Link cores at Praesepe, equal to our Link. But these have never been awakened, and it will take some time to birth and educate them."

"It seems to me," Paul said, "that by the time you can return there will be no one here to help."

"A small ship," Blackfriar said, "with food synthesizers and portable energy plants could help you preserve a small community of survivors through the winter."

"May I be blunt?" Paul asked. "Why should you care, after what we've done to you?"

Blackfriar looked up and said, "We may lose all our millions, with three thousand survivors, a few of them yours, because of one man's hatred. You may lose fifty million. We are not about to punish you."

"Could anyone inside it survive the mobile's impact?" Paul asked.

"No," Blackfriar said, "not even in the core. As it comes into your atmosphere, the habitat will be destroyed in about three seconds."

An Alexandrian Library of advanced people and knowledge was about to perish, Paul realized. Why was Blackfriar here, he asked himself, and realized that the reason, in part, was Josepha.

"You should be inside," Blackfriar said, "when the shock of high winds and heat reaches you from the other side of the world. Many of your people will survive that. Some will live through the groundshock, but then—"

As Josepha stood up from the stones and seemed anxious to speak, Paul rose with her and asked, "Are there others of your kind who might be summoned to help you . . . and us?"

"No," Blackfriar said with chilling calm. "Our tachyon transmitters are gone—but even if we could build one it would take months to sweep the sky and find another mobile. There are probably twenty others in the Galaxy, by our estimate, but they have gone their separate ways. Even if we could transmit, help might have to come from very far away. We may try after we reach Praesepe."

Paul nodded, then asked, "Can you take any of our people to safety? Perhaps a random sample of a few people from the city."

"Come with us," Josepha said suddenly.

"No," Paul said, "that would be too easy."

"Where is Josephus?" she asked.

"In a coma, and not expected to reawaken. He collapsed after the flash, when I told him you were there."

She came up close to him, and Paul saw her face clearly in the starlight, eyes wide and unblinking, free of tears.

"Do you wish to see him?" he asked, knowing that he would not let her take him away. Even the smallest chance of restoring him now struck Paul as a potential resurrection of evil.

She shook her head. "Paul, you must come with us. You should not have to face what is coming."

"I deserve to face it," he said. "I helped bring this about. Our people are innocent. I'll do what little I can." He looked to Blackfriar and said, "I'm grateful that you came to tell me." *And to let me see Josepha for the last time,* he thought.

Blackfriar came closer and stood with Josepha. "We might be able to take a dozen people," he said, "you and a few others."

"So few?" Paul asked.

"Yes," Blackfriar said. "Our means are much diminished."

"Should we issue a public warning of what is to come?" Paul asked.

"There's not much a warning could do. Is there an underground place where you could shelter a small group?"

"Would it help?" Paul asked.

Paul thought of the deep places beneath the papal palace, and felt sweat break out on his face. He thought of the millions about to die in the habitat, and the millions of his world, and felt their innocent lives condeming him.

"Come with us," Josepha repeated. "What will happen here does not need your sacrifice."

"There will be nothing you can do," Blackfriar said.

"I don't deserve to leave," Paul said. "Besides, you'll be back to help us. A month or two? Maybe some of us will last that long."

"We'll make every effort," Blackfriar said. "The library of human life is not so large that we can leave still more of it to perish."

Blackfriar's words moved Paul, but he could not answer.

"We also provoked Josephus Bely," Blackfriar said.

Paul shook his head in disagreement. "No—how could you have guessed that he would strike out so viciously when I, who knew him all his life and was once his friend, didn't suspect it? I see now that his bitterness toward death was horrendous and rare, strengthening itself with decades of self-importance and fading faith." He looked at Josepha, then back at the man from the stars. "You must never blame yourself for his envy, or for aspiring in the way that you do." He closed his eyes and tried to see the dead, and the dead to come. "I'm sorry," he said, thinking that if Josephus had truly believed in his God and in the life to come, he would not have done this terrible deed.

After a few moments, Josepha asked, "Will you be with him … at the end?"

"Yes," Paul said.

He turned away from them, as one damned turns away from the saved, and started to walk back toward the south entrance to the palace, where the long hallway would take him back to his apartment and office. There were officers and cardinals to instruct in justly useless preparations for the end of the world.

"Paul!" Josepha called after him.

He did not turn around as he walked away, but raised his hand in farewell, and for a moment feared that she would come after him. Blackfriar, if he would do her bidding, might easily overpower an old man and lead him to the flyer.

But when he heard no steps behind him, Paul knew that he had made his case with a conviction that Josepha would not dare to reverse by force.

When he reached the lighted entrance, he turned and saw the dark shape of the flyer slipping across the stars.

45

Voss peered ahead, trying to spot survivors in the tube as he ran the scooter back toward the auxiliary control area. The lack of survivors in the passage suggested that people were not leaving the levels into the tubeways in any great numbers, because they were either too injured to move or dead. The only remaining chance for the injured was to put the habitat into a safe orbit.

It was certain that even if the departure bays filled up repeatedly with survivors, there would eventually not be enough time left to carry people to the vessels standing off in sun orbit. He estimated that maybe twenty round trips would be possible, and only a small number of those individuals able to make it to the docks would be rescued in the time remaining. None of the injured and dying trapped across thirty levels would be saved, because there would be no time to bring them out. More could be saved with round trips to the planet, but that would only help the survivors if the mobile was diverted from a collision; otherwise, the rescued would only be arriving in time to die on the planet.

In any case, he doubted that the vessels standing by to receive the rescued could hold more than ten thousand individuals.

As he passed the point where Blackfriar's car had stalled, he noticed that the air was filling with strange odors, and realized that they were human smells from the dead and injured trapped in unsanitary conditions.

He heard voices, and his lights caught human figures making their way forward along the walls in zero gravity. There was no telling how far back the congestion extended or how many crossways elevators were feeding it. Faces stared into his lights as he stopped, heartened by the numbers of survivors he had not expected to see.

"Take this!" he shouted as he got off the scooter. "Extend the utility line as far back as you can and pull your group forward to the docks."

"And you?" a woman asked him.

"I'm going crossways to a control area. Let me through."

"Why?" a man asked as people made way for him.

"There's still a chance to drive us into a safe orbit!" Voss shouted.

Hands took him and gave him to other hands, lifting him high in the tunnel and passing him swiftly back toward the exit to the crossways.

"Hurry!" he shouted as he turned around at the elevator.

Its doors opened behind him and more people pushed out, jostling him as they drifted past. "There's a vehicle in the tunnel!" he shouted after them. "Add line to it, and it will tow you forward."

He pulled himself back into the elevator. The doors closed. He grasped a bar and touched for the level he wanted. Nothing happened.

He took a deep breath. The lights were still on, so there had to be enough power. He touched in the destination again, and the elevator moved, but slowly. He waited to arrive.

When the doors opened he expected to see a crowd, but there was no one. Then he reminded himself that this was engineering and maintenance, so there was no one who would have come here directly from a residential level except to reach the tubeway to rearwards.

He pushed out and the doors closed behind him. When next they opened, he feared that there would be too many people waiting, too many for the scooter to pull, too many to make it across twenty kilometers in time. This and other passages might be blocked for twenty-five kilometers from the bays. Beyond that, closer to forwards, there would be fewer able survivors.

He was certain now that the rescue shuttles would be overwhelmed. In the last moments of the mobile's life they would be forced to abandon people in the bays. If he could divert the mobile, it would suddenly become one large lifeboat; there would be time to salvage equipment and save just about everyone. The planet below would also be saved. It would not become a hell of wind, quakes, tidal waves, and fires, but a temporary refuge for his people.

It dismayed him to picture the death and destruction forward of the core, and to realize that he was one of the few survivors able even to attempt to save the habitat. Where were the others trying to do what he was about to do? The young men who were here before, where were they? They were gone by now, knowing that what he had to do would require only one person. Still, it was frightening to face the fact that so many were dead that only he and they had made it to the control area; there might easily have been no one at all.

He looked around, listening, realizing that he might die here alone. Death for him had always been a possible but unlikely accident, not something he had ever thought much about; but now he saw exactly how it might happen—and also that he had to risk it.

His life was insignificant before the millions that might be saved here on the mobile and down on the planet. He knew that if he saved their lives, he might also save his own.

But not necessarily.

To risk his life might well be a necessary condition for saving the mobile, and he might perish in the act of saving it. He had never thought of sacrificing his life for anyone or anything; it was something he had never imagined would be asked of him or anyone in the habitat. So how was it that he was asking it of himself?

He did not know how to answer or what to feel. In his linkless emptiness, he only knew what he had to do.

46

The glowing touchplates promised mastery over the vast forces of the drive generators. Voss hung over the panel, hands extended as if in prayer. One touch might accelerate the mobile past Ceti IV, or slow it into an orbit around the planet. There was no way to be sure. The damaged drive might tear the habitat apart with transient stresses or plunge it even more swiftly into the planet.

He thought of the people in the bays who might just now be

trying to leave. His action here might deny them their last chance.

"How much time?" he demanded within himself.

He waited, but there was no answer.

He looked around the chamber for a clock, spotted one, but it was not lit up. Either it was damaged or had not been set in some time. There had been little need to use this auxiliary facility. Who would have imagined that the habitat would be assaulted so decisively?

He pushed back from the temptation of the panel and tried to relax, consoling himself with the thought that people were getting away to safety with every passing minute. If he tried the drive now and it failed, he would be killing a certain number of people who might have lived; if it worked, he would save all the injured and living who could not reach a dock; a smaller number might still die from possible collision with the habitat during shuttle launch. If he was going to gamble with lives, it should be with those who would be left behind when time ran out. Every choice seemed against him.

His own pod still waited to carry him away. He would need at least fifteen minutes to reach it.

Voss waited, knowing that what was about to happen was already determined by the condition of the drive; yet he felt that he might still find some juncture, some instant of choice where his action would make the difference. Was there such a moment waiting for him to recognize it? It was an irrational thought, little more than a hope, but it held his attention as he returned to the panel.

No, he told himself as he hung over the panel, this was not an irrational hope, but a real possibility for him to seize.

He grabbed a handhold, braced himself, and touched the restart.

The panel dimmed, and the lights blinked in single color sequences, signaling the buildup toward the discharge of a gravitational wave front . . .

He waited.

Finally, the lights stopped flashing. The red touchplate glowed at the ready.

He pressed it and took a deep breath, expecting to feel a distant shudder as the mobile accelerated or decelerated.

The red light died and the board returned to restart.

He tried again, hoping that the drive would catch, if only for a few moments.

The board went through its cycle again, and the red light died.

He tried again, imagining that it might catch on the tenth, or even the twentieth try, minutes before the mobile hit the planet's atmosphere.

Again the red light winked out.

The damage was too pervasive, he realized, affecting backup systems, the power generator feeds to the drive, maybe even the power generators themselves. It was a mistake to think that because there was power in the back third of the habitat the drive generators might also work.

He let go of the handhold and drifted over the board. What did it matter now? What choices remained? He might ride his world down to death without regard for his own survival as he continued to try the drive; or he might leave and not think of all the living and injured he would leave behind. Voss felt his face flush. Moisture ran into his eyes, and he saw ahead to the emptiness that would inhabit him when his world was gone. How could he live with that, he asked himself as beads of sweat drifted near his face, sparkling as they caught the light from the board.

He looked around the drum-shaped chamber and felt weak. The air was going bad, he realized as his eyes lost focus and the chamber seemed to fill with a reddish fog.

He lost consciousness for what seemed only a few moments, then came to. Sluggishly, he grabbed whatever handholds he could reach and pulled himself toward the exit. A wash of cooler air revived him outside the chamber, and he remembered that he had to hurry to the pod. There was no way to tell how long he had been out.

One more restart, a distant voice whispered, *one more try might do it.*

He ignored the voice, insisting to himself that he would not remain conscious long enough in that chamber to carry out the procedure again.

Slowly, he crossed the engineering tunnel and found the locks that would get him back to the cradle where he had left his pod.

As he came up to the lock controls, he saw that all the touch-plates glowed red, indicating that the bank of bays was empty. All the pods had been used.

He closed his eyes and drifted, trying to think whether he should go back to the drive control chamber and cycle the board until the very end, to make his life count to the last instant . . .

He opened his eyes and looked around, listening to the whisper of air as he wondered how long he had been unconscious this time. The Link's silence inside him made him feel as if he had forgotten something.

He reached out to the panel and touched the controls to confirm their indications. The red lights blinked one by one, but the last one flickered green and stayed on.

That still might not mean anything, he told himself; red was no more to be trusted than green in a malfunction.

But he forced himself to touch the lock plate. The door slid open and he pulled himself down to the next lock. Here the indicator was also green. He pressed and waited for the lock to cycle.

He pushed forward as the door opened, and saw that his pod was still there. He pulled himself forward and up through the open bottom. It hissed shut as he touched the control.

Fresh air flooded into his lungs, clearing his brain. He strapped in and hit the eject plate, wondering how much time was left.

The pod shot out from the mobile, and the dark planet confronted him at his right. For an instant, it seemed to be attached to the ruined forwards of the habitat; but as the pod gained distance, Voss saw that planet and mobile were still separate.

He peered to his left and saw the transport shuttles—motes scattered in their orbit, glittering in the sunlight.

"Can anyone hear me?" he asked, and it seemed to him suddenly that in the deep silence within himself the Link would speak.

He turned the pod, and through its faceplate he saw his world against the planet's night. Atmosphere would soon howl into the wound of the open forwards and incinerate the dying flesh of his kind.

He closed his eyes to the sight, unable to accept what was about to happen.

47

In the large hold of the transport hauler that had taken in Voss's fleeing pod, people sat on the deck in groups of twos and threes, watching the overhead holo image.

Voss sat alone and tried to touch the Link. The foreshortening of the holo's high magnification made it seem that the ghostly habitat was pasted against the dark planet. He could not see the open forwards that faced the planet's onrushing atmosphere.

"Save us!" someone shouted in his brain.

"What is happening . . ."

"It's so cold . . ."

"I'm burning!"

Screams shot through him. Pain stabbed from behind his eyes, as if trying to escape, and Voss knew that the Link was struggling to deliver the last pleas of its dying human host, with no knowledge that its effort might damage those who had been spared.

"Be silent!" he commanded within himself, even though he had longed to hear the Link again.

"Help us!"

"We cannot see . . ."

People were holding their heads in pain. Some were lying down on the deck and moaning; others curled into fetal positions; many were already unconscious.

"Blackfriar!" Voss called out over the inner tumult, determined to make use of the Link while it lasted.

But he received no answer over the cries. He felt dizzy and leaned forward, then sat up again.

In the wispy field of the holo it seemed that the mobile was scraping across a large black stone. He closed his eyes and saw explosions. Glass ripped through his muscles. A hand closed around his heart, but he knew that the pain would end when the habitat struck the planet, silencing the Link.

He lay down on his side and waited as vermin crept through the tissues of his body, and tore at nerve endings.

"Help us!" cried the unsynchronous chorus within him.

Through teary eyes he saw the sharing of pain as people writhed around him on the deck.

"Be still," he pleaded with the Link, "convey no more. . . ."

But it was without control and did what chance permitted. Human voices flowed through its labyrinth, praying for help that it could no longer give while Voss waited patiently for the end. Nothing else would now free the linked survivors from the mind mass of injured and dying inside the habitat or prevent damage to those who were still whole.

He opened his eyes and watched the holo. The mobile was smaller, sinking forward end first into the planet's ocean of air.

Suddenly he feared that the strike would not break the Link cleanly, that there might be a jolt of nervous energy as the mobile hit, enough to cripple all of the survivors in the shuttles.

As the pain in his body swelled, he knew that the Link was still struggling. It did not feel as he felt, but it knew that its end was near, yet still it continued to feed whatever systems were open, causing unintended harm. The child of human minds, the dream of past visionaries, babbled, unable to help its people as it faced destruction.

One more restart, a distant voice whispered to him, *just one more . . .*

He lay on his side, head on the deck, watching the silent, stately inevitability with which the mobile struck the planet.

For a fraction of a second, its one-hundred-kilometer length stood up out of the shallow atmosphere.

There was no time, in the first two seconds of its fifty-kilometers-per-second rush, to fragment.

In the third second it was smashed all the way into the ground.

He sat up, suddenly relieved of pain, as the subnuclear flash shot out in all directions, ionizing the air and vaporizing everything for hundreds of kilometers around the impact with skyshine alone.

Slower shockwaves of heat went out, setting fires, and then putting them out with blasts of wind.

A big boom, he knew, was starting through the planet, rippling through its solidity, starting a dance that would wake up old volcanoes, birth new ones, and shake the ocean floors.

Antipodal vulcanism, he knew, would open huge volcanic seeps on the other continent, and the quaking would be as violent as at the impact site.

The shaking of sea bottoms would send out tidal waves more than a kilometer high to sweep the planet. . . .

All in a day . . .

There would be little life left to starve when gas and dust shut out the sun and shrouded the planet in winter.

48

"It struck the unsettled continent," Blackfriar said to the gathering in the hold of the largest surviving spacecraft. "We should send down a reconnaissance team."

Voss had come over in the pod as soon as he had learned Blackfriar's location. In every vessel, a few survivors had suffered brain damage from the Link's random feedback. Many were comatose. Most appeared unaffected, but only time would reveal if they had suffered any less obvious damage. He wondered about himself as he looked around at the group. All the Link's routine functions were gone, which meant that medical diagnosis would lose all subtlety. Informationally, the individual was now reduced to his own memory.

"What could we find down there?" a woman said sadly. "A grave. I've never seen a grave . . ."

Voss looked at a thin, long-boned woman with short brown hair and gray eyes. He did not know her. He did not know any of the people here, except for Wolt Blackfriar, and realized that all the people he had known and loved best—Loran, his best friend in childhood, Tarla Ojemi, who had first taught him mathematics, Calida . . . who had been his first physical love—might all be dead. He knew that it was likely, with so few survivors, that Wolt might be the only personal friend he had left.

"Nothing of use to us would have survived, even in the core," Blackfriar said. "But we should examine and record the site."

Voss stood up and said, "We should give detailed warning of the coming winter."

The woman who had spoken so bitterly looked up at him with uncaring eyes. Voss had never seen such a look in the face of a fellow citizen.

She asked, "Which of us will tell them? Which of us will go to see . . . what's left?"

The look of rage and dismay in her eyes meant she knew the number of the dead. Nearly twenty million individuals were gone—all the youngest and nearly all the longlived. The helpful intelligence that had been more than the habitat's nervous system was gone. The Link had grown with the mobile, becoming its shared soul and history, and it had died in every survivor—an entire living culture ripped from human minds and scattered.

"Why tell them anything," the woman said. "They'll know soon enough, when they start dying." She spoke with a restrained satisfaction.

Voss held back, trying to find an answer.

"What about us?" she asked. "What are we going to do?"

Blackfriar looked around at the saved and said, "We've already given them some warning. There's nothing anyone can do to save them from what's coming now."

Voss thought of Josepha, and wondered what the survivors from Ceti would be able to say to the survivors of his mobile.

"We are partly to blame," Blackfriar said, "but it was difficult to foresee that our very presence here would provoke an unstable leader to strike at us. The weapons were old and well hidden."

"We did not have to come here!" a young man shouted, and Voss now recognized him as one of the four he had found in the auxiliary drive chamber. Earlier, the youth had shouted the same comment, when Blackfriar had first summarized, to shocked staring faces, what had happened. Not everyone had heard all of the details through the failing Link.

Blackfriar held up his hands and said, "Ceti IV was . . . an island of humankind from Earth. It was only natural for us to have taken an interest while we constructed the new habitat. A group of us wanted to live on a planet, and this was a chance to let them go."

We should have kept our distance, Voss thought, *until we understood them better. We should not have come so close. Better to have sent in smaller vessels than to have come so close.* A million years of human skill, saved from a dying Earth, were now crushed and cooking in a cauldron of melting soil and rock.

He thought of the six hundred thousand lives lost in the virtuals when their inputs of energy had stopped. Inner suns and stars had ceased to be as minds had faded. He imagined what it had been like in the matrix tanks, as they continued to function, oblivious to events in the primary world, as the mobile struck the planet. No creative command given in the forgetful wish-worlds could have prevented the crushing intrusion from outside.

"I'm as responsible as any of the council," Blackfriar said.

We were so unsuspecting, so innocent, Voss thought, struggling with his regrets. He had known small ones in the past, never imagining that regrets might ever loom so large.

"So what now?" a man's breaking voice demanded.

49

Voss intended to inspect the strike area alone, but Josepha followed him to the flyer.

"Take me with you," she said urgently.

He looked at her with surprise, unable to understand why she would want a closer look.

"I have to see it," she said. "This is my world. My father did this. Paul admitted it to me and to Wolt Blackfriar. He planned the death of your world." She twisted her hands together and stared at him with tormented eyes.

"Your father?" Voss asked, confused. He had been assuming that Paul Anselle was her father, or at least a relation.

"The Pope," she said bitterly. "Josephus Bely, His Holiness Pope Peter III. He's my father."

Voss did not know what to say. The fact was significant, but no blame could be attached to Josepha unless she had participated in Josephus Bely's plan. Voss was suddenly afraid of learning something that would forever change his view of the Cetian woman.

"I haven't known that I was his daughter for very long," she continued. "Paul confirmed the truth to me not long after I had learned it from Bely himself, just before the arrival of your world." She closed her eyes for a moment, then opened them and said, "Take me with you, Voss. I deserve to see more of my father's handiwork."

By the broken look in her eyes, Voss felt that she was already at the disaster, her guilty imagination raising terrifying images. He wanted to refuse her request, but was suddenly alarmed at what she might do if left alone. The Link might have advised him to speak consolingly to her now, or to place her in the hands of someone wiser about the strong emotions of guilt and despair. Was she raging? Her mental universe was foreign to him, but he felt its edges expanding toward him.

"Take me with you," she insisted.

The sun was just coming up when their flyer approached the site. The great column of gas and dust stood visible for thousands of kilometers. It went straight into the sky, a roiling mountain of black and white and red, standing on a base of several thousand square kilometers of molten crust.

"It's monstrous!" Josepha cried out when they were still fifty kilometers away. "Do we have to go closer?"

"No," Voss said. "There won't be much else to see."

Twenty million people, he lamented, thinking that their loss was so much greater than what the Cetians would suffer in the next day or two. He was unable to feel otherwise as he looked at the titanic pyre, because he could not bring himself to place an equal value on the backward world that now waited to die—even though his reason insisted that only a few people were responsible for the destruction of his world. In the silence where the Link had been, he now felt a strange numbness.

As Josepha looked at him, he wondered what it was that he felt for her, and tried to set aside that she was Josephus Bely's daughter, born of the very backwardness that had reached out to take his world from him.

"Voss?" she asked. "What is it?"

Old human feelings, he realized, flowed through him now like a black river. They belonged to the ways of hatred and revenge, which had written so much of human history; and here they were within him, still under control but threatening to run wild without the Link's subtle counsels. He would soon know for himself the states that Josepha had been familiar with all her life.

"You hate us," Josepha said. "You hate me. I don't blame you."

He felt apprehensive as he thought of what might now happen to his fellow survivors. Linkless, would they learn to hate?

He touched her hand as the flyer made a wide circle before the pillar and tried to say what his mentors and Link would have urged him to say.

"No, I don't hate you, Josepha."

What he would not say to her was that at this moment he felt very little for her. The longings that had begun to grow for her had been cut short in him. They were lost somewhere in the same emptiness carved out of him by the Link's death, and he did not know whether he would ever be able to find his feelings for her again.

She looked at him uneasily.

"We must wait," he said, and saw that his words seemed to stir some hope in her eyes.

"Thank you for that," she said softly, "but I won't expect any-thing."

"Maybe sometime soon," he said, "I will explain to you."

His words surprised him, as if someone else had spoken them; and he realized that his thoughts were not in order, that he did not know what they would be when he brought them to order.

"I will explain," he said, "when I know better myself."

50

Dark clouds marbled the planet's atmosphere as the continent burned and shook. Fifty thousand kilometers above the planet's fiery nightside, the mobile's survivors, working through repair robots, assembled a makeshift starship from their smaller craft.

The vessel's core was a sluglike hull one half kilometer long. Small craft were being fitted to form chambers within the whale shape. A massive dumbbell assembly at the bow was a deflector field generator, placed to protect the living areas from hard radiation created by high-speed collisions with interstellar particles. A dual drive was being improvised: a field-effect pusher for rela-tivistic velocities, and a jump unit.

As the devastated continent rode toward daylight, a red cyclops's eye seemed to open as the clouds cleared over the area where the mobile had melted the crust.

In the forward control room, Blackfriar looked away from the sight in the holo tank and said, "Fortunately, this patchwork ship of ours will not have to work for very long."

Voss changed the view from the planet's cancerous confla-gration to one of stars. His way of life was out there, he reminded himself, growing, reproducing, diverging. *Macrolife moves like new, swift thoughts through the Galaxy,* he told himself, *even if we fail to return to it.*

"We have enough for this one passage," he said. "But we lack diagnostic links for most of our systems. We can't run sleep units, life support, and surgical units all at the same time. We have enough power, but distribution is limited by the routines we can build. We must reach Praesepe as soon as possible."

Blackfriar was silent as they looked at the stars in the tank.

Voss said, "There's just no time down there for any survivors to set up anything more than a few precarious survival redoubts. And we may not be able to get back here in time to help."

"One step at a time," Blackfriar said, and Voss felt an irrational anger. The Link had moderated internal states by providing a sense of personal security, a constant background awareness in the individual that there would always be enough resources and life to deal with anything. But now, as he lived with the fact that his world had all but died and another was dying, he began to think differently. The inward universe of Link and individuals, education and experience, growing like an infinitely branching tree of life, had been cut back to the danger point. For the first time in his life he had to live with an irreversible fact: these dead would never come again. Not even a new beginning would soften the memory. He explained to himself how it had happened, how a chain of events had led to this unforeseen disaster, but he could not rid himself of the suspicion that it might have been prevented.

"Is there something very wrong with us," he asked Blackfriar, "for this to have happened to us? Why did we not see that this could happen?"

"One envious, despairing man," Blackfriar said, "had the weapons to magnify his animosity toward us. Is there anything wrong with us? Yes—we are not all-knowing or perfectly rational, so we failed to foresee what might happen when we came so close to our own kind's living past."

"We should have left them alone," Voss said, "to grow out of their past in their own way. Josephus Bely trembled at the edge of death, and our arrival pushed him to strike at us, as we unknowingly showed him how backward he was."

"Maybe we should have given him his life," Blackfriar said. "But then that would have changed him, made him dependent on us, our puppet, and destroyed the way of life these people had set for themselves."

"It was changing anyway," Voss said, switching the view back to the ruined planet. "Anything would have been better than this!" he shouted at the red unseeing eye that gazed at him from Bely's heel.

"Bely might have struck at us later, when we were building the new mobile," Blackfriar said calmly.

Voss thought of Josepha and how the loss of her world might affect her. Would she be content never to come back here? He looked at Blackfriar sitting next to him, and the First Councilman's apparent calm seemed to say that what had happened could not have been prevented.

"We will have to come back here," Voss said, "if only to help a few."

"We will do everything we can," Blackfriar said, "one step at a time. Limit your thoughts to that."

But as he looked at the raging night face of the planet below, Voss felt a rush of desolation and loss that spoke to him wordlessly out of the human bodily past, urging him to revenge himself as Bely had done against the devils from the dark who had made him doubt his faith.

Voss closed his eyes before the burning, shaking world and recited to himself the Link lessons of his youth:

"An individual must deserve his society as much as his society must deserve the individual. One must not overwhelm the other."

He paused to remind himself that Bely's people had not deserved their ignorance. They had not deserved the short lives to which generations of priests had condemned them.

"Without knowledge, no people can know who they are," Voss continued. "History alone is not enough. Without the arrayed sciences, you will not know who you are, where you came from, and will remain powerless to choose what you might be. You will be faceless beneath your masks of mythic superstition and convenience."

Fearing the mix of knowledge and human nature that had destroyed the Earth, Ceti's generations of churchmen had chosen forgetfulness, and this had made them ignorant and fearful of losing power; and finally, in Josephus Bely, blindly envious and violent.

51

Blue-gray clouds crept in low over New Vatican. Dirty rain fell all morning. Paul Anselle sat at his desk and felt the tremors in his feet. Much of the city had been leveled by the quakes and antipodal vulcanism that Voss had warned would come, but somehow the papal palace and surrounding buildings, including the observatory, had escaped the ruinous shaking and uplifts, as if by the grace of God.

First had come the skyshine and high winds, the quakes and the ground upsurges; but the center had survived with only minor damage, protected by what Voss had described as shock cocoons, around which the ripples and volcanic shockwaves had flowed. At least for now. More was on the way very soon.

Today.

Josephus still breathed in the infirmary. Fearful, and ignorant of the meaning of what had taken place in the sky and on the far continent of their own world, the cardinals cowered in their apartments and looked to Paul to explain and lead. His very reluctance and unease in the past, which had not gone unnoticed, now made him trustworthy; yet he was still enough like them to be understandable.

But there was no time to explain what was coming to any of them. He had told de Claves, and the cardinal had passed along the relevant information. There was no time for them to take their servants and mistresses and retreat to their country villas. The palace, especially its underground levels, was as safe as anywhere.

They were down there, except for those who had tried to flee the city and were probably dead. But it would do them no good; the levels cut into the bedrock were not waterproof. He thought of going down to join the cowering clerics, but the thought of them on their knees, demeaning themselves in useless prayer, decided him to stay away. He would not add to the stone pickle jar of drowned and brined bony bodies below.

Josepha's last radio messages had pleaded with him to accept rescue, but he had refused.

Even if help came from Praesepe in the near future to save the unlikely survivors who might still be clinging to life three months from now, he could not imagine trying to outlive his shame over his failure to act against Bely. He might have said yes to Voss and Josepha's offer of rescue—and he might have taken a few of the younger palace officials with him—but this would have meant living in the prison of his rescuers' eyes.

Silence invaded his recriminations, convincing him that he had told himself the truth and was ready to accept the punishment that he deserved. He rose from his desk, knowing that he should go to Bely's bedside, because the friend of his youth might need him.

But it was not the friend of his youth who was dying, Paul told himself as he tried to open the top right hand drawer of his desk. The drawer stuck. He pulled at it roughly, and it slipped out and crashed onto the floor.

At once he knelt down, afraid that his prized possession, one of Galileo's original telescopes, had been damaged; but the instrument that had been brought from Earth by the starship captain who became Peter II appeared to be intact. Josephus Bely had given it to Paul to mark his appointment as prime minister.

As he was about to lift the drawer, Paul noticed that there was some writing inside the desk, carved into the wood where the words might be seen only with the drawer removed.

Kneeling closer, Paul read:

Angels and Devils and Snakes!
Vehes stercoris!
—Jacob Kahl

Paul laughed at the old Latin, which translated as "What a load of crap!" It was not idiomatic Latin or slang, but perfectly grammatical, and Paul wondered whether this might be Jacob Kahl's judgment of his own work, or of the subjects he had been given to depict, or maybe both.

Paul picked up the drawer and slid it in halfway, then stood up and took out the telescope. As he examined it more carefully for damage, he remembered that he had seen examples of woodcarver Kahl's writings twice before, many years ago on the backs of old work orders. It was easy to remember the man's fierce words:

"With all his great power to make a universe, I wonder how God failed to get us right. I think he gave up and started over somewhere else!"

"The sin of intellectual pride is a charge made by the stupid people who needed a smart man to invent it."

As he saw that the telescope was undamaged, Paul thought sadly that the centuries of church rule on Ceti IV had seen no Galileos, Leonardos, or Michelangelos—only mad Jacob Kahl, the secret apostate.

Paul became aware of a distant roar outside the tall, tightly shut windows behind his desk.

Today.

He turned, stepped over to the windows, and gazed out into the noonday brightness.

Beyond the ragged city stood a massive wall of water more than a kilometer high. Paul raised the telescope to his eye, and the sight produced an involuntary growl in his throat. He smiled, realizing how far he had grown from the miraculous—yet here it was.

The wave was not breaking. The water stood like a wedge, with fingers of foam reaching forward and upward as it brushed the clouds.

And behind this wave, he knew there were several others . . .

• • •

Josephus Bely opened his eyes. His mind was clear, his body free of pain, and he wondered whether he was in the hands of God or the devil.

But as he looked at the cross on the wall in the palace infirmary, he knew that his church had been taken from him. A new heaven had stolen his sky, but it was not the heaven of God, but of man—of hell.

He turned his head, expecting to see Paul sitting by him; it seemed that he had done so; but there was no one.

"You turned a heaven into a raging hell," Paul's voice seemed to say, "and that hell has descended to consume us."

"Paul!" Josephus cried, suddenly afraid once more that all his years of faith had been only a pleading with a nameless infinity that he called God to give him eternal life. . . .

Only a simple need . . .

He heard a roaring sound, drifted off, and dreamt that he could not feel his feet.

And awoke in time to die . . .

52

Josepha glanced at the timer in the cramped quarters she was sharing with Voss and saw that departure was now only a few hours away. As she sat on the edge of the lower bunk and looked around at the drab metal walls and floor of the small cabin, she realized that she might never see her world again.

Voss's people no longer offered a better life, at least not any time soon; too much of their power was gone. Her father had seen to it that both planet and habitat had been wounded, perhaps beyond recovery; but she still wanted to believe that the people of the mobile had a better chance for the future than the long, probably doomed struggle that was beginning on her home world. She had to believe that; it was all she had left.

In all likelihood, Paul and Josephus had been drowned along with everyone in the city by the huge waves that had swept across New Vatican. Voss had offered to show her a visual record of the event, but she had refused, clinging to a small girl's hope that Paul, at least, had managed to sail away somewhere before the waves arrived.

She thought of her tour through the lost habitat, the paradise in which she had begun to glimpse her new life, and wondered if the mobile had always been too good to be true, even for its own people.

She felt like an orphan taken in by an ambivalent uncle, and she saw herself becoming Voss's handmaid, his Sister of Martha, aboard this makeshift, shabby vessel of survival. After all, laundry and food would be needed, and she had no idea how his clothing would be washed or his food prepared.

The door buzzed. She got up, steadied herself in the ship's half gravity, and went over to the narrow entrance. She touched the release plate and the door slid open.

Jason stood in the passageway. He had gained weight and did not look as tall as he had seemed after the rescue; his shoulders were slumped, his face drawn and tired.

"I want to speak to you," he said sternly. "In private."

"I'm alone," she replied, stepping back.

As he came in, she recalled his questioning looks of the past few weeks. He had been saving up whatever he wanted to say to her, and now the time had come for him to unburden himself.

She returned to the edge of her bunk and looked up at him.

"Are you with Voss Rhazes?" he asked. "I must hear it from you."

"I don't know," she replied, surprising herself with the indecision in her own voice.

He smiled sadly and stepped back to lean against the door. "I'd like to think that I had a chance with you."

Again, it surprised her as she looked up at him that she was unable to say at once that he had no chance.

He stepped forward and started to turn away, but paused.

"It should be me," he said bitterly. "There will not be many of us left."

She knew his next words.

"Ondro's only chance to live is through you and me, and our world is dying!"

His words shook her, but at the same time they seemed unreal.

"Well, say something," he demanded.

"We're going to get help for our world," she said.

He waited a moment, then said, "So I've heard."

"Extended life waits for us at Praesepe," she said, "so there's no need to think of offspring, at least not now. We will grow and change within ourselves. Maybe then we'll know what to do with living."

He gazed at her with astonishment. "Is that all you have to say to me?"

"I want to believe in a new way of life," she continued, looking away from him, "and I will try to live it."

"With Voss?"

"I can achieve it myself," she said, looking up at him, "with the help that will be given to all of us at Praesepe."

"There are fourteen Cetians on this ship," he started to say resentfully, "and we may be the last. Ondro and I didn't always agree on what changes might be good for us, but I feel quite differently now. If we reach wherever we are going, and get the help we have been promised, I will command the ship that will return. And I want you to promise that you will come back with us."

"And what will you do?" she asked. "Rule a ruined world?"

"We'll start over with what's left," he said with strained conviction, "and make it the world Ondro wanted."

"There will be nothing left," she said.

"Then we'll begin with what we bring," he insisted.

"I won't want to come back," she said, thinking of the new habitat that would be built.

"But you're one of only four women in our group," he said. "Do you know what your refusal will mean?"

Anger flooded into her. He had dreamed of remaking their world, yet he still seemed only too ready to bind her and the remaining Cetian women to lives dominated by the needs of men and children. She thought of Avita Harasta and the other women of the mobile, how free they had seemed, how unlike the women of her world. Even now, in the face of disaster, Josepha could not imagine Avita calmly assenting to what anyone else thought she should do; Avita would always choose for herself, reasoning her way to decision.

"A few of these people who wanted to settle on our world may wish to come back with you," she said, suspecting that this was now unlikely.

He said, "If Ondro meant anything to you, then you must plan to come back with us."

She could not answer.

"You must decide," he said fearfully, oppressing her with his disappointment and agony.

"There's nothing for me to decide."

He rubbed his forehead and said, "Help me understand."

"The life of these people," she said, "as it was before my father destroyed it, appealed to me. When they have it back, I will be part of it."

"Your father?" he asked with surprise. "What are you saying?"

"Josephus Bely was my father. He may already be dead. To go back to his kind of world, if it survives, would mean physical and spiritual suicide. It would be actual suicide to refuse extended life. Is that what you want?"

"Your father?" Jason asked again. "How do you know?"

"He told me himself," she said, "and so did Paul."

Jason took a deep breath and leaned back against the door again, looking defeated. "We knew you were a cleric's daughter, but this—why didn't you tell me earlier?"

"It has no meaning for me now," she said. "Think instead of all the people he has killed, and all our people who will die."

Jason took a few deep breaths and seemed to be struggling to control himself. "But we can bring all this help back . . . to our people," he managed to say. "If, as you say—"

"Then you do it," she said.

He looked down at her with a sudden calm and asked, "Do you love Voss?"

"I love him," she said, unsure but hopeful of her growing feelings.

Jason stared at her, overcome with unbelief, and for a moment it seemed to her that Ondro was looking at her through his brother's eyes, accusing her of mistaking gratitude and desperation for love.

"Accept my choice, Jason," she said. "Ondro would have wanted me to be freer, as he would have come to appreciate and understand the life that had rescued him, and which he would have embraced. My father also took that from him. The only victory you and I can ever have over Josephus now is to live the kind of life he denied to Ondro, and to so many others."

Jason swallowed hard and looked down at the floor.

"You'll find your own way," she said, feeling some sympathy for his disappointment and confusion.

He looked up. "You don't understand," he said with a face that had set into a mask.

"But I do," she answered, grateful for the resolve that came into her voice. "I am not your inheritance from Ondro. I hate the world that made me. It has destroyed itself, and I will be free."

53

Voss Rhazes felt a moment of triumph as the ship's gravitational push engines came on. As stars slipped from the display tank's field of view, he felt hopeful that his kind would survive.

"We'll go in three jumps," he said. "That shouldn't overload our power draw."

The jump drive timer showed that potential would be at maximum in five minutes.

"Does everyone agree?" he asked the engine room crew.

"Ready," a man answered over the com, and Voss recognized the voice of the oldest engineer, Iannon Brunel. "Your board should show everything as on."

"It does," Voss said, and sat back with relief.

He glanced at Blackfriar next to him. A globe of Ceti IV appeared at his touch. Fires glowed on the nightside. The planet was dying, and nothing could be done about it. Voss reminded himself again of how much was gone and was about to be lost. All thought and feeling were inadequate before the unfolding fact. His life had always stood above the difficulties of decision; enough had been given to him to meet all circumstances; but now it seemed that he was reaching up from the bottom of a deep hole, and he felt that he would not always be able to grab the edge and pull himself out.

The timer reached zero.

Voss felt an instant of vertigo, and almost expected the Link to show him an accounting of the vast energy flowing into use. It had been won by the ingenuity of countless human minds as they had struggled to climb out of scarcity and constraint, and he was suddenly anxious that this legacy be used effectively—because once the instrumentalities by which power was drawn from the void were lost, they could not easily be replaced.

The stars blinked, revealing new configurations. Ceti IV was gone from the tank. The timer reset, and gave twenty-five hours as the buildup required for the next jump.

"How big is the base at Praesepe?" Voss asked.

"A globe two kilometers in diameter," Blackfriar said. "It contains full medical facilities, factories, supplies, even small vessels. Not only a base, but a seed world."

"Why was it built?" Voss asked, and for a moment, out of habit, expected the Link to answer.

"I helped set it up," Blackfriar said, "when a group of our people settled the planet there, long before your time. We decided to leave them a place to turn to if they should ever need it."

Voss felt a twinge of fear. "Then it's possible that it may have been used."

"Even if it was used," Blackfriar replied, "I doubt they could have used it all. There will probably be more than enough for us to start over with."

Voss still felt uneasy. "But it's not a certainty, is it?"

"No, it's not," Blackfriar said, leaning back at his station.

"Nothing is certain now. We may have to turn to the colony for refuge."

"If it's still there," Blackfriar said.

"And it may not welcome us."

"It's all we have left to go to," Blackfriar said.

Voss gazed at the tank, still feeling that if he searched within himself he might find the Link. A few times he had caught himself reaching out to it while he slept, only to wake up feeling lost. He longed for the return to freedom that the new mobile would bring.

The timer reached zero.

Alone this time, Voss again felt a moment of vertigo as the stars winked out and a new configuration appeared in the tank. Drive reset returned. Twenty-five hours later, all would be ready for the last step to Praesepe.

He sat back, feeling calmer and more reassured. The beauty of the drive's victory over distance filled him with confidence, and he recalled the Link's description of jump mechanics. Macroscopic quantum potentials enabled the drive to shift from the simple gravitational field-effect push to a discontinuous jump. Large amounts of power were needed to climb the mountaintop of large-scale quantum potential, from which the ship could be braked to the more level ground of normal spacetime. Wormhole theory was another way to describe the collapse of distance along a direction. Nearly all the power being drawn from the void by the makeshift starship was going into the jumps. The rest went into life support and deflection shielding.

Voss remembered again how the Link had taught him in child-hood, and he wondered how long it would be before he would achieve the same feeling of ease and character with the new Link. It would be a different intelligence, of course, that would be awak-ened to grow with the new mobile, and would not repeat exactly the previous mind's development. He thought about how much could never be regained—individuals, their art and literature, their way of looking and speaking, their loves. No single individual's memory could regain what had been lost. Even small groups of a dozen linked individuals had counted as much as whole nations in humankind's past . . .

He thought of Josepha's vulnerability, and how her losses had brought her to him. She would have so much to learn as the new mobile was being built, scarcely realizing how she might become an entirely different person, but he felt eager to help her, and the prospect that she would be with him for some indefinite time filled him with an irrational pleasure.

"Life support agrees with our bridge monitors," Blackfriar said as he sat down at his station next to Voss. Only a few minutes remained before the final jump. "We're in good shape for food, air, and water production."

It still seemed strange, Voss thought, to take over so many functions once overseen by the Link, to enter commands into primitive equipment, and to be constantly studying manuals for programs that had always run themselves. Fortunately, the effort would not have to be maintained for long.

Reset time ended.

Voss tensed, expecting vertigo, but it did not come, and the stars in the tank did not wink out. They flowed into branching treelike shapes, stopped, then flowed again. . . .

"We're not going through," Blackfriar said.

"Shut down!" Voss ordered over the com, fearing that the ship would be twisted and torn apart, compressed into small, irregular spaces by the chaos that now filled the holo tank, until all familiar experience was replaced by strangeness and agony. Leaning forward, he felt a strain in his back muscles, as if they were about to tear, and wondered if this might be the last moment of his life.

The timer again reached zero.

New stars appeared in the tank as the stress of irregular passage faded.

Voss recognized the stars of the Praesepe cluster, but they were still too distant. An accurate passage would have put the ship within ten astronomical units of the destination star, well within the open cluster.

"What happened?" Voss asked.

"It's the calibrations," Iannon Brunel's voice answered over the com. "We can try again in five or six hours."

Voss looked over at Blackfriar and said, "It's the electromagnetic flux from the thermonuclear blasts. It affected the mobile's drive and controls, and probably our calibrating equipment as well. We just can't measure jump accurately through warp."

"We may not be able to repair this," Blackfriar said.

"Let's see," Voss said, his confidence shaken. He leaned forward and entered a navigational query manually.

The answer read on the small display:

DISTANCE REMAINING: 50.36 LIGHT-YEARS

He looked at the figure with dismay, then sat back.

"Better go get some rest before the next try," Blackfriar said.

Silently, Voss got up and made his way to the narrow passage that led aft. He moved slowly in the light gravity, thinking of how much depended on the drive. The rebirth of his world and any help that might be sent back to Ceti IV required that this ship reach the double star in Praesepe—and quickly—to be of any use to survivors on Josepha's world.

He came to his cabin door. It slid open with a squeak. He went inside and saw Josepha asleep in her bunk. He gazed quietly at her youthful face, one of the last from a people now at the edge of extinction. The abyss would swallow them more quickly than his own.

"Voss," she whispered, opening her eyes.

"Go back to sleep," he said, climbing into the overhead bunk.

Sleep failed to come. Rest so often eluded him without the Link. The cave of stars around the ship grew smaller. He reached out with dream hands and felt the cave's cold, rocky walls. They moved along with the ship, and he saw no way out.

Josepha stood gazing at him. He lay awake in the upper bunk and watched her as if she were far away and could not see him.

"How long have I slept?"

"Through the night hours," she said.

He sat up, realizing that the next jump had already been made.

She stepped up on the lower bunk and touched his face with concern. "Why, you're in a cold sweat!"

"Let me up," he said.

She stepped down. He put his legs over the side and slid down to the floor.

"What is it?" she asked, stepping back.

"We didn't make the last jump completely," he said, looking away from her. "There's still trouble in the drive."

He saw the question in her eyes.

"I don't know if it can be repaired," he added.

"Voss, what if we don't get there? Will we all have to live and die on this ship?"

He nodded, feeling a knot form in his chest. She stepped forward and embraced him. "I would have died on Ceti," she said, "either from the disaster or when my life ran out."

He did not know what to say to her.

She looked up at him and half-smiled. "I was taught that the life of the flesh was not something to cling to. Each generation was one great life, a moral universe responsible for itself. You've always known that your life would reach into posterity, and that much of that posterity would be you. In my life on Ceti, we were nothing before an all-powerful divinity, and our world was nothing before the paradise of light and worship waiting for us beyond death. I lost my belief in that, but I see now what you have lost."

He looked into her eyes and felt her inwardness reaching out to him, almost as if she were about to speak within him. He felt that he knew her inside herself, and how she had grown toward a hope that would replace the faith of her world.

As she touched his cheek and he kissed her, he could not help feeling that the fatal blow against all their hopes had already been struck.

54

The suns of the Praesepe cluster blazed in the tank when Voss returned to the bridge. The holo imaging of the navigational aid showed these stars closer together than in reality, but their separations were accurate in the jump system, which did not need visuals.

"Are we there?" he asked, then saw that no star was bright enough, or near enough to show a disk.

Blackfriar did not turn around. "We're in the cluster," he said, "but still some twenty light-years from our star. It was an erratic jump. We came out too far right and below our destination."

Disappointed, Voss sat down at Blackfriar's left and gazed into the tank. The brightest suns were close enough to show smudges of gas. Fifty stars in all made up the central region of the open cluster, some thirteen light-years across, all moving together. Three hundred fifty other stars surrounded the central area of the cluster, some of them much closer than twenty light-years, but they held no prize of renewal and rebirth.

"Can we jump again?" Voss asked.

"Unreliably," Blackfriar said. "Brunel's engineers insist that another try might be extremely chaotic, and we might never find our way again. The calibration instruments are damaged at quantum levels, so we can't simply reset the drive to give us precise increments of direction."

"So what does Iannon suggest we do?" Voss asked.

"Accelerate to our destination in relativistic time," Blackfriar said. "That would take about a century, using as much power as we could draw and divert to push. Life support and shielding would have to be cut back. Our oldest people might die in that century. You'd probably live long enough; I wouldn't. But all that would count is to have a group to renew at the base."

If it's still there, Voss thought. "How many people can we put into sleep?" he asked.

"Not many, and not reliably," Blackfriar said. "This ship is nothing more than a shell with life support and a jump drive attached. It wasn't meant for a long journey. We have minimal maintenance for our power generators, much less for other systems. We couldn't count on our structural integrity at more than a quarter of light speed, and our shielding system against heavy particles is limited. The question is, could we draw enough power to do all that and run our food, air, water, and basic health systems? We can draw a lot of power, but we don't have the means of storing it, which would give us enough power. We need more than half light speed to get us there in a century, ship time."

Ship time, Voss thought, thinking of Josepha. There would be no going back to help her world any time soon. Unable to jump, this ship would become a prison.

He looked at Blackfriar and said, "Then maybe we should risk another jump."

"If it went wrong, we'd lose everything. At least now we can still aim at a clear destination."

Voss gazed at the bright stars of Praesepe and found himself unable to accept the limits that were closing in around his life.

"Iannon will work on the drive," Blackfriar continued, "but he lacks tools. Mostly he just thinks about it, trying to do the work that the Link would have done in a few moments."

"Can he accomplish anything?" Voss asked.

"Sometimes he talks as if he can, but it will take time. Some of it is his pride, which can't accept that for some problems there may be no solution, or one that will come too late."

"So we must prepare for the worst possible case," Voss said.

"Until some better course of action presents itself," Blackfriar said.

Josepha would die, Voss told himself. Lifespan for her would not exceed seventy-five years even under the best conditions. He might live to start again, just barely, if everything went well. This, he realized, was the old truth of interstellar travel, before ingenuity born of knowledge had defeated time and distance. The universe in which his people had satisfied want and desire, into which they had cast their self-reproducing worlds, had suddenly closed up into a cave. Space, across which his kind had moved like swift thoughts, had shrunk to the size of a solar system, to that of a planet, and finally to the constraints of one inadequate ship.

Feeling powerless, Voss thought of the daylight of planets. He imagined that every solar system was an exit from the vast cave of stars, and longed for the mobile's bright hollow. The loss of his world, he realized, had made his thinking sluggish, as his body fell back into another time, where survival was the central ambition of life and the world that had made him was now only a dream of the future.

55

Josepha sat, very still, in her bunk as Voss told her of the ship's predicament. When he was finished, she was silent for a long time.

"Maybe," she said at last, "we will have to learn not to hold our lives so dearly." He glimpsed resignation in her eyes. "That shouldn't be so hard for me," she continued, "because it was what I expected before you came to our world. It will be harder for you. We'll both have to give more of ourselves away."

"What do you mean?" he asked, puzzled.

"Is it possible to have children on the ship? If what you say is true, then we'll have to raise at least one generation or have no claim on the future."

"Perhaps not," he said. "We may be able to sleep, in suspension, and then renew our bodies when we reach our destination."

She looked away from him. "You may," she said. She turned toward him again, and he saw the distress in her face as she asked, "Can we have children?"

"I don't know."

"Can we all sleep?"

"It's not certain," he said, feeling that everything was still regressing, rushing toward a black pit; and once over the edge and down, there would be no way up.

"How did you have children?" she asked. "I never saw any."

"There were so few," he replied, sitting down next to her.

"How were you born?" she asked.

"We all belong to each other . . ." he started to say, then told her of the people, Blackfriar among them, who had contributed to his genetic inheritance, of the womb that had been grown for him to occupy, and the exemplar-mentors who had raised him, the Link among them. She had been told a little of this before, and he supposed that she might have found the process impersonal at first, so he emphasized how much care and attention was given to the upbringing of children.

"Do you know that you can carry a child?" he asked, shuddering at what she might suffer if she tried.

"I would have to try to know," she said.

He forced himself to smile and said, "It may not be necessary. We have a few things still left to try."

Alone, Josepha felt a moment of betrayal. Everything that was left of the mobile's promise was still endangered. She imagined her own death, which would come long before Voss's, and saw again that children might be her only victory. She imagined the years ahead, marking the distance of light-years, and she understood that Voss and his people would rediscover only what she had always known—that everyone died—and died alone. Her tormented father had faced it, had tried to cheat the dissolution that waited for him at every possible exit from his life. The window of his faith had looked out into darkness, and the door of knowledge that had opened briefly in his sky had been rudely closed in his face. Now she would have to face death in her own way.

For an instant she saw a ship of skeletons arriving at the double sun . . .

"No," she whispered as she lay down and composed herself. "Voss will find a door," she said.

56

"We'll try small jumps," Blackfriar said. "Iannon thinks this will stitch us through to our destination. Short bursts of the drive will be less dangerous than a single output of energy, which is more subject to chaotic drift."

Voss gazed at their destination, a double star that was a faint patch of light in the loose cluster. Days had passed since their last attempt. He looked at the image with a sick feeling that this was as close as they would ever get to the star.

The timer reached zero. The stars flickered, but the tank view seemed unchanged. Then the stars became distorted, as if something had smeared them.

Reset did not come back on.

"What happened?" Blackfriar demanded over the intercom.

"We made some distance," Brunel replied, "but very small. Shutting down now. There's just no reliable control left."

"Do we still have conventional push?" Voss asked.

"Yes," Brunel said. "I'm putting on constant acceleration. We must get the highest velocity possible, just in case."

Yes, Voss thought, *so we'll make the base no matter what happens, however slowly.*

"We'll hold a meeting now," Blackfriar said. "It's time everyone knew what we are facing."

Each of the ship's six main holds had been partitioned to accommodate five hundred people. Voss divided the holo tank display into six segments, so that Blackfriar would face everyone when he spoke, whether they were only listening in their cabins or watching simple screens in the common areas.

The tank filled with anxious faces.

"All of you already know our predicament," Blackfriar began. "We're nearly adrift and it doesn't appear likely that we can repair the jump drive to get us to our destination. If our conventional pusher holds up, we might get there in a century. We have no rejuvenation capability with us, so some of us may die when our bodies run beyond their current settings or acquire classic degenerative ailments. What happens will vary according to the individual, depending on when each was last treated. Still, most of us can hope to live more than a century, long enough for us to reach reversal."

All except the Cetians, Voss thought. Josepha would not outlast a century, perhaps not even seventy years.

"We might attempt to put people into cold sleep," Blackfriar continued, "but without the Link's maintenance this could be unreliable and costly in both monitoring and power use. Fortunately, sleep berths will be in short supply, so power and monitoring will not be the problem posed by the prospect of putting us all into suspension. We must consider how best to use the berths."

Josepha would need one, Voss thought.

Blackfriar said, "We will set about making the ship as fit as possible for the passage. It was not made for this relativistic passage, and we could not have fitted it for a long journey during the evacuation of the mobile. We expected to make a quick jump to Praesepe and begin our recovery."

He paused for a moment. The heads in the tank were still, watching him.

"Some of you may wish to consider having children," Blackfriar continued, "since you may not live out the journey yourselves. Unfortunately, only the bodily method is available."

"Can't the jumper be repaired?" a male head asked. Voss looked at the screen, but did not recognize the speaker.

"We will continue to study the condition of the drive," Blackfriar said. "It works, but we lack the equipment to make the correct navigational settings."

Looks of dismay and despair showed on the faces in the tank, and Voss realized that he was beginning to notice facial expressions in place of intimate link subvocalizations.

Discussion broke out among the heads. Voss recognized Avita Harasta, who was over two centuries old. When she turned her head, the view pulled back and Voss glimpsed Josepha, Jason, and a few of the other Cetians behind her. For the Cetians, he knew, there would be no other world than this vessel.

Voss recalled the apprehension that had entered his mind when he and Josepha had finally made love. At first he had thought it might be caused by Jason's resentful glances in the dining hall. But now, as he gazed at the faces that seemed to be imprisoned in the tank, he realized that for Josepha, lovemaking was not just a physical pleasure, that for her and the Cetians the moment of bodily ecstasy announced that flesh had done all that was possible to assure its future, the perpetuation of its own aspect, and it was this urgency that had come forward in his old human brain. Bodies sought to assert themselves over others, but only half of each design was passed forward in time. Jason's half might not survive. His rivalry carried itself with the strength of ancient impulses that welled up from deep structures and would not be easily denied.

There was nothing new in this, Voss told himself as he saw the look of fear and dismay in many of the faces, and he realized that the coming together of Josepha, Jason, and himself in unexpected circumstances had developed his feelings in ways that made him a partial stranger to himself. He was now an amalgam who would never have come to be if his world had not been destroyed. He was struggling to discover what his unpredictable self might do, but saw no single, clear way without the Link.

Blackfriar continued: "Form small groups, according to your knowledge and skills, and begin checking our environment for durability. Our power units are in sound condition, so we will produce air, water, and nutrients indefinitely from recycled materials. The synthesizers exist in threes within each section of the ship. If even two fail, the third can produce what we need. Our backup is to run each at half output. We have only one gravity generator, so we're going to run it at three-quarters for as long as necessary. Those of you who may choose to raise offspring will need the gravity, so that your children will not grow up physically unused to the gravity of an Earth-sized planet, or to the habitat that we will construct. It's possible that we may have to depend on the planet at our destination for some time. Although the base is sizable and will give us a good start on a new habitat, we may need the relative safety of a planet's ecology before our new mobile can function on its own. I'm assuming that the base is still there, that it hasn't been stripped. If it is not there, then we won't have access to fresh Link cores, or to rejuvenation, and the planet will be our only hope, where we will have to build anew and hope to contact another mobile. Some of you may wish to settle on the planet, but we will have to see what the colony there has to say to us."

Blackfriar paused for questions and discussion, but in the silence Voss faced the possibility that both planet and base would be gone, that there was nothing at the double star in Praesepe except a hostile planetary environment in which they might all perish.

Blackfriar said, "The oldest among us will be prepared for suspension as soon as possible. If any of you refuse, the next oldest will be offered the berths. But remember that our sleep units carry risk. You may not reawaken, or you may be revived to nothing better than what we have now . . ."

As he listened to Blackfriar's comprehensive litany of difficulties, Voss thought again of Ceti IV, whose few survivors would now have little or no chance of survival during the century or more that would pass before any help could be sent back—and he found himself beginning to mourn the loss of Josepha.

57

The oldest survivors from the mobile, only a dozen people, had been given small cabins along the central axis of the ship. As she came to Avita Harasta's door, Josepha paused, suddenly doubting her own motives for seeking out the woman. There was a self-assurance in the woman she had met in the apartments of the mobile that reminded Josepha of the nuns who had taught her in the convent school after her mother's suicide.

"You must remember," Sister Perpetua, who seemed old beyond imagining, had said to her, "that you have a benefactor who has placed you in this school. He seeks to give you the opportunity for education, here and at university. You must not grieve for your mother, humble Sister of Martha though she was, but look to be everything she could not have been."

"My benefactor?" Josepha had asked. "Is he my father?"

Sister Perpetua had ignored her question, Josepha recalled as she touched the door plate, and had never told her how her mother had died. Mercifully, Josepha had learned the truth much later.

The door slid open.

"Yes?" asked the small woman.

Josepha was again struck by the softness of Avita's large brown eyes. The woman's hair was short, but long enough to show that there was no gray in the brown that matched her eyes.

The woman smiled as Josepha said, "I'm one of the Cetians."

"Of course," Avita replied. "I remember you well, Josepha."

"May I come in and speak to you?"

Avita moved back from the door.

Josepha stepped into a cabin that was much like her own, but with room for only one bed. Avita Harasta motioned for her to sit down on the bunk, then sat down cross-legged on the floor.

"How may I help you?" the woman asked, looking up.

"You may find it strange," Josepha said cautiously, feeling uneasy sitting on the bunk, "but I want to ask you about Old Earth, about your life on the habitat, and how you see what may come . . . so that I may be able to understand better, and find my place. I'm very afraid of what is to come. You know who you are. I fear losing myself."

Avita smiled and nodded. "You remind me of the times when men and women lived quite different lives, in same-sex unions and men with women. You knew some of that on your backward world."

Backward, Josepha repeated to herself.

But the woman's voice was low, caring, without malice, and Josepha knew at once that Avita Harasta could say whatever she pleased, however harsh the words might sound, and it would not be offensive. How was she able to create such complete sympathy? It seemed to Josepha that Avita was about to take her inside her mind and show her around.

"My age alone should not impress you," Avita continued. "It's not something I can take credit for. I take satisfaction only in what I have understood in the time given to me."

"What will happen to us?" Josepha asked.

"We may all die—or regain what we have lost. I'm not fearful of dying, as long as we regain what we have lost. But until then, every individual is important, for the knowledge each carries in his or her brain and body. I've seen a lot of dying. Most of humankind died in Earth's sunspace. Some of us who survived built a new way of life, while others settled planets around other suns and took too much past with them. But we needed to see what our work would bring, so we extended our lives rather than pass on what we had gained to new, amnesiac generations. Yes, that's what they are, requiring a lot of upbringing and education. It takes a century to truly understand the character of the way we call macrolife. We wanted to be ourselves, and remain ourselves as we grew. We did not need the empty-minded, survival-driven human being who persists in nature through default programs inherited by natural selection, or even the partly educated predators of the twenty some civilizations of Earth's history—all come and gone now."

"But new people were born and raised on the mobile," Josepha said.

Avita nodded and said, "But slowly, as great works are made." She smiled sadly. "But we haven't done so well in this divergence of macrolife, have we? We're at a knothole again, struggling to slip through and make good our mistakes. And we may fail."

"You seem resigned," Josepha said, puzzled by the woman's stoicism.

"No," she said. "Elsewhere, macrolife lives and proliferates, and through my understanding I am part of it."

Josepha shrugged. "I suppose my life has been too short for me to know what you are talking about. You speak of macrolife . . ."

"A word," Avita said, "referring to a mobile as an organism comprised of human and human-derived intelligences. It's an organism because it reproduces, with its human and other elements, moves and reacts on the scale of the Galaxy. A mobile of the size you have seen is larger inside, in square kilometers, than the surface of a planet. And larger still within its minds."

Josepha smiled. "Yes, I know."

Avita said, "You're anxious to know how we will overcome our present difficulties. We will do so only by reaching the base at Praesepe."

Josepha nodded. "Will we?"

"We will try."

After a few moments of awkward silence, Josepha asked, "What was Earth like? We grew up with so little knowledge of it, and with so much disapproval."

Avita seemed to gaze into the past. "The cities of the twenty-first century were full of convenience, full of squalor and wealth, side by side. The architecture was extravagant, rising kilometers into the sky as new building materials were discovered. But more than seven billion people perished when one such building material, bulerite, became unstable. A strange physical anomaly swallowed the Moon. Nuclear war broke out in the chaos of blame that followed. Fortunately, there was enough humanity in the habitats, on Mars and the moons of Jupiter, to start over."

"Will we survive and start over?" Josepha asked.

"What we are will survive," Avita said, "even if we do not."

Josepha's heart quickened. She had never known her mother. Her father's guilt had given her what protection and privilege had been possible for a daughter who could never be acknowledged. Josepha felt weak and embarrassed suddenly, realizing that she had come here in search of another mother who might make her less afraid to face the future.

"I can't make you brave or control the future," Avita said as if reading her mind, "but I can guess at the feelings of most of us on this journey. We have lost our worlds, but our answer must be to keep growing beyond ourselves."

"Just wait, then?" Josepha asked.

"Have children, with Voss—and with anyone else you fancy. You can do that—and more later."

Josepha looked into Avita's large brown eyes, and wondered whether the woman was an individual at all, or even cared if she lived. For a moment it seemed to her that Avita Harasta was a ghost, a fragment of history that was still somehow able to speak. Where was her life, her loves?

Avita sighed, seeming impatient, as if she were still reading Josepha's mind, then said, "Let me say something more to you. The time and distance which you fear is also an inner distance through which we must pass. It is the price we must pay to regain what we have lost, and the new foundation on which we will rebuild our dedication to life. This has always been true, from the simplicity of crossing an open field or reaching out across light-years." She smiled. "Once long ago I crossed a field of weeds and dry grass to board a shuttle that took me and others to build a habitat in the Moon's orbit. I had arrived, time was short, and I had to go through a hole in a fence."

"Parables are all well and good," Josepha said, "but where do I find the conviction I need?"

"You already know enough to realize that you need it, daughter," Avita replied sternly. "If you simply try to behave as you think you should, without making the inner journey, then all the hardships that now face us will be meaningless, because even if you should survive you will not deserve the victory, not in the eyes of others, or in your own."

"But our salvation is not guaranteed," Josepha said.

"If we make this passage and reach the tools of knowledge that are waiting for us, our strength will grow from how we value the experience. If we do not rise to this ordeal, we will have nothing to start with again, even if we survive." She paused, then said, "It is possible, you know, for us to survive shamefully."

"But what must I do?" Josepha asked desperately, not quite understanding the woman's last words.

"Do what is given to you at every opportunity," Avita said, "and imagine that every positive act is a brick in a great structure that you are building within yourself."

Josepha gazed into the woman's face and knew that her father would have said, "Daughter, you are talking to a devil among devils." And one who was simply trying to make her accept the inevitable more easily.

"All life is a gamble," Avita continued. "Conscious life has sought to establish itself in greater safety and permanence, beyond simple survival. On this ship we have the beauty of a way of life to regain. We will act as we must, and so will you."

"When I think of my father's crime," Josepha said, "I wonder if it might be best for me to die by my own hand." *My mother,* she thought, *had taken her life for much less.*

Avita smiled. "A great philosopher once said about suicide that it asks a question of life, but will not stay to have an answer. You are not your father or mother, or anyone else of your world, however much you may feel them reaching after you—unless you let yourself be one of them."

"There's so little I can do," Josepha said, feeling defeated as she thought of Voss and Jason.

"It will be everything," Avita replied.

58

Iannon Brunel sat at Blackfriar's station on the bridge. Alone, Voss turned to hear what the engineer had come to say.

"I want only you and Blackfriar to know this for now," Iannon said, "because I don't wish to create false hopes. I've already spoken with him."

"I understand," Voss said.

The big engineer's large black eyes became sad, and he seemed to shrink in his seat, as if afraid of what he had to say.

"It's possible that we could take one of our two small craft and jump a few people ahead to the base," he said, looking at the tank. "They could bring back medical supplies and the equipment we'd need to recalibrate our jump drive."

Voss took a deep breath. "Can this be done?"

Iannon turned and gave him a harried look. "We're not that far from our destination, as measured by our usual capabilities. But it's not as promising as it sounds. That's why I'm restricting my conversation to you and Blackfriar. Right now we can't be sure that either small jumper would work. They might have been affected as badly as our main drive. Remember, everything was in the mobile when the thermonuclear pulse went through it. We'd have to try it once to be sure, but that's part of the problem. It might work only once, holding the chart memory for one complete round trip—maybe. Testing it would use up our one chance."

Voss nodded and was about to ask a question.

"There's more," Iannon continued. "If we test with one or more persons on board, we might lose them. If we set the craft for automatic return, unmanned, we might either lose the craft or our one chance of getting to the base, recalibrating the small jumper's throw, and getting back here to work on our main drive. Now, if we couldn't get the main to work, we could start ferrying people ahead, especially if we could repair the other small craft. It might take a while, back and forth, to get everyone there, but it would still be faster than what we're facing. What do you think?"

"Do you want to try?" Voss asked. "It seems to me that it's worth trying to get even one small craft to throw accurately, if it means we could repair our main drive and bring the ship in."

Iannon nodded. "It's tempting."

Voss said, "If it worked, even the ferrying alone would be worth it."

"True, but now we come to more problems. I want you and Blackfriar to understand them all before we even think of making a decision."

"What was Wolt's reaction?" Voss asked.

"Much like yours. But I wanted to go through it all with you alone, just to make sure I have it all clear. Without the Link's simulations, I seem to need to say things out loud, and more than once."

Without the Link's vast database, an entire universe of evolving simulation was no longer available, Voss thought. Rehearsing problems in model form was gone, the addition of each solution to still more complex models. The Link, among many other things, had been the mobile's collective experience, and its loss was clearly responsible for the constant dismay in Iannon Brunel's face. He was trying to do what no individual engineer had been asked to do in a long time.

"We've got to rule out an automatic first try because it might lose us the craft," he said. "A crew of three or four might make all the difference, but if they don't come back, you'll be losing experienced engineers." He grimaced, and Voss knew that he meant experienced in working with the Link's resources.

"Problems may occur in the years to come that we can't handle," he continued. "And their loss will decrease the number of skilled teachers we would have." He sighed and ran his fingers nervously back through his long black hair. "Mine is the best knowledge we have to make a difference aboard a small craft, yet I'm the one you can't risk."

"Can you teach someone to go in your place?" Voss asked.

"In time. But now we come to something even more tangled. The chance of the small jumper working is really not much better, in my estimate, than trying our main drive several more times. Another try might get us there, but we can't risk everything on that one chance, which might throw us somewhere from which we could never get back. I would recommend another try only if we had major problems with life support, which might very well happen in a decade or two, thus forcing us to jump or die."

Iannon stared at him with something like a perverse smile, as if he were proud of having tied up all the knots so neatly—but then Voss saw that it was not a smile. It was a grimace of fear struggling with the horror of how much would depend on his reasoning being right.

"Do you think either of the small craft can make it?" Voss asked.

"I would guess that one of the small craft can make the base," Iannon said. "Coming back is likely if the crew is able to adjust their drive at the base, to make sure it will work. But we must assume that the base is there and usable. Any number of things can go wrong all down the line. Therefore, for better or worse, we can't send our best people, even though they would be the most likely to succeed. Three would have to go at least, and we would have to be prepared to do without them."

"Can you think of anything you couldn't teach someone to handle here or in the small ship?" Voss asked.

Iannon grimaced. "No. But it will take time, and I would have to be sure of them."

"Then consider going yourself," Voss said.

Iannon seemed relieved, but the doubts showed again in his face. "I'll attempt to train people to replace me. It will take months, at least, and I may not feel that I have succeeded. We can try this at any time, you know, even years from now. I'll prepare two people to go with me."

Voss nodded. "Be sure. Take all the time you need."

"I'm torn about going, Voss, but . . . I see myself doing it, getting there and bringing back all the help we'll need to get through. I dream about it . . . as if the Link were still there showing it to me." He looked at Voss, and for a moment his black eyes seemed calm as he said, "I'll get back."

"You'll save us a century," Voss said.

59

Josepha was about to enter her cabin when she saw Jason coming down the passageway. "I have to speak to you," he said almost casually.

She looked away as he stopped at her side. "I must talk to you," he continued calmly. "It's important."

She turned her head and looked at him, unsure of what to say. He had not shaved in a while and looked tired, but seemed otherwise composed.

"Are you alone?" he asked, looking at the door. "Is he in there? I can come back later."

She hesitated, then told herself that this was Ondro's brother Jason, and that she had no reason to fear him. He had never been violent. "Come in," she said at last, touching the plate. The door slid open and she went inside, then turned around to face him. "What is it, Jason?"

The door slid shut. He backed up against it and slid down to sit on the floor. Strain showed in his face. Concerned and startled, she retreated to her bunk, sat down nervously, and waited for him to speak.

He closed his eyes and said, "What right have they to decide anything for us? Their decision has condemned us to death." She saw that he was angry.

"What are you saying?" she asked, knowing full well what he meant.

He opened his eyes and grimaced. "There won't be any sleep for us. Their oldest people will get those berths."

"There aren't enough berths for them, either," she said.

"All of us will die," he said, "but you'll get through. He'll see to that." He laughed. "It'll serve you right if the chamber fails and you wake up dead."

She tried to control her reaction. "But what else can be done? You know the chambers may not work very well."

"They might have offered a lottery," he said, "for hibernating in shifts, maybe."

"That would only put more people at risk," she said.

"It would be better than chance," he said. His eyes opened wide and stared at her. "We can jump. I've heard that the main system is still operational, but they're afraid to try it."

"It's too dangerous, Jason. We might get lost—and then even the chances still open to us would be gone."

"But it's a chance for us," he said. "Our people will certainly die aboard this ship if we don't take chances now."

"You would have died on the islands," she said, "or from the effects of the collision. Voss and I got you out."

"And look how many are left!" Jason cried. "They promised so much, but it's always out of reach. If they had not come here—"

"You would have died on the islands," she said, "and I would have died in the city. Another jump would risk all the life on this ship. You know that."

He shook his head and smiled bitterly. "It's not the same for us as it is for them. They're willing to die for their way of life, if that will get them through." He looked at her for a moment, then said in a voice that broke with pity, "Don't you see? There will be no more of our kind?"

She looked at him carefully, without fear, and a distant part of her wondered about her lack of feeling. "What do you want?" she asked, knowing that he was in agony over her.

He smiled despairingly. "You, for one thing—but I'll settle for another jump and the chance to extend my life."

"You don't understand the dangers of a jump," she said.

"You believe what he tells you?" he asked. "Yes, I see that he's explained it to you. With him, you don't have to consider what anyone else thinks or feels."

"Jason, I think for myself, and I know that we can't risk everything."

"We? You count yourself with them? You and Voss probably have a nice safe sleeper ready somewhere!" His eyes were wild now, fixing her with his resentment, and she expected that he would suddenly get up. "There are so few of us, but we're not important to them! Josepha, we won't last a century. We're useless. They should never have visited our world." He covered his face with one hand.

Josepha felt the silence come alive between them, filling with their fears. She knew that he feared becoming violent toward her, and she was afraid that he was right about everything.

"Talk to Wolt Blackfriar," she said softly. "Try to understand more."

"Just like your father," he muttered into his hand. "No good for your own kind. You'll help finish what he started."

"That's not fair," she tried to say, but her throat was dry and the words came out in a loud whisper.

"Fair?" He looked up, as if sensing her weakness. "We're being mistreated every day!"

"How?" she demanded, regaining her voice.

"Oh, they give us food and living quarters, but we're nothing to them. We can't be useful, because we don't know enough. It's another prison."

"Have you tried to know some of them?"

"Their women avoid us," he said, glaring at her, and Ondro was in his eyes, trapped there, unable to reach her. In a moment he would speak in Ondro's voice; he would smile and it would be Ondro's smile. He would stand up and come to her, and it would be Ondro touching her, but Jason hitting her.

"I'll speak for you," she said, trembling as if in a dream.

He grimaced, and it was Jason's face that said, "What does he want you for? Love? Children—so his kind can live again? Would you have chosen Voss if Ondro had lived?"

Josepha went cold with doubt as she gazed into his mocking face. Would Ondro have mocked her?

"I'll speak for all of us," she said, getting up and coming toward him. "I'll try to present your views."

He embraced her hips, buried his face in her belly, and she touched his head gently as he wept.

"My poor brother," he whispered. "What did he do to be rescued from one grave, only to die in another?"

Hatred of her father swelled in Josepha's breast as she held Jason's head in her hands.

"I'll speak for all of us," she said again.

60

Iannon Brunel's party consisted of one other man and two women, Narilla Zora and Neva Hedron. All three, Voss knew, had been tutored by Iannon in life support and propulsion systems, with the help of as many texts as could be retrieved and displayed for study.

Voss came with Josepha and Blackfriar to see the team off in the departure bay. He had come to know the three younger people only a little, and now realized why he had kept his distance; he had lost too many friends already.

Everything that needed to be said had been said, Voss thought as he stood before the impassive engineer and his team. The four would reach the base, adjust their drive if necessary, and return as soon as possible with the needed equipment and supplies. The working intelligence at the base would link to them when they arrived. Voss suddenly wished he were going along, if only to link again and feel the presence of past and knowledge at the ready again within himself.

"Farewell," Josepha said in a solemn voice.

Next to her, Blackfriar only nodded.

Iannon took a deep breath and turned away. Voss looked for a moment into the youthful faces of Narilla, Neva, and Amon. They seemed to be smiling, but they had to know full well that they might never come back. He had thought it would be easier for someone who had lived a century or two to be braver than a younger person, but had finally concluded that an older one might cling more to safety, knowing just how much might be lost. A younger one like himself might be more willing to risk the unknown.

Then he reminded himself that there was little enough chance for all of them.

The three younger people turned and followed Iannon into the lock. It closed, sealing off the bay.

Voss looked at Josepha. She still seemed troubled about something, but he knew that she was not ready to tell him.

"I hope they make it," she said with faint hope in her voice.

Wolt said, "We will continue to plan according to the worst possible case, namely that we'll be on this ship for nearly a century."

What was it like for her to know, Voss asked himself, *that their lives were draining away like blood from an open wound, that she and the Cetians would die, while he might just be able to reach renewal at Praesepe?*

He thought again of Paul Anselle, and knew that Josepha was also troubled about him. She was hoping that he was still alive, but in all likelihood Ceti's few survivors would die waiting for help that would never arrive.

They watched the small craft shrink away on the utility screen. After a minute there was a faint flash in the starry black, signaling a jump.

Voss took Josepha's hand and leaped ahead of the small ship in his mind, and imagined its arrival at the cache of treasures that he and she might never see.

61

"Do you think they got there?" Josepha asked.

Voss lay in his bunk as she dressed, unsure of how to answer her. The ten-day return period was drawn to a close. He thought of what might have gone wrong. The base might not have been there. Iannon and his people might have been thrown into distant spaces on the outward jump, or on the way back. The ship was coming back in short jumps because that was all it could handle. Any number of things might have happened, and there was nothing to do but wait.

"If they don't come back," she said, pulling on her coveralls, "we'll have to raise children, teach them while we live, and die. You will outlive me, won't you?"

She stood still, looking at him, waiting for his answer.

"Yes," he said, "that's likely, and still might not be enough. No one, including our children, may last the time we might need to get there."

"But you said a century."

"Time and achievable velocity," he said. "Our measurements may be off. Sublight travel . . ."

"So it's possible that everyone will die?" she asked.

"I still think we'll make it, one way or another. All of us, or some of us."

"It frightens me," she said.

"If the ship lasts long enough to support a new population," he said, thinking of what it would take to birth, educate, and leave on its own even a group of a few hundred. He and Blackfriar met daily with the specialists to attempt projections of resources and the maintenance of equipment—and always there was something missing, some device or program that had not been taken from the mobile before its death. Voss wondered if he could bring children to be on their own in such a desperate situation.

"Any more word on the number of sleep berths?"

"There won't be enough for more than two dozen people," he

said, "and the systems are unreliable now. People will die. We would need hundreds of berths to even think of setting up shifts."

She did not answer him. He sat up, got down from the bunk, and embraced her. She came into his arms uneasily, but held him after a moment.

"I regret our blindness," he said, "in the way we came to visit your world."

"What could you have done?" she asked. "You could either have come or stayed away."

"We might have stood off," he said, "further off in your sun-space, and sent in small craft to visit. We might have learned more and been more careful with your . . . Pontiff."

"You had no reason to be suspicious," she said. "It was all one man who did this. We were struggling to change. Ondro and Jason and countless others knew what was wrong with our world. I grew up hoping for and expecting change."

He held her close. "And you would have had time to change if we hadn't arrived in time to provoke your father."

She pulled free and looked into his eyes, and he knew that she did not want him to blame himself or his world.

"He was to blame," she said, "because he acted deliberately to do harm. Your world did not."

And for a moment he felt again that his reason was crumbling. He missed the Link, the inner world of knowledge and discussion into which he might retreat in moments of fear and doubt, where he had always found modes of analysis and decision, and the continuing ideals of a way of life whose ruins now stood as much within him as in the makeshift vessel around him. Only the hope of regaining the lost way of life kept him going. Josepha, no matter how much or how little he cared for her, was unimportant before his loss.

"I know," Josepha said, "that you are just as wounded as I am."

He looked down at her calmly, thinking of the release that she had given him from his fears, but wondered whether he truly loved her. He had wanted to give her the servant Link, the assurance of life for as long as they might wish it, and a universe to explore and feel at home in. Now, without the inwardness of his world, without the treasure of centuries, to which they would have added together, he saw the confidence that had been his, and his to give, diminishing until it died.

"I saw enough," she said, "to know the life we might have had, and might still have."

She looked up at him, waiting for his answer.

"I know too much," he said, "to hope blindly. But I still hope."

She kissed him quickly. "I have something to arrange," she said and turned to the door.

Alone, he climbed back into his bunk, determined to confront and set right what seemed to be happening within him without his consent.

He lay there, listening to the ventilators, and remembered when Josepha had told him about prayer. Paul had told her it was a way of organizing one's will and intellect to deal with loss and responsibility.

I had the Link to help me do that, he had told her.

Now, as he considered once again the loss of his lifespan and the deterioration of his body, he wondered at the feelings that stuck to the simple perception of facts. All the strengths of mind and ingenuity that had made more of human life than the fleeing shadows Josepha had known on her world were slipping away. The security of the mobile's life had proven impermanent, and he feared the weakening of his body that would bring states of regretful sentiment and longing—until at last he welcomed death. His people would die nobly, but without the nobility of what had been lost. Shadows would visit his eyes more often as he aged, until his sight blackened and his limbs were stilled.

"No," he said out loud, and sat up and looked around what Josepha had called, in bitter moments, the coffin of their cabin.

He would live to see the last of pity, and the start of recovery. A Link would join him again, bringing all the hoard of knowledge humankind had won from time, and he would share it with Josepha.

62

The survivors from Ceti's penal islands gathered amidships, in one of the large storage bays just off the long axis. Josepha had insisted that Jason arrange the meeting. She tried to look confident as she entered the bay. Some of the men looked away from her. All fourteen Cetians, counting herself, were present, sitting on the floor, on containers, and standing near the bulkhead. She stopped and realized with a shock that she was looking at what might be the last of her people, and that they no longer regarded her as one of them.

Jason sat alone on the floor against a large carton, looking away from her.

She stopped under the single white square of light in the low ceiling and said, "I want to hear your complaints, alone, before Voss and Wolt get here. You can speak freely to me. I will take nothing amiss, however mistaken I might think it to be."

"How considerate of you!" Pietro Lukis shouted derisively, showing his teeth.

"I am one of you," she replied sternly.

"Bely's brat is one of us!" Lemuel Annan shouted, and Josepha cringed inwardly, wishing that Jason had not revealed the fact.

"Shut up, Lemuel," Jason said, looking at her with regret. "I thought we had all agreed that she had nothing to do with him."

"So you keep saying," Lemuel muttered.

Josepha looked around at the skeptical faces of the nine men and four women, most of whom still looked thin and unwell, and said, "Think what you will of me, but these people are not like us. They don't act from greed or distrust, but from what's constructive and possible."

Jason squinted up at her. "You're so very sure of their motives."

"If their motives had been so bad," she said, "they would never have come close enough for the Pontiff to destroy them. Remember, it was he who did this to you."

Jason said, "No one knew what Bely had in his hands to use against them. These starpeople came to show off, and were too careless about it."

"None of that matters now," she said. "Nothing is more important now than getting this ship to the base in Praesepe. They don't have enough sleep facilities for their own people, much less for us. Many of them face death as we do."

"But more of them will live!" Lemuel shouted.

"Their lifespans are longer, to be fair," Jason said.

"Let's be fair!" Lemuel cried, half laughing. "They want us to whelp children and die."

"They will also have offspring—" she started to say.

"What?" Lemuel asked. "You mean they know how?"

"They have offspring," she said, "but not only as a means of securing the future."

Lemuel laughed loudly. Jason raised a hand for silence and

said, "This is all beside the point. What I question is their decisions concerning us."

"If you tried to understand what kind of people they are—" Josepha began, and stopped. "What do you think should be done?"

"That's clear enough," Jason said. "Risk more jumps and avoid a century of travel." He looked directly at her, as if saying, *Agree with me now.*

"But you don't understand," she pleaded, looking from one face to another. "It would be foolish to risk everything. There would be no way to save the situation if a jump threw us at random."

"Who's to say?" Jason said. "It might work out fine."

"It's not that simple," Josepha said.

What do you know? Jason's look asked her.

"Who cares if we make their base!" Lemuel shouted, then leaned back against a storage case. "There's worlds out there. We could find one and make a new life for ourselves."

Josepha took a deep breath, appalled at the man's ignorance. "Even if you looked for a thousand years," she said, "the chances of finding a world where we could live, breathe, and eat are almost zero. And we would be starting with no technical base to help us, like our ancestors had on Ceti. They had a starship full of help. We'd have nothing."

Lemuel licked his lips, obviously shaken.

"Let's get back to the point," Jason said. "We can't live for a century. We can't be what these people are, and that includes you, Josepha. You're asking us to contribute to their future, not ours."

"I'd rather die under an open sky," Terence Ohar said with sorrow in his voice. Josepha looked at the young man for a moment, and then at Beata Lorenz, who sat with him on the floor and stared at Josepha with old, tired eyes.

"What I am saying," Josepha said, "is that there is no choice but to make the best of things as they are. This applies to everyone on this ship. Don't you think they would prefer to have it otherwise?"

"Do you know that?" Lemuel asked. "How can you be sure?"

"She talks fancy," a small, bent old man sitting in the shadow between two crates said sadly. "I don't understand a word." Josepha recognized Padraic Tolen.

"They saved you from the storm," Josepha said.

"They wouldn't have," Jason answered, "if you had not persuaded Voss Rhazes."

There was a long silence, but she realized that Jason's words had helped her, by reminding everyone here that she had helped save their lives.

"How far can we be from our destination?" young Terence Ohar asked hopefully.

Josepha took a deep breath. "I know it's hard for us to understand travel between stars. The distances are greater than anything we've known."

"But you've had it explained to you," Jason said.

"It would take thousands of years to reach even the nearest star to Ceti," she said. "We're much closer than that. Everything that can be done is being done."

"Screw you, bitch!" Lemuel shouted. "You're going to whelp bastards for them, then sleep it off! Why can't you stick to your own kind?"

Josepha's heart fluttered before the force of Lemuel's words, but she was determined not to show her humiliation. She looked at Jason, but he would not meet her eyes as he stood up and leaned against a crate. His posture still reminded her of Ondro. She felt his bitter confusion, and wanted to help him, to help all these people whose lives had been wrecked by Josephus Bely.

"What can we do?" she asked. "We're from a backward world, where life was ignorant and short. You knew that when you opposed Bely, and he exiled you for it. He destroyed the life of these people after they had rescued you from certain death."

"Gratitude must end somewhere," Jason said.

"We have our lives," Josepha said, "and we're all in this together."

Lemuel sighed. "That's just it," he said tiredly, "we're not all in this together, not in the same way. How much can we mean to them? Fourteen of us and some three thousand of them?" He looked at her reproachfully and said, "You're the only one of us who means anything to them."

Josepha tensed, and for an instant she saw a look of sympathy on Jason's face.

Bent old Padraic Tolen grinned at her toothlessly. "They're soft," he said. "Just give me a few moments alone with Rhazes or Blackfriar and we'd have what we want."

"Shut up!" Jason shouted.

"You're in love with her," the old man shot back, "so you'll take her part in the end. It might be your ticket into a sleeper berth."

Jason gave her a look of defeat.

"Josepha's right about one thing," Lemuel said. "They're not like us. They can't know what we've lived through, how we feel and think. Makes it easier to let us die. What's thirteen lives against three thousand to them?"

"They're stuck with us!" toothless Padraic cried out.

It had all been too much for them, Josepha thought, the change from the islands to the habitat, the struggle to reach the rear docks after the explosions—and now this ship, with its metal corridors, harsh lighting, and hopeless journey through a darkness without daylight.

She said, "You must believe that I am with you," but looking at their faces, she couldn't tell what they were thinking.

"She's sincere enough," Jason said, "as far as it goes." He looked unsure suddenly, searching for his words. "They're not really our enemy, not the way Bely was. They just want to make it to their base so they can start over. Nothing wrong with that. We'll gain if that happens, even if it's only through some of our children. It's not their fault we're here, caught in the middle. It's not their fault that there's fourteen of us, who can't be as important as three thousand and what's waiting for them. It's not their fault our lives are so short. Thank the likes of Bely and those before him who made life the way it's been for us, when so much more was possible."

Josepha looked around at the faces as Jason spoke, and for a moment she began to believe that a real discussion was beginning. But she also saw that their fears could have no answer. This small group could never be whole again. By exiling them, her father had taken family and friends from them. And her rescue of the exiles had come, if not to nothing, then to very little, bringing death to most of them when Bely had loosed his weapons against the mobile. A double amputation had left only bits and pieces of the people they had once been. She could not expect them to speak to her as fair-minded souls, or view her with anything but skepticism and contempt. All this she would have to make Voss and Wolt Blackfriar understand.

The door slid open behind her.

"We've come to listen to you," Voss said behind her.

She turned in time to see Blackfriar come up next to him.

"Please speak freely," Blackfriar said.

Josepha felt her stomach tighten as she sat down on a cylindrical container.

"You must understand," Jason said as he came forward, "what our position on this ship is."

"Please explain," Blackfriar said.

She saw Jason smile, and realized with dismay that they would not know how to talk to each other.

"We'll die off," Jason said, "with no chance at the longlife that waits for you, no chance of living long enough to get there, no chance at sleep."

"Only a few of any of us will sleep," Voss said.

Jason glanced at Josepha, and the regret that she saw in his eyes seemed beyond help. "From what I understand," he said, "many of you will live long enough to get there without sleep. Our world is gone, while you still have something of yours left, and a hope. If we survive the next century by mating with your kind, there will be nothing of us left. We will become you, and help you rebuild your way of life."

"There is a planet," Blackfriar said, "where those of you who might still be alive can settle with your children."

Jason looked around and asked, "How many of us will still be alive?"

"We can rejuvenate any survivors," Voss said. "And they can have children, as you can now."

Jason looked around and said softly, "That would be hard on our five women. Will we be permitted to have offspring with yours? And whose children would they be then?"

"You can have a variety of your own children," Blackfriar said.

Jason looked puzzled.

"We can combine enough of your hereditary materials," Blackfriar explained, "to start fetuses, store them, and bring them to term in better times. We can still regain that capacity. No women, yours or ours, need carry young in their bodies unless they can and wish to do so."

Jason looked around the group, then back at Voss and Blackfriar. "If this is true—" Jason started to say.

"There is some hope," Voss said, "that we won't have to reproduce to survive. We've sent a shuttle ahead to Praesepe, and it may bring back whatever we need to repair this ship's drive, long before aging becomes a problem."

"You've sent a vessel ahead?" Jason asked with surprise. "With a jump drive?"

Voss nodded. "No word from them yet, but we expect them back soon."

"You have nothing to fear from us," Blackfriar said. "When we begin to rebuild and grow again, you may even have a chance to go back and help your world."

Jason glanced at Josepha, and she saw that he still doubted. He was struggling to control his feelings, to prevent them from drowning his reason in what he saw as credulity.

"And what if the shuttle does not return?" he asked. "And why are you afraid of trying further jumps?"

"We would all risk losing everything," Voss said.

"There may be no help at Praesepe," Jason continued.

"That's possible, but unlikely," Blackfriar said.

"Another jump might be no more a risk than others," Lemuel added.

"It's our lives," Jason said, "those of us in this bay—that's what we're worried about. What chance have we got doing it the sure way? We're not very important to you, are we?"

"I'd like to die in daylight!" old Padraic rasped.

They were right, Josepha thought. It was going to be too late for the faces staring with hope and fear at Voss and Blackfriar.

Blackfriar nodded. "We will take the best solution for the greatest number, despite the cost to you or the rest of us."

"I told you so," Lemuel said.

Jason was silent for a while. "I do realize," he said finally, "that there may be no happy solution. We may gain, through our children, only if you succeed, but your success will be too late for . . . most of us here. But the shuttle's return may solve all our difficulties. When did you say it will return?"

"In several days," Voss said. Josepha was surprised by his vagueness, then realized that it was deliberate.

Jason looked around at the gathering and Josepha knew that there would be no more discussion. They had all been worn down by the hope and fear of words, enough to see that only events would decide the future.

"We'll wait," Jason said with a nod so much like Ondro's, and Josepha heard only defeat in his voice. What else was there to do but wait? What else would there be for any of them if the shuttle failed to return? It had all been said.

63

Jason went to see Voss in the forward control area on the day after the meeting with the Cetians. He had agreed, at Josepha's urging, to find out as much as he could about the ship's predicament. He had decided to go despite Lemuel's charge that he was planning to join the enemy because it would be his only chance to live.

The baseless accusation had infuriated Jason. "You don't think I remember you," he had said to Lemuel, "but I do. And I know that you were a thief and common criminal, not a courier for the resisters as you claim."

"What do you know?" Lemuel had jeered. "What do you remember?"

"I saw you pick up that knife on the hill just before Rhazes rescued us. What were you thinking? That you'd have a better chance at being saved if you made room for yourself by killing a few others? You should have cut your own throat!"

Lemuel looked surprised. "What?"

"During the storm," Jason said, remembering that he had expected Lemuel to attack him, but for some reason the man had held back, shaking and looking pale, as if he might be ill, and Jason had glimpsed the fear inside him. The truth was that the man had planned to kill himself.

"Well?" Jason asked. "Do I go to the control area to see what's what?"

"They'll turn him!" Lemuel had shouted, but the faces of the others had told him to go.

"We're all agreed, then," Jason had said, but Lemuel had turned away, hugging himself as if he had caught a chill.

Voss showed Jason to the second station in front of the panel, then sat down next to him. "We're putting as much power as we can into continuous thrust," Voss explained. "That means our speed will keep increasing for as long as we exert force. At large speeds we can make the passage to Praesepe in a shorter experienced time."

"I don't understand," Jason said, remembering Lemuel's warning that it would be easy for Rhazes to deceive the ignorant.

"It's a fact of nature," Voss said, "that faster moving clocks run slower in relation to their point of origin. That also holds for your heartbeat, since your body is a natural clock."

"There's no doubt of this?" Jason asked, looking carefully at the man who was his rival for Josepha. Maybe Lemuel was right—maybe she wanted him only for purely practical reasons of survival. As he sat next to the man, Jason realized that he couldn't read him at all.

"The theory was proven a long time ago," Voss said, "by countless experiments. Relativistic travel was the first method of interstellar travel, but too costly in energy and time—and dangerous. For example, we have the power to accelerate, but we have to provide adequate shielding to protect the ship at even ten percent of light speed. At very high fractions of light speed, every bit of gas and dust becomes a deadly missile, wearing away at the ship and producing hard radiation in the collisions. We're trying to sustain a force shield ahead of us even as we accelerate. If we don't get well above half light speed, our relativistic journey will take more than a century. Even the most longlived among us cannot last a century and a half without treatment, which means, as you know, that only our children and the sleepers will get to Praesepe."

"You will just have to take his word for it," Lemuel had said, but to Jason it all had the ring of truth. If there was a deception, what was its purpose?

"But isn't there any circumstance," Jason asked, "under which you would try the drive again?"

"If our life support systems were failing," Voss said, "if we had other massive breakdowns we couldn't repair, if we were so hard-pressed that there would be nothing to lose by jumping—those would be reasons to take the risk."

Jason looked at the stars in the tank. There was not the slightest sign that the ship was moving, and he wondered at the reality of distances so great that all comparisons were lost.

"But the shuttle's return would make all this unnecessary," Jason said. "Should it have been back by now?"

Voss nodded. "It's already late."

"How late?" Jason asked.

"It should have been back in ten days, if everything had gone as it should have."

"And how long will we—" he started to ask, then realized the uselessness of his question.

"We will have to wait while preparing for the worst," Voss said. "Supplies and equipment for growing food will last more than a century, or longer, as will our basic medical facilities. But the renewal of our bodies requires a link intelligence to send small machines into our bodies to make repairs at the molecular and genetic level, in effect rebuilding aged structures as cell division is restarted. We can't do any of it on this ship, and there was no way to save any of the needed systems before the mobile struck Ceti."

Jason saw that Voss was trying to explain things to him as well and as clearly as he could.

"There's no partial or piecemeal way to do any of this?" Jason asked.

"That's a good question, but no," Voss said. "We must reach Praesepe, and get there while everyone is still in reasonably good enough condition to benefit from the procedures."

"And you are certain of these constraints?" Jason asked.

"I wish I weren't, and there are other problems. We can't carry on the manufacture of many other things, since most of the work was done by replicators—again, small machines working at molecular and atomic scales. In the mobile we had large industrial systems, where we could grow or build whatever we needed, from biologicals to mechanical and electrical devices. We can still do a few of the basic things, but until we have a full habitat again we'll have to depend on tools, and even on human machine-tool craftsmanship, which is an inefficient and labor-intensive way of doing things, but the only way when you have no choice."

Jason sat back in the station chair and tried to imagine the truth of what he was being told. It was clear to him that no one individual could grasp it all, and even on the mobile no one had ever been called upon to do more than a small part of anything.

"The greatest difficulty for us," Voss said, "is being cut off from our knowledge base. We have much of it with us, but it's not as accessible as it was through the Link. We have to search out everything laboriously, using simple and slow retrieval programs, using people who don't know enough to do it quickly and effi-ciently. No one had to specialize in the kind of direct access which the Link gave us, and in which we now have to specialize."

"Can you ever get back everything?" Jason asked, feeling overwhelmed by Voss's description of the problem.

"Another mobile may be able to give us an infusion of data equal to what we lost, updating whatever new knowledge has been gained in the time it takes us to reach Praesepe and build a new mobile. Most of our scientists, doctors, historians, and psy-chologists are dead, and the few who still live do not have their Link. Our culture did not live in its individuals, but in the very structure of the mobile's social container, which can accommo-date any kind of culture or subcultures within the secure eco-nomic framework."

"But it wasn't secure enough," Jason said, "because you were vulnerable to an unexpected attack."

"Yes," Voss said. "It was both unforeseen and unimaginable, and unforeseen because we could not imagine it."

"Now imagine our plight," Jason said, seeing his chance. "Think how our small group feels in your midst, with all our hopes gone, and yours in peril. The help that was held out to us when you took us away from the islands now seems a cruel joke."

He looked into Voss's eyes and hoped to guess at the man's trustworthiness, what his father had called character. Voss gazed back at him, but Jason was unable to see into him—and for a moment he suspected that what sat before him was not a man at all, but something that had lived according to the rules of a now-dead god called the Link, without which the human shape was only a feeble fragment of that lost awareness.

"We will do what we can to keep your group alive," Voss said.

"What can you do? By your own admission, you can't keep everyone alive for the time that might be needed."

"Everyone will live for as long as possible," Voss said, sounding both methodical and insistent. "The oldest and most vulnerable will sleep. In time we may be able to try blind rejuvenations. Some of us will die in sleep and in the blind tries. But enough of us should live to reach Praesepe and rebuild."

Jason stared ahead at the stars in the tank. "Don't you see? If it's so difficult for three thousand of you, what chance do fourteen Cetians have?"

"Your children will live," Voss said. "That much is nearly certain."

"But they won't be ours!" Jason shouted, hearing Lemuel within himself. "They'll grow up looking to your way of life." He felt bitterness climbing into him, reminding him that Josepha had chosen this man. It seemed impossible that he had chosen her with any passion or love. Josepha would get everything Voss could give her to keep alive, Jason told himself, while he grew old and died.

He sat in silence, struggling both to calm himself and to find what he must say. "Sleep seems the surest way to survive," he said at last without looking at his rival.

"But it's not reliable, and we can't sleep many. We need everyone who knows anything and has any necessary skills to monitor and maintain the ship, even among the oldest."

"Then put all of us from Ceti into sleep, since we know the least," Jason said.

"Let me explain again," Voss said. "You might all die in sleep. Only the oldest, who have nothing to lose, and when their lifespan is coming to an end, decades from now, when there is no other choice, should risk going into sleep."

"No one goes now?" Jason asked, turning to face him.

"We won't even begin to think about it until the shuttle returns and Iannon Brunel tells me what is possible. When and if that happens, we may not have that many problems left."

Jason waited a moment, then said, "I'm sorry to be so insistent. I did not quite understand."

"It is often difficult," Voss said, "for me to keep so much distinct in my own head, without the Link."

"Was it a great help to you?" Jason asked, grateful to have something of the man's feelings.

"Yes. I had never really been alone before—inside myself."

Jason waited another moment, then said, "You must know that I love Josepha and want her." He waited for Voss's reaction, but the look on the other man's face seemed to be one of curiosity, not surprise or angry jealousy. "Do you understand?"

"I have no objection—" Voss started to say as the door slid open behind them.

They both swiveled around at their stations and saw Josepha standing in the entrance, staring ahead nervously. She came forward stiffly, and Jason saw the thin wire drawn tightly around her neck.

"Don't move," Lemuel said. "She'll die with one twist!"

Jason and Voss stood up as the rest of the Cetians came in, took up positions around the drum-shaped bridge, and the door slid shut.

"Sit down!" Lemuel shouted to Voss.

Voss obeyed. Jason saw that Josepha was staring upward, unable to move her head.

"We're all here," Lemuel said, "so there's not one of us your people can threaten in return."

Josepha's mouth opened to get some air.

"Let her go," Jason said, still standing.

"We're not listening to you any more," Lemuel said. "They'll make you over, just like her, so we have to look out for ourselves now."

"Are you hurt?" Jason asked Josepha.

"No—" she managed to whisper.

"Sit down!" Lemuel ordered.

Jason sat down.

Lemuel glared at Voss and said, "You will do as we say or she dies."

Voss did not reply. Jason looked at the faces of his people as they stood around the drum, and saw by the resignation in them that Lemuel was in complete control. It had been a mistake to humiliate him in front of the others, he realized.

"You will jump this ship—or whatever it is that you do—

to its destination, right now. Clear enough? Right now."

Voss said calmly, "You don't appreciate the dangers."

"Anything's better than dying on this ship!"

"You're endangering three thousand lives," Voss said calmly.

Lemuel gazed at him with contempt. "We don't care about your three thousand lives. She dies in front of you if you don't do it."

Jason tensed. Josepha's head was tilted back and he could no longer see her eyes.

"If she dies," Jason said, "you won't get anything of what you want."

"But she'll be dead. Do you want that?"

"No," Voss said calmly.

"We have nothing to lose," Lemuel added, "and we don't care." Behind him, old Padraic was grinning with pleasure, and Jason reminded himself again that not all the outcasts of the islands had been political prisoners. He had never met Padraic, but he seemed to be neither a member of some political cadre nor a religious heretic. All such distinctions had been lost during the comradeship of imprisonment and in the exhilaration of escape.

"Prepare to jump!" Lemuel cried, shaking, and Jason saw the strain in the man's face.

The door slid open again. Lemuel tugged on Josepha's wire, forcing her to move with him.

Blackfriar's tall figure entered the control room.

"Now the gang's all here!" Lemuel cried. "Sit down on the floor!"

Blackfriar surveyed the room, then lowered himself to the deck, assuming a cross-legged position.

Josepha gasped and was struggling to get her fingers under the wire around her neck. "She's choking!" Jason cried.

Lemuel loosened the noose. Josepha gasped and took a deep breath.

"They insist that we jump," Voss said to Blackfriar.

Blackfriar nodded. "One more try might not make any difference," he said, turning toward Lemuel. "Will that satisfy you? It will pose a danger."

Lemuel nodded.

"Listen to me," Jason said to him. "I've learned enough to know that you'll be risking even our smallest hope, not just theirs. If we're thrown distantly, no one of us will ever have a chance to see a world again."

Lemuel clenched his jaw and said, "We don't care. Trying anything is better than doing nothing, living for nothing, being nothing in these people's eyes. Get that through your lovesick head."

"Lemuel, listen to me," Jason continued, looking around at the four Cetian women, hoping to find more reason among them. "We can make a community for ourselves on this ship, raise children. There are ways to help us have them, believe me. These people are not our enemies."

"You've gone soft and stupid!"

"You should consider," Voss said calmly, "that if we succeed in shifting our position, the shuttle won't be able to find us on its way back."

"It's never coming back," Lemuel answered, "if one was ever sent."

Blackfriar said, "But if it does return, it may solve all our problems—and you would never know, would you?"

Lemuel seemed to consider this as his free hand gripped Josepha's shoulder. She turned her head to one side, and for a moment Jason saw how she might look with her neck broken in the wire garrote.

"Lemuel," Jason said, "if you hurt her, I'll choke you myself until your eyes burst. I promise you that. Whatever happens, you won't be able to stand there forever."

Lemuel smiled. "You don't frighten me. Nothing can frighten me. If the jump works or even if it doesn't, we can kill all of you in here and run the ship our way. We'll have that for sure one way or the other. These people are so cooperative, so full of their own brains." He smiled again. "All that power and knowledge—and old Bely did them in."

Jason looked around at his fellow Cetians. Their faces still seemed resolved, but he was certain that walls of suffering hid their doubt. If only he had known some of them better on the islands, they might have been more willing to listen to him; but these had kept away from the political prisoners, and chance had permitted them to survive Bely's bombs. The promise of health and a new life had also faded from their minds, taken away by the same man who had imprisoned them; yet they blamed the people of the mobile. He knew their confused feelings—but Josepha and Voss had pulled him into the middle position, where he could do nothing.

"Set up the jump!" Lemuel shrieked.

Voss looked to Blackfriar, and Jason hoped that the older man would not say, "You have to let her die, if need be, because it's one life against the whole ship."

Blackfriar said, "They know that if they kill her they will lose their hostage. Therefore they will not kill her if we refuse their demand."

Jason tensed, knowing that Josepha would die.

"Oh?" Lemuel asked. "We don't care what happens after she's dead. All you can do is kill us. But she'll go before we do!"

Lemuel had convinced them that they had nothing to lose, no matter what they did.

"Do it now!" Lemuel shouted.

Blackfriar finally nodded to Voss, and Jason relaxed slightly.

Voss now turned to the panel before the tank and began entering program commands. "It'll take a few minutes to ready the energy outlay," he murmured.

"Don't stall!" Lemuel barked, tightening the noose. Josepha cried out softly.

"It's true!" Jason answered.

"Four minutes," Voss said, hunched over the panel.

"See! See!" Lemuel chided his followers. "See how they obey. I told you. Old Padraic told you they would obey."

The old man cackled behind him.

Blackfriar said, "Now you'll see what we're up against out there."

"Shut up!" Lemuel answered. "What kind of people are you? Don't you ever take a chance? Cowards!"

"Lemuel," Jason pleaded as he looked at Josepha, "stop and think of the risk."

Lemuel spat on the deck. "Voss there wouldn't be doing this if it were that dangerous, not for one life."

Voss said, "We'll lose the shuttle. It will come back to the expected coordinates, but we won't be there."

And Jason knew that Lemuel was at least half-right. Voss would not risk Josepha's life. He was acting without thinking, hoping that the danger would not be too great, that the shuttle would still find its ship, and that the ship would not be thrown so far into the dark desert of space that it would fail to find its way to Praesepe.

Lemuel stood very still, the wire turned tightly in his right hand, and Jason was shamed by a brief impulse to choose Josepha's death and save the greater number of lives, or to live with the fact that he had seen what was coming and done nothing to stop it.

"Reset is on," Voss said. "Here we go."

Jason felt a moment of vertigo.

The stars flickered in the tank.

Three Cetians fell to the deck, holding their stomachs and moaning.

"It's malfunctioning," Voss said. "There should be no extreme bodily reactions."

We're lost, Jason thought, thinking that Bely would have been pleased to know that his daughter had unbalanced the judgment of the same Voss Rhazes who had denied him life.

The stars steadied in the tank.

"Have we jumped?" Lemuel asked.

"No," Voss replied. "The timer is at zero and the stars have not shifted position."

"Do it again," Lemuel said, unshaken.

"Not for five hours," Blackfriar announced.

"I don't believe you," Lemuel said.

"It's true, Lemuel," Jason said.

Lemuel looked around at his people. The four on the floor were sitting up, as if recovering. He tugged on Josepha's noose. "Sit down, we're going to wait."

They lowered themselves to the floor. Lemuel looked directly at Jason and said, "Don't even think of it. The wire will slice through her neck before you can reach me, and she'll bleed to death even if you get me."

Voss said, "Lemuel, you don't really want to kill her, do you?"

"Ah, the other lover speaks! So both of you really do want her."

"Surely you now see the dangers in what you're forcing us to do," Voss said.

"I've got nothing to lose."

"It only seems that way to you," Voss said. "But you can't change physical facts."

"So you say."

"They know more about it than you do," Jason added, convinced now that everything would be lost because both sides were fools—and he could not bring himself to act.

"We'll get you there," Lemuel said to him. "You'll see."

64

As they waited for the reset, Lemuel loosened the noose around Josepha's neck. She began to breathe more easily, and watched as Jason tried to engage her captor in conversation, but the man refused all words. Lemuel sat staring at the screen, ignoring her, as if fearful of losing his resolve.

The rest of the Cetians sat on the deck, becoming more impatient with each quarter hour. Josepha avoided Jason's eyes, fearing that he might act impulsively if he saw her fear. She could not guess what Voss and Wolt were thinking, but she was sure that they were unused to physical violence. She had never seen any enforcement of civil order on the habitat, and there was no police force of any kind on the ship. She had been told that the Link had a means of restraining individuals by inducing sleep, but that it had been rarely used—and the Link was dead.

She sat very still and tried to breathe normally, thinking of what she could say or do that might help—and whether anyone had thought it would be best to let her die.

Slowly, the screen timer was counting down to zero. The wire, she noticed, was loose in Lemuel's hands. Being this close to him, she saw that he looked old and tired, and pitiably stoic, but his physique was thin and wiry, with more strength than was apparent.

As she looked around at Lemuel's group of Cetians, she realized that he was clearly their leader and had probably always been a leader, even on the island. From the time when they had realized that they were different from the political exiles, this group had kept together—and that might be why they had survived the mobile's destruction. They had been together somewhere, probably in the hollow, the environment most like their world, when the explosion came.

"It's time," Voss said.

Josepha tensed as the timer reached zero and the stars flickered in the navigation tank.

Lemuel groaned. Josepha noticed that he seemed suddenly ill, and felt his grip loosen on the wire.

Jason leaped out of his station and caught Lemuel's hand. Josepha felt the wire constrict as she was pulled down. Voss was suddenly next to her, working his fingers in between her neck and the wire.

"Stop them!" Lemuel cried.

She felt blood running down her neck. Then, as Jason worked to pry Lemuel's fingers from the wire, she glimpsed the tank. The universe of stars seemed to be going through a strange agony as Jason separated Lemuel's hand from the wire, threw him back, and sprang forward to pin him down on the deck. Voss managed to remove the noose and freed her hands from behind her back.

"The neck wounds are superficial," Voss said, examining her.

"Get him off me!" Lemuel cried as Jason held him down.

There were too many, Josepha thought. Even with her help, Voss and Wolt would not be able to overcome all the Cetians. Four men were on their feet. Lemuel cursed as Jason pinned him.

"We've jumped!" Blackfriar shouted as he got to his feet.

Voss helped Josepha into his station chair, then sat down in the other and examined the readings.

"Yes!" he shouted. "We're now twenty-five light-years nearer."

"Do it again," Lemuel said bitterly, "and we'll get there yet."

Josepha turned around as Jason raised Lemuel to his feet and held his hands behind his back.

"It was a fluke," Blackfriar said, "but we'll get there sooner."

"How long?" Lemuel demanded.

"In fifty or sixty years," Blackfriar said.

Lemuel laughed grotesquely and spat on the deck. "If it hadn't been for us," he said, "you wouldn't have even tried."

"It was only chance," Blackfriar said, "that it worked."

"So you say. Try again."

"We might still be thrown at random," Voss said, "and lose every gain we've made."

Josepha touched the drying blood on her neck. Jason was looking at her, and she knew his thoughts. He had defended her, but she would not be his.

"Try again!" Lemuel shouted, his face full of hate as he struggled in Jason's grip.

"It can't work," Voss said calmly.

"I don't believe you!" Lemuel cried.

"Why should we lie to you?" Voss asked. "We want to get there as much as you do."

"After we're all dead!"

Josepha looked around at the other Cetians. They seemed lost, unable to decide what to do. Even the old fool Padraic was silent. No one moved to help Lemuel.

"Try again!" he shouted. "Cowards! Fools!"

"Nothing will happen," Voss said. "Look—we don't even have time left to reset."

"You won't make happen what they can't do themselves," Beata Lorenz said to Lemuel.

"Do it!" Lemuel shrieked, as Jason restrained him.

Blackfriar said, "Show him. It can't hurt now."

Voss turned to the controls and touched in the commands.

The stars remained steady in the tank.

"Even if we could get reset, nothing would work," Voss said. "What happened was a freak effect. It can't happen again."

"So what now?" Terence Ohar asked.

"We'll get there," Blackfriar said, "but we'll still have to do it the hard way."

Lemuel roared like a wild animal, broke free of Jason's grasp, and stood up defiantly in the center of the deck. "I got us closer! I did it!"

"That you did," Blackfriar said. "Now quit while you're ahead, and no one's dead."

"He's right," Jason said.

Josepha took a deep breath and knew that an agreement of some kind had been reached.

65

When he imagined how the social prosthetic that was his ship might look from afar, Voss Rhazes knew that it would always seem lost. Powerless to subvert spacetime, the patchwork vessel pulled along on its gravitational oars, determined to cross the cave of stars to its port, however slowly and modestly. An objective observer might have concluded that the voyagers had been very foolish, or very brave, to have come out into the night at such an agonizing pace.

But the pace quickened as ways were found to shield the ship. Five decades of slow, dying life came to an end one day. The narrow bridge of patience was crossed—into sunlight.

Brightness flooded the bridge from the tank as Voss adjusted the glare and scanned for the inner planets of the double star.

Josepha stood next to him, frail but still healthy. Next to her stood their son, Ardys, tall and thin at fifty-three; his son, Axel, seemed youthful at thirty, and was taller than his father. Josepha's granddaughter, Lucina, sat next to Voss. She was expecting a child, but had insisted on coming to the bridge to see the entrance into the sunspace of the double star.

Jason was nearly eighty now. Ondro, his son by Josepha, stood by his side with his wife, Adria, and their three grown daughters, Perenna, Antonia, and Ariadne.

Voss remembered the dead. More than half the people of the

mobile were gone, among them Wolt Blackfriar. Wolt's son, James, was now captain of the ship. He stood to one side of the tank, rather than sitting at the command station, in deference to the expectant mother, Lucina.

All the Cetians, except for Jason and Josepha, had lived out their lives, but a few had left children. Voss remembered his first daughter, also named Lucina, who had died of a malformed heart. He had mourned for years, much longer than Josepha, unable to accept the fact that growing her a new heart had been impossible.

The oldest from the mobile were still in cold sleep; no one had wished to see their years perish, despite the seeming unfairness of giving them preference over others, but it was still uncertain how many would awaken. Their privilege waited to pay a price.

"Is the base there?" Ardys asked eagerly.

James said, "Orbiting the fifth planet at two hundred thousand kilometers. No answer from it yet, or from the planetary colony."

Voss felt an old stirring within himself, and realized that it was the base Link reaching out with test routines. He answered subvocally with basic information, then asked about the shuttle.

"There has been no vessel arriving from you," the Link replied, and Voss felt that he was hearing from an old friend, now somewhat unfamiliar, but unmistakable.

At the same time, he realized that the shuttle must have been thrown randomly on the leg out and had never been able to find its way back. For a moment he saw Iannon Brunel and his team struggling to set and reset the drive, and each time finding unfamiliar stars in their tank. If he had lived, Lemuel Annan would have learned that it was unclear whether he had been responsible for losing the shuttle, since it had never arrived at the base; so its presumed inability to find its way back to the ship on its previous course after the two wild jumps might not have been the cause of its disappearance.

And yet, Voss thought, it might have returned to the ship's first position from some far space, and might still be drifting there with its dead, having been unable to jump again. There was no way to be sure except by going out and finding it.

"I hope the planet is livable," Josepha said. "I've been so long without outdoors and daylight."

"Still no answer from the planetary colony," James said, and Voss realized that there might have been something about the planet that had made it unlivable.

As he looked at Josepha's long gray hair, Voss felt the mystery of having loved her, and it seemed to him that he would not mind if death took him now, near this life's end.

But the voice of the new Link, much like that of the one he had lost, whispered to him, saying that the body's ancient ways dulled the caring of those who reproduced, preparing them for death. Soon now, the Link assured him, he would defeat this anesthetic longing with a new beginning. He looked over at James and saw Blackfriar rebuilt in his son; but James was not Wolt.

We will grow again, Voss told himself, cheered by the electric yellow-white glare of the double star—and by the returning presence of the Link within himself. *We'll build,* he said silently, *until our shard of macrolife plays again on the great galactic stage.*

66

The growing mobile became a new star in the fifth planet's night sky, eventually outshining both the starship and the globe of the base-depot. As the resources of the base and starship were exhausted, tugships went out into the sunspace and diverted metal-rich asteroids. Construction machines reproduced and maintained themselves as needed, and the base Link directed them into ever more subtle tasks.

The new mobile's Link began to develop after a deposit of the old one's fragments was made into a fresh brain core, adapting to the needs of the survivors.

There were setbacks in the decade that it took to make the new mobile functional and capable of further growth. The reversal of aging was not entirely successful with several hundred of the survivors. Half the sleepers failed to revive, and as a last effort, some of their personality patterns were turned into the Link, in the hope that their experience would not be entirely lost.

James Blackfriar joined the new colony on the fifth planet, named Lea. The settlement consisted of those survivors who had been denied the chance to settle on Ceti IV and a number of those whose bodies had not responded well to rejuvenation and who now wanted to start families before dying. Exploration teams failed to find any signs of the previous colony.

When the mobile was complete, with one asteroid core and ten shells, Voss restocked the base, overhauled the patchwork starship, and left it in high planetary orbit; the time might come when the surface colony would need them both.

On the day before the mobile's departure, Voss and Josepha went down to Lea and visited with James Blackfriar and his family in their wooden home, lingering with their good-byes until the slow mill of the night ground the bright stars into an ashen dawn.

67

Josepha, in the first years of her renewed life, sought a better understanding of what had happened to the world of her birth. She constructed a record that presented the observations, thoughts, and feelings of all the survivors, and arranged these echoes of the catastrophe, through the Link, into an artifact that might reveal hidden relationships and provoke understanding.

She shaped it into a whole, then recast it several times to include second thoughts, qualifications, and even the most irrational judgments. This virtual history, accessible to all through the Link, revealed the events at Tau Ceti, the interstellar passage, and the new beginning at the double sun in Praesepe.

Characters flickered in the forever-incomplete fluidity, analogs of the living and the dead. One day she hoped to add the stored personalities and question them. As she worked on the past in this way, the effort burned away her feelings of pity and regret, and she began to doubt both the accuracy and necessity of her efforts. The dead spoke, but the complex infrastructures of endless motives and actions always seemed to elude her. She wore the faces of others; figures walked within her; thoughts swirled; places poured in like rivers. The death of her birth world played itself out again in endless variants, affirming and denying her previous convictions and feelings. Her effort at truth, her hope for a permanent bridge with the past, threatened to collapse.

But there were moments when her recreation seemed better than the truth:

"We did nothing to deserve destruction," Voss's simulacrum said bitterly.

"You humiliated an old man who feared death," she heard herself reply boldly. "And a man is a world in himself."

"That's only a confused way of speaking," Voss said coldly.

"These ghosts you've summoned live in hell," her father said, fixing her with his gaze. "And you live in a mock-heaven devised by the damned to keep you from the fellowship of God!"

She shaped the field, unfolding the story's variants and contradictions, until its figures cried for peace. The enormity of suffering and loss was always the same.

The inwardness of the hopes for Lea also eluded her. One group had settled the planet; the rest reached out again to macro-life; but the divisions were never decisive. Lingering doubts and curiosities about natural planets carried into new ages of macrolife, never quite succumbing. The communal-conscious of the mobiles always retained a love of the artful, communal-unconscious of sunlit worlds.

One day, Josepha asked the echo of Avita Harasta for a lasting judgment.

"The crossing was brave," replied the pattern of the lost old woman, "but don't make an *Aeneid* out of it. Look ahead now."

Josepha laughed, and suddenly the fever of shaping left her.

68

Jason, as he retreated in delighted wonder from death, saw that his new life gave him more than he and Ondro might ever have achieved in their dreamed of revolt against Josephus Bely. At least Ondro had lived to see something of what was possible, only a few steps up from humanity's past. Young Ondro seemed very much like the brother Jason had lost.

There was no point in returning to Ceti. Either there would be no one left alive, or the survivors would be well into a new age that might not welcome another intrusion. The passage of time, so much greater there than aboard the relativistic starship, might have already played out a new epic of conflict between angels and devils.

Jason wanted no part of it, and in time he let his memories go, until they existed only in Josepha's hyper-tapestry, now lost in the Link's often scholastic continuum of knowledge and personalities, where she sang of the painful love of a worn-out past.

He let go because pasts do wear out. Human nature hits a wall, and will pass through only by loosening its previous constraints, by leaving its given humanity behind for a greater humanity.

He let go because the lessons of his past became so small one day that he could safely forget them. Earlier, he had become alienated from his past because he knew it too well, but had still concluded, out of insecurity, that alienation and forgetting would yield no future. Finally, he saw that alienation and some remembrance would help make his future.

But with his ongoing future made, he routinely let dissolve the lowest standing layer of remembrance.

69

Voss Rhazes held on longest to the memory of the crossing to the double star in Praesepe, when time had become a stone wall to

wear away, space a cave of stars, and consciousness a mote slipping toward death. He wanted to keep, for a time, something of
the bravery common to all shortlived creatures who yearned use-
lessly to step out from the abyss of themselves.

In Josepha's virtuals, she asked him, "What have we learned
here?"

And he said, "We knew again what we had not properly left
behind, the tenacity of a past that reached into our lighted future
with a murderous rage. We should never have stepped into its
shadow, but instead left it to fade away."

"And now?" she asked.

"Forget what cannot come again. Drown all sorrows and
pities offered by broken constancies. . . ."

"And where will we cross to now?" she asked.

"To the inconstancies of joy," Voss had said—and it took her
a long time to find him in "The Inconstancies"—virtual islands of
mad love and ecstasy—served by a great link from Procyon,
where she sometimes visited him through a tachyon hookup.

70

Finally, only the Link retained the record of Ceti's ruin, the passage to Praesepe's double sun, the settling of Lea, and the rebirth
of the lost mobile's life from a handful of individuals.

The Link searched the sky for other mobiles, saying, "We are
here. We have not perished. Where are you?"

Josepha's graceful effort at remembrance and understanding
reached its moments of greatest interest during the passage to a
meeting of mobiles at Sirius. Later, her work became a curiosity

even to her, a file of puzzling traumas long ago redeemed by time.

The discarding of memories was common among the human macrolife of this period, and a necessity until the capacity of the old brain was increased to complement the indefinite renewals of the body; but even when memory could be continuous, few individuals chose to maintain full detail.

For the longlived, another kind of death became necessary. It was not quite death and not quite sleep. But it was also an answer to the question of how to use the past, especially when pasts refused to stay past even when they were all used up. When too much living remained motionless, when life went on indefinitely with too much that was unbearable or painful, then another kind of confession was practiced—confession into the void.

Mosaics of retained memory in the longlived became an expression of steadfast character and style; but unlike the amnesia of generations arising from sexual reproduction's punctuated immortality, this death without dying became an art, a dance of deletions and additions that slowly brought forth new personalities.

Josepha, once she had understood what the mobile had lost in its encounter with her father, came to the deeper question: what to do with life that stood outside of nature's time of simple survival?

Macrolife sought greater survival and development, to discover what a permanent culture would achieve in the ways of inward and outward knowledge. They were nomads of knowledge, these people she had joined, set to seek beyond the past's horizons, determined to awake into ever greater dreams.

Still, something of her chose not to lose her memories entirely. She stored them in the Link's inner landscapes, in a dusty warehouse, near a calm sea, where she sometimes came to wander, and to forget again.

About the Author

George Zebrowski's thirty-five books include novels, short fiction collections, anthologies, and a book of essays.

Science fiction writer Greg Bear calls him "one of those rare speculators who bases his dreams on science as well as inspiration," and the late Terry Carr, one of the most influential science fiction editors of recent years, described him as "an authority in the SF field." Zebrowski has published more than sixty-five works of short fiction and more than a hundred and forty articles and essays, and has written about science for *Omni* magazine. His short fiction and essays have appeared in every major science fiction magazine, including *Amazing Stories*, the *Magazine of Fantasy & Science Fiction*, *Science Fiction Age*, and in the *Bertrand Russell Society News*.

His best known novel is *Macrolife*, which Arthur C. Clarke described as "a worthy successor to Olaf Stapledon's *Star Maker*. It's been years since I was so impressed. One of the few books I intend to read again." *Library Journal* chose *Macrolife* as one of the one hundred best science fiction novels, and the *Easton Press* included it in its "masterpieces of science fiction" series. Zebrowski's stories and novels have been translated into a half-dozen languages; his short fiction has been nominated for the Nebula Award and the Theodore Sturgeon Memorial Award. *Stranger Suns* was a *New York Times* Notable Book of the Year. *The Killing Star*, written with scientist/author Charles Pellegrino, received unanimous praise in national newspapers and magazines. *The New York Times Book Review*, which included *The Killing Star* on its recommended summer reading list, called it "a novel of such conceptual ferocity and scientific plausibility that it amounts to a reinvention of that old Wellsian staple, [alien invasion] . . ." The *Washington Post Book World* described the novel as "a classic SF theme pushed logically to its ultimate conclusions."

The Borgo Press brought out *The Work of George Zebrowski: An Annotated Bibliography and Literary Guide* (third edition) and *Beneath the Red Star*, his collection of essays on international SF, in conjunction with his appearance as guest of honor at the Science Fiction Research Association Conference.

Brute Orbits (1998), an uncompromising novel about the future of the penal system, was praised by reviewers for its characters, originality, and thought. Paul Di Filippo, in *Asimov's Science Fiction*, said that "Zebrowski never ceases to invest his individual characters with three-dimensional roundness . . . startling, sobering, provocative," while *Publishers Weekly* called this novel "boldly speculative." The book was also the winner of the John W. Campbell Memorial Award for Best Novel of the Year in 1999.

Forthcoming in 2000 is *Skylife: Visions of Our Homes in Space*, an anthology edited by George Zebrowski and Gregory Benford (Harcourt Brace).

George Zebrowski's World Wide Web site is located at: http://ebbs.english.vt.edu/alt/projects/zebrowski